THE
CRYSTAL GAZE

BOOK 1

H. D. GIDWANI

H. D. GIDWANI

For information, permissions, or licensing, contact:
h.d.gidwani.official@gmail.com

ISBN: 979-8-9994866-0-8 (paperback)

THE CRYSTAL GAZE

H. D. GIDWANI

For my parents,
Without you, I'd be a crystal statue.

PREFACE

Hannah could hear every minuscule sound that reverberated through the chamber: the drips of the cold water webs, the small pattering of footsteps from distant parts of the cave, the horribly pleasant sound of crystals clinking...

The hair-raising, bone-chilling, inhuman sounds that resonated through her skull.

Her shoulders sagged, her heart pounded, and her eyes burned to squeeze shut.

Pure agony ran through her body, leaving her scared, bruised, and so exposed to all the horrors of the world.

Her fingers curled instinctively around the cold, lethal object, forcing her out of her shock. She stared down at it in surprise, her heart twisting at the sight. The jagged, crystal edges of the blade reflected the gold piles around her.

It reflected her hazel eyes.

Hannah felt a pang as she studied herself in the reflection. The girl staring back at her wasn't her. Her eyes were wide with terror, and several bruises and cuts decorated the side of her face.

She swiped a thumb against the cut striking through her lip, smearing some blood as it began to sting in protest.

Hannah glanced up, watching the cave shudder around her. She still had a few minutes left. That wouldn't be enough, but she'd have to make do.

Hannah felt herself draw the Orb out of her pocket. It felt like ice on her skin. A small, feeble part of her brain suggested using it like an ice pack. She banished it away before she could get distracted.

For the first time since she'd left home, her mind was blissfully yet unhelpfully empty. She watched the purple fog swirl inside the Orb, entranced. This was it.

This was supposed to be the end of *it*.

Magic curled around corners, death lurked in the shadows, and above all, a huge monster loomed somewhere around her, waiting, saliva dripping from its jagged teeth, claws gleaming, traces of blood spilled across it.

Whatever courage she had was gone, and now Hannah clenched her teeth, trying to find any ounce of bravery or wit, because that was what was going to help her survive...

Or die.

LORE

In every world, light and shadow dance in endless balance—forces of good and evil forever intertwined, like two halves of a single whole.

But when one side falters, the scales tip, and the world trembles.

Here, two ancient Orbs embody this fragile equilibrium: one glowing purple, the other green.

As they draw near, their colors swirl and merge, and a chill spreads through the air. Yet one always grows larger — a silent sign that balance has shattered.

The purple Orb steals souls, turning those it claims into living crystal– frozen, silent, lost. Those crystal statues can be given orders, can move, and can steal. They just cannot feel.

The green Orb holds the power to restore what's been lost, breathing life back into flesh and bone.

But now, only the purple Orb has awakened.

Cities grow still as people morph into crystal, then vanish. Governments deny it. Fear silences the truth.

And if good has to prevail in its ever-lasting conflict with evil, it must do it soon. Otherwise, all that is living will be lost to crystal.

Forever.

CHAPTER I

HANNAH

Grief is quiet, cold, and– if one is less fortunate–
made of crystal.

And the girl was well-versed in it. She'd become
acquainted with it the moment a crystal statue had been
perched on her driveway, eyes frozen in melancholy, barely
gleaming in the brightening morning light.

Her world hadn't ended with a bang– it had ended
with the barest glimmer. And it had vaporized, leaving
without an explanation.

The same way the frozen bird across the driveway had
vanished.

***

Hannah might've been a reckless girl, but she wasn't ignorant either.

Or even close to foolhardy.

No, she was simply willing to risk her life to glimpse *it*, even for thirty very fleeting seconds.

So out she crept, when the mists had just begun to blanket over the neighborhood and the sun began climbing its way up into the sky. Streaks of its light lazily painted across the brightening canvas, symmetric to Hannah's careful steps as she softly closed the door, wincing when the tiny *click* echoed through the air.

Nevertheless, she was out.

Cautiously peering for spying neighbors, she broke into a brisk walk down her driveway.

A statue was once here. Made entirely out of precisely chiseled crystal. It had captured his features perfectly, as though he had turned to it.

Hannah paused, her eyes scanning over the spot she'd seen a hundred times previously. Nothing had changed.

The statue of her father had looked to be expertly crafted, yet no one could've moved it to her driveway. And her father had recently left home...

Her dad had stood here. In the very spot where Hannah was now.

He didn't even get to warn his wife and six-year-old daughter. Didn't get to shout. He'd been crystallized. And then—

"Gone," Hannah murmured. A rustle of wind swept around her, prompting Hannah to uproot her legs and move forward. She padded down the path, halting instantly at the sight of the bird.

Crystal, just like that statue had been.

She crouched to lift it, cradling the delicate bird in her palm. It refracted against the strengthening light, sending tiny spots dancing on her surroundings.

A stray breeze shoved her light brown hair into Hannah's hazel brown eyes, momentarily blinding her as she swept the strands back.

In her sudden distraction, Hannah didn't realize when the bird had melted in a swirl of green, leaving behind a pocket of air and a mourning girl.

She closed her fists, darting several more glances around, except this time her eyes were peeled for something else.

Something that was turning people into crystal statues.

Okay, *now* she was being careless.

With her hands tucked into the pockets of her hoodie, Hannah half-heartedly walked back to her home.

Whatever portion of her father's wealth had also magically disappeared, leaving them with a house, a car, and her mother's money.

The house was still soaked in silence when she stepped over the threshold.

Hannah crept in, releasing a breath as the door successfully clicked shut. When she whirled around, she was met by a wall of fabric.

"Whoa– Mom?"

Mrs. Thorne raised an eyebrow at her. "What were you doing?"

Hannah grimaced, fully aware of how much her mother would hate her next words. But she said them nonetheless.

"Crystal-hunting."

On cue, her mom's face tightened. The lines in her face deepened as she turned away and headed to the kitchen. Hannah watched her go, her stomach widening with guilt.

Tentatively, she followed and sank into a chair, watching as her mother began cooking breakfast.

"I thought we had decided to stop that." Mrs. Thorne said, undeniable pain lacing the words. Hannah winced.

"It was just this one time," she said defensively, picking at a splinter in the table.

"You say that every time."

Her mother cracked an egg on the pan. Hannah watched as the yolk and whites spilled out onto the heated surface and began to crackle, developing a brown film on the edges.

"I know... but I need to figure out how it happened."

Mrs. Thorne huffed, shifting into her regular, crabby demeanor. "Hannah, we've talked about this. You need to let it go."

She faltered, perhaps realizing her words came off too harsh, and went over to cup Hannah's chin. Hannah looked up at her mother, allowing herself to feel shame. Mrs. Thorne's face was a canvas of lines, framed by soft brown hair similar to Hannah's. But her eyes were a gorgeous hue of green, and often Hannah found herself wishing she'd received them. But alas, she'd inherited her father's hazel eyes—not terrible, but they served as an agonizing reminder whenever she looked in a mirror.

Her mother's lips tilted in a small smile before she kissed her daughter's forehead and returned to the bubbling omelet.

Hannah's eyes tracked her as longing resurfaced, this time in the form of cold, returning grief.

"I miss him," she whispered, her gaze landing on the pendant swinging down from her neck. It was a tiny silver heart with a small *H* engraved on it, gifted to her by her parents on her sixth birthday. They had meant to save it for when older, but little Hannah had been excellent at sniffing out secrets.

Or so she'd been told.

Mrs. Thorne flipped the omelet, her attention purposefully diverted when she said, "I know, hon."

Hannah plucked at the splinter on the table again, steadily working it free.

Mrs. Thorne sighed, turning to face her daughter. Hannah looked up glumly, slouching in a way that her mother would probably scold her for.

But instead, she said, "I have to go meet with a client today. So... I'll drop you off at the library before I leave."

The words took a minute to register, but when they did, Hannah's lips stretched in a wide smile. She straightened.

"Wait– really?"

Mrs. Thorne huffed. "Don't make me regret it." She returned to the omelet, oblivious to a beaming Hannah.

Her mother rarely permitted Hannah to go, since each time her daughter came home with a stack of books taller than her.

As for Hannah, she adored the stocky building. She would lose herself in the aisles, drawing out more words and stories than she could count. Able to escape all sense of reality between the pages of perfectly crafted books.

"When should I get ready?"

***

A boy was bent over the desk, his chocolate-colored hair spilling into his face, concealing his equally dark eyes. The moment Hannah had entered the library and spotted him, her face brightened with undeniable enthusiasm. Discreetly, she headed over to where he was, fingers curled around the strap of her shoulder bag in concentration to remain silent.

He glanced up, a brief flicker of a smirk appearing on his face before his attention was redirected. "Hi, Hannah."

Hannah scowled. "How'd you know it was me?"

He grinned to himself, tucking a card into a spare book. "Please, I'd recognize your footsteps anywhere."

"Nice to see you too, Jax."

Jax set aside his work, leaning forward on his arms to offer his undivided attention. "So whatcha here for?"

Hannah pursed her lips, pausing to consider his question– it was majorly abstract, and Jax himself knew it. Hannah could show up one day to search for true crime, and another day for fantasy.

She settled for the truth: "I don't actually know."

Jax's smirk faltered, and he leaned back, straightening slightly. "I have to show you something."

Hannah raised an eyebrow. "What is it?"

"Follow me."

He weaved through the aisles, not bothering to check whether Hannah was following him or not. Puffing out a breath, she impatiently padded after him, dodging shelves and librarians while keeping her eyes pinned on his tall frame.

Jax was only two years older than she was, but they'd been friends for much longer than that. Most of his summers were spent in the library due to his mother's job here, and though it seemed infinitely boring at times, Jax always enjoyed assisting.

Hannah's thoughts were interrupted by the sudden collision of her and Jax's back after his abrupt halt. Jax turned to steady her, and Hannah fought a blush off her face.

"Sorry," she mumbled, straightening her hair. Jax chuckled, waving away her unnecessary apology. They both were aware of the clumsiness written in her genes.

Hannah cleared her throat. "So what are you going to show me?"

Her gaze washed over the simple wooden structures bearing a plethora of books, all falling under the category of *Animals.*

Jax marched to the end of the aisle, his eyes pinned on the empty wall. Hannah eyed him uncertainly.

He glanced at her and reached for Hannah. She attempted to hide the hammering of her pulse as he grasped her palm, clasping their hands together as his other palm came to rest against the beige wall.

Without offering any warning, the plaster and wood crumbled into a shower of green light, crackling away into tiny particles.

Hannah's eyes widened, and her entire attention was pegged onto the fading wall. It dissolved without noise, brilliant light emitting from the spectacle. Hannah distantly wondered if anyone else even noticed the sight before her.

Because after it eradicated itself completely, it displayed not the exterior of the building, but rather a secluded room.

Something akin to awe accompanied shock as Hannah fuzzily stepped into the little section. Her brain was in a frenzy– disbelief and excitement warring with one another.

The room was filled to the brim with weathered and warped books. The covers were bound in leather, titles scrawled with pen and printer. The pages were slightly creased, maybe even yellowing. Some, however, were propped open on pedestals, looking significantly fresher than their superiors.

And most stupefying of all were the crystals encased in glass and metal frames, pegged to the shelves like eerie trophies.

And this place was a secret—until now.

Dumbfounded, Hannah stared at Jax.

"What—how—?"

His footsteps slowed as they neared the first row of towering, dust-covered shelves.

"Stay close," he muttered, voice unusually tight. "This isn't just any library."

Hannah blinked, speechless.

"If you ever need to come here, ask me first," he added, turning to face her.

"Does it only open for you?" she asked, eyes darting over the secluded, otherworldly space.

Jax cringed. "No. You place your palm on the wall and imagine pulling a handle. That's how you get in."

Hannah nodded slowly, still processing.

Jax chuckled, some of his wariness easing as he squeezed her hand, then let go. "It's a secret, okay?"

She shook her head hazily. "How... from where did this come from?"

"From wherever or whatever the crystal disappearances originate."

His voice gentled, understanding her surfacing dread. "It's all magic, Han. I found it like this. The same way... the same way you found your father."

She sucked in a quick breath, her ribs tightening against the reminder. Hannah bit the inside of her cheek, her fingers absently clenching around her pendant. She glanced behind, noting the rematerializing wall sealing them shut in here.

In this private library.

In this secret library.

In this *magic* library.

She'd never been opposed to the idea of mystical elements— in fact, Hannah even had fantasies of delving into worlds of magic. But now...

She turned back to the front, her eyes falling on the nearest shard of crystal.

Now...

Now, what was the point of inhibitions seizing her?

Now, she had none.

The crystal soldiers couldn't have been created through a human's creation.

They were a product of magic.

And so was this little haven of books.

CHAPTER 2

HANNAH

The smell of ink had always been one of Hannah's favorites. And when printed on paper, it was undeniably satisfying.

Except when it was smeared across her fingers, staining her fingernails and skin.

Muttering under her breath, Hannah dropped the filthy book and fished for a tissue, hoping to clean off the sticky substance before it branded itself into her hands.

The ink itself had come from a greasy, small, leather-bound diary. The pages were smudged and even shredded at sporadic intervals. Cringing, Hannah threw a glance over to the untouched pile of books atop the table.

After she'd spent her sweet time collecting novels, journals, and scrolls– practically anything that snagged her attention– she'd made her way into an isolated corner of the main library and dumped them on a little table. Jax had excused himself to assist his mother, but she suspected he wanted to let Hannah pore over the books in peace.

A shame; she could've used his help now.

After deeming her fingers free of wet ink, Hannah seized the greasy book, with the tissue in hand, and frowned at it.

Its condition was worse up close, and an odor of iron wafted from it. Wrinkling her nose, Hannah held it at arm's length and hastily made her way toward the *Animals* Section.

***

The aisle was just as she and Jax had left it: empty and unbothered. Hannah stepped into it, palm already outstretched to place against the plaster...

Only before her skin could come in contact with the wall, it had already begun to dematerialize.

It crumbled in a shower of green light, unchanging from the first time Hannah had seen it, only this time, there was something behind it.

Something massive.

Gray fur covered its body, only leaving its palms bare. Two trunk-like feet were planted firmly against the wooden floor of the hidden library, each one taller than Hannah.

She watched, transfixed and rooted to the ground, as the rest of the wall faded. Hannah's gaze inched higher, curiosity clashing against pure, unbidden terror.

The thing was so massive that the rest of it was obscured behind the library walls, which Hannah realized were too thin.

And defenseless.

The book landed with a thump on the ground.

Her breath hitched as her gaze locked on what appeared to be its knee. A growl that sounded like it originated from the depths of *evil* resonated through the room. The air was submerged in cold, like spirits drifted around in a haze.

Only when there was movement did something inside her click.

A word formed in her mind.

Run

Hannah took off, sprinting through shelves and past people. The world melted into a blur, rapidly evolving into emerald lawns and pavement after she burst out of the library, still running ceaselessly.

Her lungs screamed to stop.

Her brain screamed to keep going.

The adrenaline prompted her forward. Her footsteps pounded against the asphalt, only reducing to a brisk walk as she rounded a corner and the library vanished from sight.

It's okay.

You're safe.

She needed to get away. Hannah wasn't sure what that thing was and didn't want to find out.

Shivers dragged down her spine at the memory of its enormous, slightly concealed form. Hannah didn't have enough time to see its face, which she assumed was behind the wall. She just sprinted out of there, suddenly fearing for her life.

And *why*?

Was it because of the enormity and absurdity of the creature?

Her splitting nerves?

Or was it–?

"Duck!"

Hannah whipped her head up, gaining enough time to see a flash of yellow hurtling towards her before agony exploded in her head and the ground tipped forward.

And then her vision went black.

***

"She's gonna be okay. Probably a mild concussion..."

"Good." An exhale of relief.

"This is all your fault, Dee!"

"I'm sorry..."

"You could've *exposed* us."

"I–"

The voices were hazy, breaching the ringing in Hannah's skull so that she could feebly focus on them. They continued, muffled, now that a headache throbbed behind her eyes, distorting blobs of color once she peeled them open.

A woman was standing near her, arguing with her daughter, it appeared. They both had jet-black hair and pale skin. But the girl's features were sharper, more alert, and the woman's were softer. Anger didn't look common for her, but exasperation did.

The girl's gaze betrayed her mother to lie on Hannah for a minute, and when it did, her gray eyes widened.

"Mom, look!"

The woman turned, a relieved smile tugging at her lips. Her eyes were ocean blue, contrasting with her daughter's. They surveyed Hannah, who blinked back, unsure if she was hallucinating. She was lying on a bed. How she got there, Hannah also didn't know.

"Hello, darling," The lady said softly, "Are you feeling okay? What's your name?"

Her headache flared when Hannah attempted a nod, so she settled for a simple: "I'm Hannah. And... I think I'm okay."

The woman shifted, raising her hand above Hannah's head, but not quite touching her. Hannah nodded in permission, despite the aching in her skull persisting, and the lady gently pressed her fingers against Hannah's forehead.

"Does it hurt here?"

Hannah swallowed. "Yes."

"Poor girl. Hold on."

The woman reached for a pill and a glass of water. Despite all her better judgment, Hannah sat up and drank it.

After a couple of minutes, her headache reduced to a dull pulsing, easily ignorable if Hannah wanted to.

"Thank you," she told her.

The lady grinned. "I'll explain everything in a couple of minutes, but first..."

She raised an eyebrow toward the shadow lurking in the corner. Her daughter stepped out, looking uncomfortable and avoiding Hannah's gaze as she fidgeted with her fingers.

"I'm sorry," she mumbled, "I kinda... hit you with a tennis ball. Really hard."

A strange laugh bubbled in Hannah's throat, but she smothered it. Out of all the things that could've rendered her unconscious, a tennis ball was not one she was expecting.

Suddenly fascinated, Hannah studied the girl closely. She was likely the same age as Hannah, maybe a couple of months older, but she was stunningly pretty– in a fierce kind of way. This girl was the opposite of anything dainty or cute. She looked demanding and impatient. Devilish and fiery.

Yet now, she was uncomfortable and guilty.

"What's your name?" Hannah asked.

The girl looked up, taken aback. "Diana. But most people call me Dee."

Hannah grinned widely. She wasn't even sure why she was so thrilled with the prospect of meeting a girl who lived near her, but something about her compelled Hannah to want to know her.

"Thanks for the apology, Dee." Hannah swung her feet off the tiny bed, wincing when her head throbbed again. "And the tennis ball."

A tiny smirk crawled to Dee's face, which immediately morphed into sheepishness. "And that, too."

She gestured to Hannah's forehead. Frowning, Hannah glanced in the mirror to see a massive bruise on the side of her head.

Dee's mom sighed. "I'll get some ice for that."

Hannah nodded. "Thanks, Mrs–?"

"Adrane. Sarah Adrane."

"Thanks."

She received a tight smile before Mrs. Adrane abandoned the room. Dee pushed her chin-length hair out of her face and said, "I hope you don't mind... staying for a little while. Well, mostly I feel guilty and need to find a way to make it up to you."

Stay? Hannah pondered it, unsure whether or not to entertain her. Staying meant leaving Jax, those books, her home, and whatever half-baked plan she had formed in her head.

Which, to be fair, was no plan.

Staying also meant leaving behind whatever monster she'd seen at the library.

And her mother wasn't even home today, so Hannah might as well find something else to do.

A feeble part of her brain reminded her about not trusting strangers, but this was the same thing as hanging out with a new friend, right?

"Okay." Hannah decided. "I'll stay,"

Dee's eyes lit up, but before she could say anything, the door was flung open.

A young girl, probably seven or eight years old, sprang into the room. She had black hair but sky blue eyes, unlike her sister. In her fist was a small pack of ice.

"Are you Hannah?" She asked curiously.

Hannah nodded, a little startled. "Yes, I am," she hesitated. "Who are you?"

The girl beamed. "I'm Pelli." She waddled up to Hannah and handed her the ice pack.

"Mama told me to tell you to ice your head. She'll be back soon." Pelli paused. "She also says it's okay if you stay. Can you please stay? Dee doesn't bring home many friends."

Dee frowned. "Yes, I do."

Pelli blinked back at her, as though she forgot Dee was there. She turned back to Hannah, seemingly ignoring her older sister's claim.

Hannah couldn't help but grin. "Yeah, I'll stay for a couple of hours." She glanced up. "If that's okay?"

Dee nodded. "Of course it is. And whenever you're feeling strong enough to stand, I can show you the tennis ball you got hit with."

Hannah winced, fighting back a grin. "I would like that."

CHAPTER 3

HANNAH

Despite having plenty of distance between her and the library, lingering panic still surfaced when she stood on her weary feet.

Deciding it was best to forget it, Hannah followed Dee, trying to pay attention as she explained what had happened when Hannah was unconscious. Mostly, it was Mrs. Adrane who panicked and had Dee haul Hannah to the guest bedroom, where she'd stayed.

Dee made several remarks on Hannah's apparent haste to wherever she was heading, which Hannah made no effort to entertain. She wasn't sure what she saw. Safe to say Hannah had been pretty shaken up.

The Adranes' house was magnificently large and practically screamed *rich*. It had glass chandeliers, mahogany finishes, and glossy tiles. Hannah had seen these regal homes whenever she and her mother drove past, but she'd never expected to be in one. Her mother always told Hannah to be grateful for their more-than-adequate home.

And she was.

At the reminder of Mrs. Thorne, Hannah grimaced. She'd forgotten to call Jax and her mom to let them know where she was. Absently, her fingers tangled in the hair at the back of her neck.

And froze.

Dee glanced back. "What's wrong?"

"My... necklace," despite her searching, no silver chain met her hand. "It's gone."

Dee frowned. "Did you drop it somewhere?"

"I don't think so..." Panic reared its reckless head. Where was it?

Her phone buzzed in her shoulder bag. Hannah pulled it out and answered the call.

"Hello?"

"Hi Hannah," Jax said from the other line, "Where'd you go? I found your necklace here."

Relief charged through her. "Really? Thanks, Jax. I'll come get it."

She set the phone down, breathing a sigh of relief.

Dee watched her. "You found it?"

Hannah nodded. "It's at the library."

An image of the creature flashed into her mind, rousing a shudder. But Hannah ignored it. Her pendant was important to her, and if Jax hadn't called her screaming about some monster, she'd likely imagined the whole ordeal.

Stupid.

"Hold on, I'll go tell my mom we're heading to the library," Dee told her, then dashed off.

Upon seeing her sister's absence, Pelli quickly stepped in.

"Do you want to play with me? I'm bored."

Hannah blinked. "Er, maybe later, Pelli. Your sister and I have to go somewhere."

Pelli looked disappointed but nodded and left Hannah alone, who fought back another headache. She groaned, pinching the bridge of her nose, and turned around, hoping Mrs. Adrane would bring some of those pills again.

But it was just her in the foyer.

Hannah mulled over her choices. She could either wait here for Dee or go and grab another pill.

The insistent ache made her choose the latter.

She began walking to where she thought was the guest bedroom, but instead emerged near the stairs. Huffing, she chose a hallway at random and padded through it.

Her thoughtlessness led her to a dark room.

Hannah ran her fingers on the wall, feeling around for a light switch. They snagged onto one and flicked it up.

Golden chandeliers powered, distributing their glow, highlighting this beautiful room.

Acrylic paintings were bordered by golden frames that hung on the wall, covering the pristine white paneling. The tile here was accentuated with gold, matching the large futon in the center. Everything was covered in a thin film of dust, as though the room hadn't been disturbed for a while now.

Hannah knew she should leave. But her feet carried her forward to examine the paintings, her headache forgotten.

The portraits depicted various figures, mostly revolving around a woman beside another man. They both had jet-black hair, but the woman had blue eyes, whereas the man had gray ones. They both were grinning at the painter as he meticulously sculpted them to life.

In another frame, the couple was holding a baby, who appeared alone in the next painting as well. He had dark curls strewn across his forehead and glacial blue eyes.

Next to that painting was another with a young, gray-eyed girl grinning at something in the distance.

But despite her attentiveness, Hannah's gaze almost always made its way back to the young boy.

"Who are you?"

Hannah whirled around, and her eyes clashed with the boy's blue ones. Vaguely, she recognized them but was too surprised to say much.

Behind her, the painting clunked off a hook and tipped forward. Before Hannah could react, the boy surged forward and gripped it against the wall.

Sandwiching Hannah between it and him.

Her heart hammered in her chest, her eyes transfixed on him. He was even more gorgeous up close, and their proximity allowed her to count the dark eyelashes framing his eyes. Count the barely perceptible gray flecks in them.

And he seemed equally as stunned with... whatever this was. His eyes were glued to Hannah's, his arms pressed on either side of her as he propped the painting up.

Hannah was the first to look away, confident her face was flaming. The boy tore his eyes away from her and inched the painting back on the hook. It landed with a quick snap.

Now less-than-occupied, he stared down at her. Hannah glanced to either side, at the arms pressing her against the painting.

"Sorry..." She murmured, inching forward to loosen them from this awkward position. She slipped underneath his arm, allowing him to disentangle his limbs as Hannah stood to the side, eyes averted.

The boy was silent, but she could feel his gaze pinned on her.

A moment later, he laughed quietly. "Sorry about that. I've always told my mom to get these paintings fastened firmly."

Mom?

Hannah stared. "You're Dee's brother?"

He nodded, before hesitantly asking: "Who are you?" Then his face hardened. "Wait a minute. What are you doing here?"

Hannah's cheeks were flaming again. "I... got lost," she said stupidly.

He blinked, opening and then closing his mouth. Finally, he glanced back and pulled a startled Hannah out of the room.

"That room is kinda... private." He explained, darting an uncomfortable glance back.

Hannah's ears turned red, and she was grateful for her hair obscuring them. "I'm sorry. I didn't realize–"

"No, it's okay."

Simultaneously, both of their gazes dropped to their still-clasped hands. He hastily let go at the same time Hannah pulled back.

The silence was thick. Hannah's brain screamed a jumble of words she couldn't even decipher.

"So..."

Hannah snapped her gaze up when he spoke.

"...who are you again? I didn't catch your name."

She cleared her throat. "I'm Hannah."

He raised his eyebrows. "Dee's friend?"

She shrugged, then mentally kicked herself.

Words! Use words!

"I kinda... met her today," Hannah explained, pushing her hair back.

He cocked his head to the side, making her heart do an involuntary flutter. "Oh. Where is she then?"

"Hannah! My mom said we can go!" Dee shouted, running into the room.

She halted at the sight before her, glancing back and forth. Hannah stared at her, then her brother, then at her again. Heat crawled to her face.

But Dee just nodded. "Hannah, meet my older brother Adrian. Adrian, meet Hannah."

He blinked. "We've met. Where are you two going?"

"Library,"

Adrian raised an eyebrow. "Alone?"

Dee rolled her eyes. "Want to join?"

"I'm good." Adrian turned back to Hannah, whose heart thumped erratically when his blue eyes pierced her.

"I'll see you later, Hannah. If you're staying." He offered a small smile before exiting the foyer.

Dee waited until he was gone before turning to Hannah, beaming. "Let's go get your necklace."

***

The pendant was lying on the same table she'd dumped the books on, with no sign of Jax. Hannah fastened it on her neck, relieved to see it was still intact. Her senses hummed with anticipation she couldn't speak for.

Nothing seemed off aside from Jax's absence. Both were things Hannah hadn't expected. Everyone seemed to carry on with their lives, fully convincing her she'd fantasized the enormous thing.

Dee plopped down on a chair, poking at a journal. Hannah bit the inside of her cheek, realizing her foolishness had nearly exposed Jax's secret resources.

"What are these?" Dee asked curiously.

Hannah snatched up the book before she could see it fully. "Just some... research."

Research that gave her a concussion, although that was mainly her fault. She sighed, rubbing her head.

Hannah's imagination would be the end of her.

Dee rose to her feet. "Hannah?" She asked quietly.

"Hmm?" She didn't bother to glance back as she collected the weathered scrolls.

"Look."

Hannah turned around. Her heart lurched with alarm.

Sitting there, perfectly innocent, was the evidence confirming that what she'd seen was true. It allowed her carefully confined theories to spring out, letting her mind run wild.

Because standing there before her was a tiny crystal dog.

CHAPTER 4

HANNAH

Dee gaped, awe lining her voice when she said, "It's beautiful."

And it was.

It was a sickening sort of pretty.

A cruel sort of stunning.

Hannah watched, her pulse humming, as Dee kneeled next to it. But before she could touch it, the dog melted in a flurry of green, just as something in Hannah's arms began to glow.

Dee jumped to her feet, her gray eyes wide. Hannah let all the books topple from her arms, except one.

It was a black book with a fuzzy green light shimmering around it in a halo. Hannah stumbled back, half-tossing, half-dropping the book on the table.

It fell flat in the center of the table, opened at the midpoint of its blank pages. The green light thickened.

"Whoa–"

Hannah jumped back, startled, as a blonde-haired girl fell into step beside them. In her hands was an identical book, only it glowed purple. It slammed down beside Hannah's book, and they both conjured up a sea of light, nearly engulfing the texts.

The three girls watched, stunned, as the glow surged up...

And then died down, leaving behind gifts.

Where Hannah's book had been was a crystal orb and a scrap of paper. Both couldn't have been larger than her palm, although the orb was significantly denser. It was the size of a softball, except translucent and smooth.

The other book had stayed, except this time there were words scrawled across the sand-colored, flimsy paper. In addition, there was a folded piece of parchment.

Nobody moved.

Then, after a stretch of heavy silence, Dee spoke.

"So... we all saw that, right?" She laughed nervously.

The blonde girl frowned at her. "What kind of idiot are you? Yes, we all saw that."

Dee bristled. "Idiot? It was a simple question."

"A dumb one."

"Who asked y–"

"What's your name?" Hannah interrupted, tossing a meaningful glance at Dee.

The blonde turned to her. She had intelligent turquoise eyes framed by gold, thin, rounded glasses. "I'm Ara."

"I'm Hannah."

They both shook hands while Dee glared.

"Hello? Magic glowing books and thingies." She reminded them.

That jarred Hannah back to the situation at hand.

Her eyes switched between the items, unsure of what to do next.

The Orb gleamed, sparkling in the sunlight that filtered through the window. Light refracted off of it, sending sparkles splayed across their surroundings.

Tentatively, Hannah reached forward. She knew she shouldn't, yet something within urged her to pick it up. To discover what it contained.

Where did it come from?

What can it do?

Her fingers closed around the sphere, clutching it to eye level.

Instantly, the Orb burned to life. Green smoke erupted within the crystal vessel, clashing against its restraints and swirling as though awakening.

A shower of sparks rained down on her. It coiled into a simmering crystal of gold and shot straight into the scrap of paper. The parchment uncoiled, revealing fresh writing scrawled across it. It floated toward Hannah, hovering in mid-air until she plucked it out.

Dear person(s),
The Orb in your clutches is no less than a weapon. Its true purpose will remain hidden unless you take full responsibility and power upon yourself. Unless you make it your companion, your curse, your burden, you cannot gain true power from it.
As all balance requires, a yin exists to both oppose and accept this Orb; its enemy. Its brother.
Another Orb.
Its brother Orb is purple. As the two spheres come near one another, the greater their colors will mix, until they are their opposite hues. Their temperatures will drop too.
The person who has picked it up first has been chosen and will now carry the weight of it. If that person wishes to, they may embrace the full power the Orb may contain. But as it is with the world, consequences come threaded with greatness.
The Orb will never leave you, even if it is lost in the depths of the ocean or cast away in a desert. It will never break until it is with its brother. It can also help you advance closer to its duplicate, but only once. Call "Orb, Advance" to use it.
Once you are ready, seek tools from this Orb.
Abuses of power will destroy the world.
There is not much time left.

It occurred to Hannah that she wasn't breathing.

Her lungs strained as they fought to pass the air. What used to be an unconscious habit was now a chore.

She felt weightless. The world had tuned out, blocking out Dee's murmured words of surprise, ignoring Ara's sharp inhale. Hannah was staring, eyes transfixed on words that seemed to bleed through the paper. Words that granted her what looked to be a curse.

And then it all came crashing back to her.

The green Orb had floated into the air, shimmering innocently, tempting Hannah. She felt herself collect it in her hand, fingers curling around the smooth crystal Orb.

A blonde lock of hair fell before her as Ara peered over her shoulder, adjusting her glasses as she read over the note again. Dee's hand crept onto Hannah's shoulder as she copied Ara.

Leaving Hannah to drown in her thoughts. Her gaze fell on Ozzie as she turned it over in her hand.

There were a few things she truly wanted.

First and foremost, she wanted her father back. She wanted him pure and alive and everything that was the opposite of crystal.

Number two, she wanted her family beside her at all times.

Number three, she always wanted her pendant with her.

And number four, Hannah wanted her and her parents to be safe.

What she didn't want was a curse on her head, an Orb stuck with her, a monster/creature/*thing* appearing at random, and crystal statues.

"The crystallizations are real..." Dee murmured to herself. Both Ara and Hannah glanced at her.

Dee looked back. "I've been hearing stories about them."

Ara pressed her lips together, tight. "Reporters are already coming up with fake news."

"I've seen it," Hannah mumbled.

Instantly, two pairs of eyes were trained on her.

Shrinking under their gazes, Hannah continued. "My father. When I was much younger. Also, I've seen small birds and animals crystallized, too."

"But where do they go?" Dee pressed.

"And how does it happen to them?" Ara questioned.

"I don't know," Hannah admitted. "I've seen them disappear into flashes of green light. It's kind of unnerving."

Dee scoffed. "Kind of?"

"Very." She amended, feeling something heavy settle in her stomach.

All three girls stared at each other.

"This is very, *very* weird," Dee muttered.

"Where did you get the book?" Hannah asked suddenly, dread firing up within her.

Ara crossed her arms. "Where'd *you* get *yours?*"

Both girls stared at each other, neither of them willing to reveal the truth. Hannah could practically feel the tension weighing on them.

But then Ara said, "I just found it. When it started glowing."

"Me too," Hannah confirmed. The disappearance of the crystal dog must've caused both books to glow.

"Guys, what's that?" Dee interjected, pointing at the parchment on Ara's side. Ara snatched it up and unfolded it, displaying–

"A map?" Dee asked dubiously, staring at the ink marks. Hannah frowned, tentatively plucking it from Ara's hands to study it better.

The brown paper was coarse, the dry ink crumbly. A loose version of the right half of America was sketched, border lines undefined.

Hannah turned the parchment over in her hands, its glowing outline still pulsing with quiet magic. It had come straight from Ara's book— not a relic, not something she'd found or stolen, but something given. That made it worse.

Why her?

Why now?

The map was simple, yet impossibly specific: two glowing dots, one green, pulsing in Michigan, and the other purple, burning in Florida.

Was it a warning? A lure? Or... an invitation?

She swallowed, fingers tightening on the edges. Whatever the book wanted, it had chosen her to see it.

"That's where its twin is." Dee pointed at Purple. "That's what will be destroyed by this... thing." She gestured to Green and frowned.

"Can we name it something? I want to name it."

Both Hannah and Ara turned to look at Dee, their eyebrows raised.

"What?" Dee shrugged. "Just a suggestion."

"Well, suggest it later." Ara slid into the seat beside Hannah and grabbed the propped-open book. She flipped to the front, where a cover had been drawn– gold bordering framing the words *YIN*– and turned to the first page.

"*The purple Orb, otherwise known as Yin, is the negative counterpart to its twin, Yang.*" Ara read aloud, "*It possesses one of many powers, unique to its kind. Where Earth fills one with life, color, emotions, and vulnerability, the purple Orb erases each one, leaving all beings a mere shell of what they once were.*"

"The crystal statues," Dee nodded, making Hannah flinch. She couldn't fathom how easily Dee had adjusted to the whole prospect of a mystical, crystallizing Orb-thing.

Ara plowed on. "*One sight of Yin will crystallize organic matter.*"

In the margins were the scribbled words: *Exempting plants.*

Someone had already discovered this book and compromised it.

A jolt shuddered through Hannah. *The Monster.* It had been in the secret library, and though she doubted it would be able to write with its claws, this Orb proved anything could be possible.

So they were dealing with a creature, a mystical crystalizing Orb, and its twin sitting in Hannah's palm.

"I'm naming it Ozzie." She blurted impulsively.

"What?" Ara looked aghast. "Sure. Whatever. Anyway..." She cleared her throat and continued: "*Once the Orb has been bonded, like now, full power will be at the disposal of the one bound. Teleportation is one of the key abilities, and those who have been drained by Yin can equip it too.*"

Dee furrowed her brows, leaning over Ara's shoulder– much to her obvious irritation– and reread the words.

"What does that mean?"

"The crystal statues," Ara gritted out, "They can teleport."

"So that's how it happens..." Hannah trailed off, a swish of green flashing behind her eyes. She didn't even have to attempt to remember the acidic light as it crumbled away, taking her father with it.

When she returned to the present, both Dee and Ara were staring at her. Ara's brows were pressed together, almost concerned, and Dee blinked.

"I feel like we need to regulate what we're doing here," Ara murmured after a moment, setting the book down. All three girls exchanged glances.

"We just walked into something massive," Dee admitted, finally taking a seat.

"Wait, wait. What is it exactly we're doing here?" Hannah rubbed her pendant anxiously, trying to dispel her mounting heart rate.

Ara scoffed. "Well, let's see." She shifted so that she was facing Hannah and held up her fingers, ticking them off.

"One, we just got introduced to glowing books, orbs, and text. Two, we just discovered that the crystal abductions are real, and how they are happening–"

"Not to mention Hannah and I saw one." Dee supplied.

Ara's vexation faded for a moment, and she stared at them, her checklist forgotten. "Where? And when?"

"Right here, before the books started glowing."

Hannah bit her tongue to keep from talking about the mysterious creature. They hadn't necessarily found out how the crystallizations were happening, considering the purple Orb was in Florida and the green one– Ozzie– was here.

"Wait, does the book say anything about the purple Orb's bearer?" Hannah interjected, "Because it kept mentioning that it was already 'bonded'."

"Hm, let me check." Ara reopened the text and skimmed through it, murmuring words under her breath as she read them. A tense silence hung in the air, mostly consisting of Hannah rubbing her pendant and Dee chewing on her knuckle. Even though she didn't look it, Hannah could tell Ara was hurriedly searching for the answer.

"At the end, it just says 'Beast', but that could mean anything." She concluded, eyes still scanning the text.

Yes, it could mean anything. But a sinking suspicion told Hannah otherwise. The monster's body flashed in her memory again. But how could it be the bearer of the Orb if it could move freely, but the Orb was in Florida?

"I don't want to be involved in this," Hannah said suddenly. Adrenaline and terror climbed onto her shoulders, forcing her to stand up. To step away from this. Grabbing her bag, she backed away.

Ozzie floated in the air, zooming towards her.

Ara looked up from her text. Dee hopped to her feet, eyes concerned.

Hannah shook her head, dodging Ozzie as it nudged her temple.

"Hannah, you're the least able person out of all three of us to back away." Ara informed her, standing up too, "You've supposedly been 'chosen' by this Orb– Ozzie, whatever you want to call it. You're its burden as much as it is yours."

"But I don't want it!" Fully aware of the consequences of yelling in the library, Hannah did nothing to stop her voice from projecting, desperation and alarm fueling her.

Ara winced, glancing around furtively before stepping forward. "Let's figure something out, okay? Please."

"Please," Dee echoed, her stance tense, as though ready to lunge for Hannah if she attempted to run.

That unspoken threat alone sent her stumbling back into her chair, Ozzie perched on her head. She stuffed it in her bag and zipped it up, uninterested in seeing it.

Ever.

Dee and Ara followed suit warily, only breaking eye contact when Dee accidentally stepped on Ara's foot.

Ara swore under her breath. "Watch where you're stepping, airhead!"

"Airhead? *I'm* the airhead? First of all, you show up out of *nowhere*–"

"I was right here–"

"–and then you call me stupid names–"

"'Cause you're an idiot."

"–and you're only doing that because you don't even know my real name!"

"I bet it's something dumb, like Fiona."

"Diana." Dee gritted out, hatred sizzling in her gray eyes. "My name is Diana."

"Nice to meet you, *Dora*," Ara shot back.

"Guys! Focus!" Hannah couldn't believe that she— who was on the verge of a breakdown a few minutes ago— was telling *them* to concentrate.

The world really had gone crazy.

Reluctantly, they settled in their seats, both of them glaring at one another.

"Ara, is there any way to get rid of the bondage?" Hannah asked, partially desperate and partially willing to steer the conversation in a different direction.

Ara broke eye contact with Dee to turn to her and the book. "I read through some of it, and no. But even then, your bondage with Ozzie hasn't been completed unless you accept full power. Do you?"

"Absolutely not," Hannah said, repulsed by the mere thought.

Ara looked slightly relieved. "Good, because it seems that once you've accepted full power, your life is tied to its life."

Dee chewed on her knuckle, eyes flashing. "And if you wanted to, how would you accept full power?"

Ara's face instantly hardened upon hearing Dee's voice, but she still answered after referencing the book. "It's unclear. Does the note say anything?"

Hannah checked it, rereading the ominous words before setting it down again. "No."

Dee sighed and leaned back in her chair, her posture suggesting they were discussing taxes rather than magic. "So... now what?"

Hannah stared, her gaze flicking between both of them. Sure, major revelations had been thrust upon them; what were they going to do after learning them? Report it to the police under 'paranormal activity'? Hannah might've laughed if this situation weren't so stressful.

"Maybe everything will stop if we ignore it," Dee suggested, ever the optimist.

A ghost of a smile tugged at Hannah's lips but died away. She settled for a stoic expression.

"I guess there's not much we can do," Ara admitted reluctantly, her shoulders sagging. She didn't look thrilled with the prospect of magic, though. Only disappointed because she couldn't figure something out.

"I guess we have to go then?" Hannah suggested. Then bit her tongue. She hardly knew Ara, or even Dee, for that matter. She'd been acquainted for what, an hour? Maybe two? That wasn't enough to get all chummy with them.

Jax. She had to talk to him. Let him know everything she did. She imagined he wouldn't be very thrilled about Ozzie either.

"Yeah, I guess so," Dee muttered, clambering to her feet. Hannah averted her gaze; she'd have to say goodbye to her, too. She couldn't stand being in this library for much longer– unless it was to talk to Jax, that is.

"Wait, before you go," Ara pulled out her phone and unlocked it, holding out the keypad for Hannah. "Keep in touch. I want to know if anything happens."

"Me too." Dee butted in, "I don't have a phone, but I do have a smartwatch."

"Good enough," Ara said, haughtiness creeping into her voice. Whether or not she intended it, Hannah wasn't sure. Scoffing, Dee held out her watch for Hannah to type her phone number in. She did, and instantly received two text messages.

"Alright. Cool. Now who's gonna take what?" Hannah gestured to the smatter of mystically-charged items.

"Yeah, I'm not taking anything. I'm gonna lose it, or my sister will take it, or my mom will take it. I'm not risking anything." Dee declared, stepping back.

"I can keep the map and book." Ara offered after a moment.

"I'll keep the note and– and Ozzie," Hannah said, hating her voice crack.

Ara pretended not to notice. "I'll text you later. I'll do some more digging."

Please don't, Hannah wanted to say. But she held her tongue and nodded.

"I'll call my mom to pick us up," Dee suggested.

"No, that's okay. I have a friend here, and he's probably gonna drop me home. But thanks, though." Hannah replied, feeling a twinge of guilt at Dee's disappointed face.

"Of course. No problem." Dee nodded, feigning indifference.

Ara stared at both of them. "You guys live nearby?"

Hannah nodded. "Yeah. Don't you?"

"I live in Australia."

Dee nearly choked. "And you came here for the library? Wow, this city should feel flattered."

Ara tossed her a disgruntled look. "No, I live in Australia, but I'm here for–" She winced, biting her tongue. "For my father's vacation."

Dee stared. "You guys vacation in Grand Rapids?"

Ara raised her brows, crossing her arms. "It's a nice city."

"Yeah, but still–"

"Well, I'm glad you're here," Hannah interjected, "We should meet up sometime again."

Ara looked as comfortable with that as Hannah felt, but nodded politely. "Sure."

Dee scoffed. "And get a couple of boxing mitts since you like fighting so much."

Ara turned to her sharply. "What was that?"

"Hmm?" Dee feigned innocence, "I have no idea."

Hannah sighed, rubbing her temples. In her bag, Ozzie chirped sympathetically.

This day was just getting better and better.

CHAPTER 5

HANNAH

Just like Ara had promised, a text pinged onto Hannah's phone the next morning. She opened it to see a politely worded text from Ara, asking how things were going with Ozzie. Not feeling compelled enough to reply properly, Hannah just sent back a *Good*, plus a smiley-face emoji.

Setting her phone down, she released a groan and flopped back down on her bed. Mrs. Thorne's footsteps approached her a minute later.

"Wake up, Han." She said, planting a kiss on top of Hannah's head before opening the blinds.

Hannah squinted against the sudden light pouring into her room. "I'm awake, Ma,"

"Then get up. It's late, especially for you."

Hannah groaned into her pillow but made no effort to get up.

Mrs. Thorne's footsteps padded around her room. "Wait... Hannah, what's this?"

Alarm shot through her bones, causing Hannah to jerk up. Ozzie was somewhere in her room, and despite everything, Hannah couldn't bring herself to explain it all to her mom yesterday.

But upon seeing her pendant clutched in her mom's hand, she relaxed. Slightly.

"What was this doing on the floor?" Mrs. Thorne demanded.

Hannah shook her head. "I don't know. The chain loosened yesterday, too. I'll try and fix it today."

Mrs. Thorne nodded, her eyes clouding slightly as she set the necklace on Hannah's nightstand. Her daughter watched as Mrs. Thorne continued to caress it with her gaze.

"You know your father was the one who picked it out." She murmured.

Pain twitched in Hannah's heart. "I know, Mom."

"He pulled it out of the jewelry rack and showed it to me. Said 'This is cute and sweet, just like our Hannah. We should give it to her.' And I responded with, 'She's much too young for jewelry.' But your father insisted we give it to you, later, if not at the moment. I agreed."

Hannah's chest was tight. "You told me before, Ma."

Mrs. Thorne laughed softly, eyes still pinned to the little heart. "But you found it. And you always wore it since."

Her smile turned sad, and a minute later, she said. "He would've loved to see you wear it every day."

To that, Hannah had no response.

Mrs. Thorne cleared her throat. "Come down for breakfast soon." She offered a little nod and left the room.

Breathing heavily, Hannah glanced toward her shoulder bag, which still contained a magical Ozzie. Its twin did this to them. Ripped out a hole in their hearts.

And Hannah had no idea what to make of that.

***

Hannah was sitting cross-legged on the floor in her pajamas, eating yogurt, and flicking through things to watch on the TV. So far, nothing snagged her interest. Her mind kept returning to the neglected Orb sitting in her bag upstairs.

Not important! She wanted to shout, but instead switched the TV off, glancing around in search of something to do.

There was a bang at the front door, causing both Hannah and her mother, who was getting ready to meet a client, to jump.

They exchanged looks. Hannah shrugged, heading to greet their visitor.

Scratch that– visitors.

At the door was Dee, Ara– both of them struggling to shove past the other and reach first– and an exasperated, slightly guilty, Jax.

Hannah blinked, suddenly very self-conscious of her pink pajamas.

"Who is it, Hannah?" Her mother shouted from the living room. Hannah turned around to see Mrs. Thorne clasping a gold watch to her wrist as she strolled towards the door. At the sight of the three guests, she stopped.

She stared.

Jax offered a polite, weary smile and wave. "Morning, Mrs. Thorne."

"Good morning, Jax." Mrs. Thorne frowned at Dee and Ara, two people she'd never seen before, in company with their most frequent visitor.

"Friends of yours?" She asked Hannah uncertainly.

Despite the redness on Hannah's face, she nodded, unable to say much else. She was very acutely aware of everyone's casual day outfit, exempting her mother, who was dressed formally.

She was the only one in pajamas.

In front of Ara, Dee, and Jax.

Ara shoved Dee aside and gathered a moment to look professional, before plastering a no-nonsense, stoic expression on her face.

"Sorry to bother you, Mrs. Thorne. I was wondering if Hannah has a moment. I need to discuss something with her."

Mrs. Thorne blinked. "I—yes, of course. Are you all staying?"

Hannah wanted to hide.

Far away.

Jax gave her an easy grin. "If that's not too big a deal. The girls needed to talk to Hannah, and well–" he gave Hannah a smirk, "I was just hoping to hang out."

"Oh... of course." Mrs. Thorne turned to Hannah, eyebrows raised. No doubt she was criticizing Hannah's lack of neatness at the moment, which was absurd since she was always neat. Today, though, it took a ridiculous amount of effort to pry herself from the bed, let alone change clothes.

"Are you okay with staying alone with your friends?" She asked, brows still drawn.

Hannah forced a nod. "We'll be fine, Ma. Jax is with us."

Jax nodded, flashing another wide grin. "I'll make sure they don't do anything stupid, Mrs. Thorne."

Hannah scowled. He was milking it, that's for sure. Between the two of them, he always did the stupid things.

Mrs. Thorne smiled back. "Alright, then. I'll leave you to it."

***

Ten minutes later, they were all gathered around the coffee table, lemonade in hand.

And much to her dismay, Hannah was still in her pajamas.

Her mother had left promptly after the whole debacle, allowing Hannah to drag in her 'friends' and seat them in her home.

A flurry of questions swam in her head, but the most cardinal was:

"How did you guys find my house?" Hannah demanded, deciding to forget about her attire completely.

Ara adjusted the collar of her jacket, which was much too elaborate for a teenager, and took a sip of lemonade before saying:

"Dalila will explain."

Dee turned to glare at her. "Why me? Also, it's pronounced *Diana*, or *Dee*, if the first one is too hard for you."

"How would you know how it's pronounced?" Ara replied, taking another sip, "You need to sound out the syllables to speak full sentences."

"Okay, new plan," Hannah proclaimed, clapping her hands to drown out Dee's reply, "Jax, start."

Jax set his drink down, lazily tracing the rim of the glass. "Apparently, they both have something very important to tell you. Or so I hear. They both came running over to the library, where they somehow found me, and asked for your address. I wasn't going to give it at first, but they convinced me, and I brought them here."

"Why didn't they text me?" Hannah asked, flummoxed.

Now both Dee and Ara frowned at her.

"We did." Dee said spitefully, swishing her lemonade, "But you didn't answer."

Guilt crept up her neck. She *had* been neglecting everything, and her phone was one of them.

"And so," Ara drained her glass, "After numerous *failed* attempts at trying to contact you, I recalled your friend you had mentioned. The one who stays at the library."

"That's me," Jax murmured absently, raising his arm.

Ara hardly acknowledged him. "So then, I headed to the library to find him, where I met Debra–"

Dee made an angered noise at the back of her throat.

"–who was also looking for you. For, it seems, the same reason."

Dee scoffed. "Yeah, that pretty much sums it up."

Hannah sighed, leaning her chin down on her wrist. "Fine. Now that you two are here, enlighten me. What was so important?"

Ara opened her mouth, then glanced at Jax and closed it. Hannah rolled her eyes.

"You can talk in front of him. I trust him enough not to panic."

"Panic? About what?" Jax straightened, looking unusually intrigued.

Hannah fixed him with a flat look. "The crystallizations."

"Oh."

"Yeah. Anyway, Ara, you were saying?"

Ara rummaged through her bag and retrieved a notebook and pen. She flipped it open to pages bearing a plethora of notes and numbers penned in cohesive sections.

"It is unreliable and inexact to discover how many people are being crystallized each day, but if we look at police records for 'missing person' and search for abnormalities, we can estimate the number.

"Firstly, I filtered through the most prominent section, something like this would be labeled for. Within that, I examined it for shifts in status."

Ara leaned forward, circling a box with her pen. "It has been noticed that once one family member has 'disappeared', so too, does the rest soon after. After the entire family has vanished, their files are either declared closed or resolved.

"After developing a pattern, I began to note down the average number of crystallizations per day." She pointed at a number in her notebook, "Of course, this number has been derived from a singular county– here, actually– so if we multiply that with all counties in America, assuming the average remains, we get this number–" She pointed at a slightly larger number– discreet enough to be unnoticed by the authorities.

"But then again, America is only a country with this population. So after more calculating– using populations– I have concluded."

Ara paused to glance at each baffled and alarmed person around the table before saying, "The entire human race will be crystal within eight days."

Silence fell.

The tension spoke louder than their thoughts.

Hannah was drowning in it, her heart thudding against her chest as she looked over the notebook once more. The information was organized, reliable, and very, *very* real.

A flurry of questions erupted within her mind, theories strangling, spiraling, and wrestling. Emotions materializing, clashing, and flickering.

Eight days.

Eight days until what had happened to her father... happened to the entire world.

With a rush of nerves, she realized eight days of dodging, hiding, and peeking.

Because she'd be crystal, too.

Frozen.

Forgotten.

"How did you gain access to these undoubtedly classified records?" Jax asked suddenly. When Hannah looked at him, she noted his widened eyes and incessant drumming on the table with his fingers. He was appalled.

Ara looked uncomfortable. "You needn't know that."

"No, seriously. Where'd you get it from?" Jax pressed.

She grimaced. "My father is... very rich. I might've... used bribery to acquire these." Her gaze hardened. "And that's all I'm saying."

Hannah was confounded. And here she was, thinking Ara was a regular teenage girl who had accidentally stepped foot into something mystical. As she had, Hannah assumed Ara would just back out. Forget it ever occurred.

Obviously, she was extremely far off.

And just now discovering the lengths this girl was willing to go to– *bribery*– made Hannah realize she really *didn't* know what was going on around her.

She's rich. Hannah jotted in her mental notes. *Inquisitive and sharp. Wears sophisticated clothes.*

"That *was* important..." Jax mumbled to himself.

Ara gave him a sharp stare. "You thought I was lying?"

Jax shook his head. "Just registering everything you said, that's all." He inhaled deeply before turning to Hannah. "I'm guessing you have a lot to catch me up on?"

Hannah nodded begrudgingly.

"Hold on! You didn't even hear what I had to say," Dee intruded, splaying her hands in the air.

Back up, Hannah.

"Right. Of course." Hannah nodded. "Tell me."

"Okay," Dee lowered her hands, ignoring the bouncing of her knee, and said, "Yesterday, when I was outside, I saw a crystal statue.

"Only this one didn't melt away like the ones we've seen before. This statue had a bunch of money and gold in its arms, and it *moved.*

"I was obviously shocked when I saw it walk. But it barely did. Only a couple of steps– as it exited someone's house– and *then* it disappeared."

Hannah stared.

This had gone beyond unnerving.

It even went past shocking.

Now it was just straight-up *weird*.

Jax raised his eyebrows. "And you're sure this happened?"

Dee stiffened. "Are you doubting me?"

"Yeesh, what is with you people? I was just asking."

Dee tilted her head in an exaggerated nod. "It happened."

At this point, the weirdness threatened to swallow Hannah up.

"Anyone up for refills?" She asked suddenly, still mulling over the revelations of the last few minutes.

Three pairs of eyes stared at her.

"Right. Not the time." Hannah shrank in her seat, reaching up to squeeze her newly mended pendant.

"Now what I don't understand is how this is happening." Ara started. She began speaking about physics and scientific principles, but Hannah barely heard her. None of that mattered when magic– clear, corrosive, damaging magic– lingered in the air.

"–but despite this, I'm sure my calculations are correct–"

Abruptly, the front door unlatched and swung open, revealing Mrs. Thorne leaning back precariously, carrying a massive bag of groceries. Ara fell silent when she walked in.

"Oh, hello. Are you all still here?" She set the bag down with a relieved exhale.

Reluctantly, all four teens nodded.

Mrs. Thorne stretched her neck. "My client postponed last minute, so I just got groceries." She told Hannah.

Her daughter nodded. "Okay, Mom."

"I'll go get the rest. And the mail." She departed with an easy smile.

Hannah turned back to her friends, but Ara was already looking at her.

"Where's the Orb?"

"Ozzie," Dee corrected.

Ara shot her a disgruntled look. "Yes, where is it?"

"Orb?" Jax asked, clearly perplexed.

Hannah sighed. "I'll go get it." She retrieved Ozzie and its ominous note and dropped it on the table.

Jax regarded it with wonder and poked it once. It rolled across the table before Dee blocked it from falling.

Ara examined the note, no doubt searching for hidden clues. "It turns purple when it meets its twin..."

"Twin?" Jax glanced up, abandoning Ozzie, "There's another?"

Hannah tilted her head in confirmation. "It's big and purple."

Jax's eyes widened, and he leaned forward. "Really? What does it do?"

Ara's face was grave when she answered, "It does the crystallizations."

Dee swatted Ozzie from side to side, apparently uninterested in their conversation.

Jax returned his focus to the green Orb before him. "And what does this do?"

"We don't know, since it's not bonded completely."

Jax raised his brows. "And that means...?"

Hannah opened her mouth to respond when–

"Um, guys." Dee stared down at Ozzie, whose smoke had turned fully purple, "Something's wrong."

Ara frowned, rechecking the note. "It shouldn't be purple, unless..."

A strangled gasp caught in Hannah's throat as she leaped to her feet. "The crystallization? It's happening? Right now?"

Ara copied her, shoulders tensing as her brows furrowed. "But... I don't understand. Today's quota should be filled..."

Jax stumbled out of his chair, too. "Maybe you calculated wrong?"

The blonde shot him a dirty look. "No, that can't be it. Something different must be happening today."

Dee attempted to lift Ozzie but hissed and drew her hand back. "It's freezing cold!" She exclaimed, hopping beside Hannah.

Hannah turned to Ara, eyes wide and flashing with panic. "Different how?"

They burst outside just as the air drew its breath. The world skidded to silence.

Crystal statues.

Everywhere.

On their driveways and lawns. In cars, on roads. Some were in their houses. Some bearing gold.

Everyone was crystal.

Not a single soul was spared.

Except for them.

And on Hannah's driveway...

"No," She whispered. Ice had secured her feet to the ground and steadily crept up. It froze her waist, traveling higher, anchoring her shoulders.

Goosebumps broke out on the back of her neck. The ice had reached her face now, clouding out her vision, encasing her in its irreparable, eternal frost.

She heard herself scream. The ice faded. She shoved herself forward.

Distantly, Hannah heard Jax cry her name. But she was too deep in to care.

I'll go get the rest, she had said with a smile. *And the mail.*

No, she wouldn't.

Hannah's mother was crystal.

Hannah stumbled over to where Mrs. Thorne's statue was standing, face unchanged except for the absence of warmth her eyes once contained.

If it had been a clever trick, a joke, even, Hannah might've admired the statue's beauty. It looked like an ice sculpture without the threat of melting. The face was carved into the most intricate of details. It had framed her in time, exactly how she would've looked if frozen.

Yet the eyes. No matter what they did, Hannah suspected they could never replicate the gentleness in there.

Without even her realizing it, tears began to splatter Hannah's cheeks. The air had turned stale, mirroring what had occurred seven years ago. Only that time, Hannah had been too young to be aware of it.

Now, however, she was old enough to shoulder the pain.

Strong enough, though?

She didn't know.

A torrent of tears poured down her face. Each one, splattering the asphalt. Each one the outcome of a burden forced upon her. Each one heavier than the last.

Warm arms encircled her shoulders, pulling Hannah flush against a strong chest. She melted into the embrace, letting out deep, gut-wrenching sobs.

It was the same as before.

It was different.

The situations paralleled.

Did they, though?

The first time it was at dawn. She was six years old. She followed her mother outside and saw it. Her heart had cracked.

Now it was a little past noon. She was thirteen years old. Her heart was thoroughly shattered.

A warm hand stroked her hair. Soft words followed–gentle, desperate, possibly lies. She couldn't bring herself to hear them. *Couldn't* hear them over the sound of her own heart imploding.

"Hannah, please. Look at me." She squeezed her eyes shut, afraid to see the statue again.

"Look at me. Not the statue. Just me. I'm here, right?"

Tentatively, she pried her eyes open. Jax tilted her chin up higher, his own eyes moist.

"You're going to be fine," He whispered, his voice washing over her like an enchantment, "We'll find a way to fix this..."

Yes, she would.

Hannah was unsure about many things, but now she'd been tied to the Orb. Silently and subconsciously, thoughts were adding up. Feckless plans were piecing together. Within the span of a minute, she'd come to terms with it.

Hannah wouldn't rest, wouldn't let down her guard, until she destroyed Ozzie's counterpart. Until she brought her mother and father back.

But for now, she just let Jax hold her while she wept.

CHAPTER 6

HANNAH

Everyone in the city had become crystal.

It took a surprisingly long time for the news to reach the press, but once it did, reporters swarmed from every neighboring area to cover the disappearing statues.

That was another thing that was taking a long time: the dissolving of statues.

Numbly, Hannah was seated on her couch, staring forward at nothing. Her face was stained with dried tears, and she was sure everything had collapsed. The world had drowned in tangible silence.

Jax approached with a cup of tea, dredging her out of her stupor. Her eyes snapped up to watery ones.

He was probably mourning the loss of his family, too.

Slowly, her gaze flickered over to the other silent souls in the room. Dee was in the armchair, face gaunt with horror. Ara, for her part, remained solemnly stoic.

"Take it," Jax murmured, lowering himself beside Hannah. Clumsily, she accepted the tea, bringing the rim to her lips.

"What do we do now?" Dee asked, her gray eyes tinted red. She looked around the room, only to be met with silence.

Hannah took a slow sip, attempting to extract whatever feeble warmth the tea supposedly provided. She imagined it seeping into her bones, winding its way to her chest, trying to mend the shattered remains there.

To no avail.

Because, alas, tea is tea.

And crystal is crystal.

DIANA

No one had yet answered her question.

Dee was drowning in denial, refusing to believe her family, who lived in the same city, had been crystallized too.

And now they were gone.

Only yesterday, Dee was getting used to the fact that there was some magical *thing* turning people to crystal, then causing them to vanish.

One day wasn't enough time for *this*.

Her gaze washed over Hannah, noting the haunted look on her face. The dullness in her eyes. Her cheeks were painted with the ghost of tears. Dee couldn't even imagine the emotional agony she was experiencing; first her father, now her mom.

Somehow, she had both more and less to lose.

We were supposed to be safe here! Dee wanted to scream. But she and her family had only been liberated for a couple of years. Now, they were all in danger.

Correction: Dee was the only one left to be exposed to danger.

She needed to get her sword.

AMARA

Ara was a terrible person.

She knew she should feel some kind of grief over the fact that her father had crystallized, seeing as he was the only *close* living relative she had.

But in all honesty? She cared more about her dog's crystallization than his.

Her father was a famous actor, meaning he had little to no time for Ara. It was part of the reason why he got Goldie, her golden retriever, for her.

The reminder of Goldie sent a flash of accusatory hurt aimed at her. Perhaps if she'd brought Goldie, she'd still be alive.

But that's another thing; why did everyone else get affected except for them? Whatever was controlling the magic was doing it tactically. Or giving them a sign.

Now, looking around the room, all Ara felt was diluted sorrow gnawing on her insides. Hannah was numb, Jax was barely holding it together, and Dee was submerged in denial.

So Ara had to form a plan.

HANNAH

She had a white-knuckled fist around her pendant. An even tighter grip around Ozzie.

It had hovered into her palm at some point, as though offering sympathy. Hannah felt none.

"Hannah," Jax ventured gently, "I know everything is... a lot, but I need to know how this–" he gestured toward Ozzie, "–came to be."

Hannah nodded, opening her mouth. But no sound came out. Pitifully, she closed it again just as Ara filled in. While she brought Jax to the same page as all three of them, Hannah drank her tea.

When she had finished, the cup was empty.

"So now what?" Dee hugged her knees, still seated beside the table, "We're all alone."

Hannah flinched, and somehow, her grip became even more unforgiving on the necklace.

Ara surveyed the room with her acute, callous blue eyes. "Hannah set Ozzie here with the note."

Hannah complied, stumbling over and dropping the green Orb on the wood. The note flapped beside it.

From her bag, Ara extracted the book and map and then spread both atop the surface. Jax and Dee scooted closer, both still teeming with grief but curious as to what Ara was doing.

The blonde pried open the book and flipped through the pages, frowning. When she reached her desired mark, she looked up at them.

"I did some more reading yesterday–"

"Dude, how much research did you do?" Dee asked impulsively. Her voice was thick and recovering, but Hannah knew hers would be even worse if she tried it.

Ara scowled. "A lot. Now pay attention.

"I found something new in the book. As we read before, the Yin Orb drains life, emotions, vulnerability, and color. However, those four aspects comprise a soul; therefore, we can assume the Orb is taking souls out of people.

"If we manage to destroy Yin, the souls should theoretically restore themselves in their respective bodies. However, since this is a rise to full, unfiltered power, and it is like the souls are being collected–"

"So we can only decrystallize people before every single soul is taken. Which is in eight days." Hannah mumbled, her voice hoarse and raw, lifting her head to meet everyone's eyes.

She didn't like the way they were staring at her; genuinely surprised. It made her realize the extent to which emotions had overpowered her, displayed for everyone to see.

Ara pushed up her glasses with her knuckle. "Yes, that's about it."

Dee leaned forward, hardened anger chiseling her face. "So then what are we waiting for? Let's go and destroy the stupid Yin thing."

Jax blanched. "You did see its location, right?" He gestured exaggeratedly to the map. "And even then, you think it's just gonna be sitting in one spot? It is probably guarded or something."

Lightning seized Hannah as a realization overcame her. Gasping, she sat up straight.

"The monster! It's guarding the Orb!"

Ara frowned. "Wha–?"

"When I was walking down the street yesterday," Hannah interrupted, turning to Dee, "Did I look tense? Uncertain?"

Dee blinked. "I didn't really have enough time to see before you got hit by the tennis ball, which, by the way, didn't even leave a big enough bruise. It's already fading."

She pointed at her head, but Hannah had already moved on. "Yesterday, when I was heading to the hidden library," She told Jax, "I went to disable the wall, but before I could, it crumbled by itself."

The memory was vivid, lined in gold now that it carried significance. Hannah could remember it acutely, down to the most vivid of details. The deformed body, the enormous shadow. The way her eyes never reached past its torso, as she had already begun running.

They stared at her intensely as she recollected what had occurred. And to her surprise, nobody called a bluff.

Dee was baffled.

Ara was alarmed.

And Jax looked downright horrified.

Hannah turned to him. "Jax, you just said something may be guarding Yin. That is what's guarding it. It even said it in the book: The Beast."

The name sent a tremor around the room. Each person shuddered unpleasantly.

"That... complicates things," Ara said finally, attention on the book again.

Dee scoffed. "So? Let's fight it and get it over with."

"Did you even listen to Hannah? She said its waist began where her height ended." Ara snapped.

"But what if we made it?" Jax tapped his finger against Ozzie. "Say, by some miracle we make it. Then will Ozzie destroy it?"

He received a tight nod.

"And then everyone who was ever crystal will come back." He slumped back in his chair, eyes bright with the intensity of the revelation. Jax turned to Hannah, wide-eyed. "Do you realize what this means? You can have your parents back!"

Yes, Hannah had processed the words exchanged at the table. She'd pieced together this far-fetched tale. But her emotions were dappled with dread.

The whole thing was ludicrous.

Ara and Dee had both taken to studying their items. Dee dragged a finger from Michigan to Florida on the map, mouthing words under her breath. Ara was scouring the book for hidden clues.

"We're just four kids," Hannah whispered, though nobody heard her.

How were they supposed to stop *this*?

She squeezed her pendant, wondering how durable the tiny heart really was. If she pressed too hard, would it crack?

Her mother would've done it for her. She would've upended any Beast or Orb to safeguard them. So too would her father.

And if they failed, they would become crystal anyway. No one else was there to save her. She was alone.

Jax gave her shoulder a comforting squeeze, likely noticing her sudden silence.

Okay, maybe I'm not entirely alone.

Dee and Ara were more acquaintances, but for the sake of whatever they were about to attempt, she'd consider them friends.

A pretty cover-up for their rushed relationships.

Oh, how messy it would look when juxtaposed.

The noise had swelled around Hannah, mostly consisting of Dee and Ara's debating, occasionally broken by Jax's comments. Her thoughts rang just as loud.

"Okay," She murmured.

The noise stopped.

The silence nearly rendered her speechless.

Hannah straightened as much as her crumbling spine could muster before it dissipated.

"We'll go to Florida," She said, hoping her voice didn't waver, "We will find this Orb. And we will destroy it."

CHAPTER 7

HANNAH

They were all presumed dead.

That was a major inconvenience.

Alongside news coverage, police from neighboring stations entered Grand Rapids to check for survivors.

They had knocked on doors and searched for moving cars. Hannah and her friends ducked behind the table when they arrived at her house, afraid the cops would cart them into custody if they discovered the only survivors. Then their already half-baked plan would perish.

The report came a few hours later– everyone in the city had disappeared. Or died.

Hannah focused on the first one.

They were still crowded around the coffee table, this time with more notebooks, pens, and devices. However, once they'd realized their phones were trackable, they were immediately discarded.

Except for Ara's. Technically, she was still in Australia, since everyone was unaware that she and her father were in Grand Rapids. Accidentally, she had let this fact slip, then proceeded to explain the status of her father's job.

An amazing actor. But a horrible father.

Ara didn't mention that last part, but Hannah could tell from the way her tone turned bitter when talking about him.

Unsteadily, a plan was hatched.

Under the alias of a reporter, they would book a taxi to pick them up from Hannah's house. No doubt, a single cab driving through the streets would be extremely suspicious, but the city was already buzzing with journalists. Hannah figured the taxi would go unnoticed as long as it looked simple enough.

Assuming all went well, the taxi would drop them off in Cincinnati, Ohio. There, they would get another taxi to drop them off in Georgia, where they would take a train to Florida.

All the money would be unabashedly charged from Ara's father's wallet, which, yes, could be potentially tracked. But by the time they would get caught, they would either be crystal or conquerors.

Slowly, a fantasy was unwinding in Hannah's mind. She did not know if she believed it, but it was difficult to shove away the visions of her parents hugging her. Wrapping her up in arms that would never let go.

Hope was a strange, fickle thing.

Most of the practical planning was done by Ara, with occasional intervals of Jax's suggestions. Dee attempted to help but got bored after the first few minutes.

As for Hannah, she tried to help. But mostly she succumbed to the nerves threatening to swallow her whole every time her mouth opened. So she settled for just listening.

That was something she was good at: listening.

Their journey would begin tomorrow, since it would be reckless to leave now, with half the day gone. No, it was better to prepare today and trek tomorrow. Besides, the night would conceal anyone who needed to get anything from home, although Dee's house, they discovered, was the closest to Hannah's.

Still, if she needed anything, she had that option. Otherwise, they all intended to sleep over at Hannah's, seeing as leaving would be too risky. And though nobody voiced it, Hannah knew they were reluctant to be home alone with numerous threats upon them.

This was going to be the weirdest sleepover she'd ever have.

Around eight p.m., Dee slipped out of Hannah's home. She returned an hour later with a bulging duffle bag slung over her shoulder and a conflicted look on her face.

"I wasn't captured," She offered when she caught Hannah's eye.

"We noticed," Ara grumbled from the kitchen. But despite her indifference, she plopped down a stack of sandwiches, freshly made, before them a few minutes later.

Hannah nibbled numbly at the sandwich. Ara's cooking was perfect—but her stomach was tight with nerves and dulled grief.

When they had finished eating, nobody spoke. Stillness hovered in the air, leaving everyone quiet and mourning. The lights were mostly off, the curtains drawn so as not to create suspicion for anybody outside.

Dee had made herself comfortable on the couch and was using her duffle bag as a pillow. Ara was still awake and at the coffee table, shining her phone's flashlight on the book. Jax was on the floor, turning Ozzie over in his hands, and the green, glowing smoke bathed the room in its light. Wordlessly, Hannah went to sit beside him.

"You okay?" He whispered, rolling Ozzie toward her.

It bumped gently against her knee. She picked it up, letting the silence stretch before she answered. "I'm not going to lie to you, Jax. So I won't answer that question."

His head bobbed in a nod. "I know... just... just asking."

Hannah felt a stab of guilt. Here he was, worrying about her emotional state while his parents, too, had disappeared. "I'm sorry. I didn't ask before. How are you doing?"

Jax let out a quiet, pain-filled laugh, dragging a hand through his hair. "To be honest? It all feels surreal. As in, I cannot believe it's happening."

He quieted, eyes following the Orb. "Everything changed... in *one* day."

"Yeah..." Sobs threatened to rise, sending tremors through Hannah's chest. She tensed, wishing them away. Jax hopped to his feet abruptly, pulling her up with him.

"Go to bed. I'll stay down here." He urged softly.

His face had blurred from the tears pooling in her eyes, though Hannah attempted to see past them. "That's gonna look rude. I can't leave all of you to camp down here while I sleep up in my bed."

Jax furrowed his brows, thinking. "Fine. Dee has already taken one couch, and Ara can take the other. You and I can use sleeping bags."

"Hannah, go upstairs and sleep in your bed." Ara intruded suddenly, looking up from her work, "It's already big that you're letting us stay here tonight. You deserve a good night's sleep."

"But... you and Dee–"

"We'll be fine. Ara can take the other couch." Dee assured her, "And Jax... Jax can take the guest bedroom?"

"Yeah, I'll figure something out." Jax turned to Hannah, plastering on a reassuring smile. She faltered, but too tired to argue, she nodded and headed up.

She slipped under the covers, desperate to drown in the expanse of sleep. Yet the Orb beside her burned in her thoughts, preventing her from doing so. With a fatigued sigh, she sat up and tugged the blanket around her shoulders, turning Ozzie over in her hands.

A light flashed, and the note from earlier fluttered open. It turned over, on its blank side, and new words began to ink themselves onto the page.

The Chosen are not random. The Orb seeks what the world lacks: courage, grief, hope, and pain. When Yin awakens first, Yang must wait. The green Orb seeks not a fighter, but a healer. Not one who breaks—but one who rebuilds.

She stared, a breath caught in her chest.

Bonding does not require belief. Only contact and a moment of willingness. Even fear will suffice, so long as the soul is open.

"So... I didn't choose this?" She whispered, not knowing what she expected of the note.

You did not. But you cannot stop it. You are the bearer now. The more you resist it, the more it resists you. The more you accept it, the stronger your connection becomes.

"Can I unbond from it?" She asked, her voice meek. The parchment stilled, and then–

Only if the other Orb accepts you instead. And it never will.

With that, the parchment dimmed and folded up on its own accord. Hannah placed it beside Ozzie on her nightstand, her mind reeling as she lay down again.

She was tethered to a mysterious force now, her life entwined with it. And the only way out, it seemed, was to destroy it. But to do so, the Orb needed to be broken by its brother, Yin.

Hannah had been caught in something vast and inescapable. And she doubted it had only just begun.

Exhaustion rippled through her body. She let loose a half-sob, half-sigh.

She didn't even bother to take off her pendant, clutching it as an anchor. As though she were caught in a typhoon, and it was the only thing grounding her.

Hannah was certain sleep wouldn't claim her tonight, yet steadily, its long arms grasped her until she was dragged under its spell, drowning in darkness.

AMARA

She squinted in the light of her phone, making out a few words in the text before copying them down in her notebook. The ink swam across the pages, mirroring her gaze.

Ara blinked once, twice, then set to more writing.

The only noises were the sounds of her pen scratching along the paper, the shifting of pages, and the steady breathing of Dee as she slumbered away on the couch. Jax was absent, likely in the guest bedroom upstairs. And Hannah...

Ara felt a twinge of sympathy for her. She was being crushed by responsibilities she hadn't asked for. So Ara insisted she take the bed, hoping it would ease even a fraction of the weight, just for a night.

Or whatever was close to comfortable. Ara just hoped Hannah would succumb to sleep in general.

Despite their uncertain partnership, something about Hannah compelled her to watch over her. Unlike her, Hannah didn't have trouble expressing emotions, and perhaps that was something Ara admired about her.

Her pen skirted off the line, causing Ara a great deal of annoyance when she saw the strayed ink. She blinked, and this time her eyelids stuck together for a moment before torturously prying themselves open.

What time was it?

A glance at her phone screen told her that it was around one in the morning. They'd have to leave at eight a.m., give or take. This allowed Ara only six hours to slumber if she succumbed to sleep this very moment.

Sighing in defeat, she set the pen down and turned off her phone light. Ara dragged herself toward the only unoccupied couch and laid down, resting her head on its arm. There were extra blankets in the little basket beside her, but Ara was already too hot for any extra warmth.

Still, she shrugged off her white collared jacket and draped it across her torso, the added weight providing a sense of comfort as she tried to achieve what she never got: A good night's sleep.

DIANA

Her breathing mimicked deep slumber.

But Dee was wide awake.

Her thoughts were a tumble of emotions mixed with memories.

That tennis ball, the one she had hit Hannah with, was not hers. It was Adrian's. She had stolen it from him to see how hard and far Dee could hit it. Hannah just happened to step into the way.

Sorrow dimmed whatever amusement had lingered in that memory. Dee had never been able to return that ball to him. She'd meant to do it yesterday, but one thing led to another, and now she found herself on Hannah's sofa, pretending to sleep in a city haunted by the people who used to live here—people who had turned to crystal, and then vanished.

Dee's duffle bag dug into the back of her neck, eliciting a series of silent grumbles she would've let out. If only Ara weren't there, she would've shoved away the bag entirely.

Because Dee had gotten what she'd left for: her sword. It was currently concealed underneath the couch. Hopefully, tomorrow morning, she'll be able to brandish it to everyone. Hopefully, they wouldn't freak out.

The sound of Ara shifting wrenched Dee back to the present. She stayed extra still until she was sure Ara had gone to sleep.

Dee let out a breath so soft it barely counted.

Despite herself, she couldn't help but anticipate what the morning would bring to them.

HANNAH

Time slipped by, and suddenly, it was morning.

Hannah slid various items into her shoulder bag– a water bottle, a food bar. Ozzie and its note. Her room was melancholy and dull, the sun barely filtering in through the closed blinds.

After she'd finished, Hannah changed into simple yet comforting clothes. A light pink long-sleeve top tucked into jeans. Her hair was open and loose, but Hannah slid extra hair ties into her bag, just to be cautious. And as always, her silver necklace hung around her neck.

Vaguely, she put on socks and sneakers. Checked her reflection in the mirror one more time. Then she set off downstairs.

Everyone else had already assembled in the living room, munching on fruits and whatever snacks they could find. Ara was typing something on her phone, Dee sat on the floor, her back against the couch, while she inhaled a granola bar. Jax was on the counter, eating an apple, and was the first to spot Hannah. He shot her a tiny grin that Hannah could barely reciprocate.

"The cab is arriving in ten minutes," Ara announced, setting her phone down.

"' Morning," Dee told Hannah.

Hannah nodded, her throat unable to form proper words.

Dee's duffle bag looked much thinner than yesterday, the bulge gone. She'd changed clothes, now donning a navy blue t-shirt and black jeans. Her hair was swept back carelessly.

Ara had also changed, though where she'd gotten the outfit, Hannah wasn't sure. She was wearing a mint green shirt and another white jacket paired with trousers. Jax had rolled up the sleeves of his dark shirt, but otherwise, his outfit remained the same.

Hannah tore her gaze away to get a drink of water. While she tipped it into her mouth, Dee cleared her throat.

"Um... look what I got, guys." She extracted something from underneath the couch and hefted it up.

Hannah spat the water into the sink, coughed, and turned. She blinked once. Twice.

Nope, still there.

A giant silver blade was balanced in Dee's hands while she attempted a friendly grin.

"What the..." Jax hopped off the counter, his face alarmed. Ara snapped her gaze up to the sword, and her eyes widened slightly.

"It's a sword," Dee said brightly.

"Yeah, no kidding," Hannah murmured, squinting against the glint of the blade. It was entirely silver, excluding the hilt, which was midnight blue. It looked beautiful and very real.

"Dee..." Jax started slowly, his eyes tracing the sword, "Where'd you get that?"

Dee's expression faltered. "I... just own it."

"Do you even know how to use that?" Ara asked, scowling.

Dee looked affronted. "Duh. Why would I bring it if I didn't know how to use it?"

"I don't know, why do you bring your brain if you don't know how to use it?" Ara muttered, eyes still on the map.

"Don't you have a sheath for that?" Hannah interjected, voice flat.

Dee grinned. "Yeah, I do. "Think the driver will notice if I wear it across my back?"

"*No*, because you are not taking that thing with us," Ara said firmly.

Dee scoffed. "And how do you plan on stopping the guard of Yin?"

"By sneaking past it, if it's even there. Not by fighting it." Ara said it like a well-rehearsed statement.

"How about Dee just keeps it hidden?" Jax proposed, "Then even if we're in danger, she can use it."

"I second that idea." Hannah jumped in.

Ara scowled but didn't argue.

Dee beamed.

Jax and Hannah exchanged looks.

"Okay," Ara said, standing up. She folded the map and placed it with the book inside her bag. "Are we all ready?"

And just like that, the room was reminded: this wasn't a game. This was real. And they weren't prepared in the slightest.

But of course, Hannah wouldn't say that.

So instead, she straightened and nodded. "We're ready."

Abruptly, Hannah's shoulder bag whined. She frowned and unzipped it to extract Ozzie. Its normal smoke has shifted into pearly white and swirled abnormally fast, triggering Hannah to set it on the counter.

The beam of light enlarged, making Hannah squint against its sheer brightness.

She reached out to the dim it— then the light devoured them.

CHAPTER 8

HANNAH

Someone yelled. Hannah didn't know who. Her eyes were glued shut, covered by her palm with extra protection as she slowly stepped forward. Her other arm was outstretched, swiping for Ozzie.

But before her skin could come in contact with the Orb, the light had switched off. Hannah pried her open to see Ozzie sitting innocently on the counter, back to standard green smoke.

Nothing seemed out of the ordinary, that is, until she turned to her friends.

New artifacts hovered in the air beside them, triggering surprised remarks from everyone in the room.

In front of Dee, there was a ring. It had a silver band

with deep blue, glossy enamel. Silver lines slashed through the blue, creating a bold outlook on the ring. Dee slid it on her finger curiously.

Her sword evaporated into shimmering threads and wove itself into the ring. Dee frowned, tapping the band, only to have it spring out again.

Who needed a sheath? No, the ring would conceal it perfectly.

Highly impressed, Dee transformed the sword back into the ring and grinned up at them.

"I love magic." She declared.

"Your turn, Ara," Jax urged. The blonde turned to her gift and plucked it gingerly from the air. It was a gold monocle, the frame mimicking the same thinness and color of her regular glasses. The lens dangled from a gold chain, which she tucked into the pocket of her blazer.

"Thanks, Orb," She told Ozzie, "I'll be sure to use it sooner or later."

"My turn," Jax interrupted, cupping the thin mirror he received. It had a smooth crystal frame and an ethereal glow emitted from the surface.

He frowned, tilting it in his hands. Then he slipped it into his pocket with a shrug.

"Hannah, what'd you get?"

She raised her brows at the leather holster belt she'd received. It was nothing special, unlike the other presents her friends had received, and was the same color and material as her shoulder bag. Connected to the holster was a small pouch that looked perfectly Orb-sized.

Hannah glanced at Ozzie, then strapped on the empty holster. She plopped Ozzie in the pouch.

"Do you have a blade too?" Dee asked excitedly.

Hannah shook her head. "I don't know why the holster looks like that, but it will be easier to carry Ozzie in it, so..." She shrugged. The belt was comfortable enough for Hannah to forget she was wearing it, so no harm was done by keeping it on.

"Guys, the taxi is here," Ara told them.

"Right," Dee flipped the ring between her fingers. "Let's go to–" She paused, glancing their way.

"Where are we stopping, again?"

Ara sighed. "Cincinnati?"

"Yes, that."

Hannah's stomach churned, but she ignored the queasiness, preferring to keep the meager contents of her breakfast in. She looked at each of them — her friends, her team. They were all watching her, even Ara, as though she expected Hannah to lead.

None of them were prepared for what lay ahead.

But that didn't matter.

What mattered was that they had someone willing to take the first step.

She met Jax's gaze, then turned toward the door.

"Time to go," she said softly. Not as a question– as an assertion.

***

In her dream, Hannah was falling.

She didn't know where or how. Just that gravity was wrenching her down into a dark abyss. Just when she was going to meet the end, the scene changed.

Crystal statues were surrounding her. Some were shifting towards her. Others stared blankly. A shadowed figure loomed over her. She could barely see it through the crystal bodies around her.

A huge fist swung towards her–

"You good?"

Hannah gasped, jumping in her seat. Her eyes flew open, and her hand leaped to her pendant.

"Are you good?" Dee repeated. She blinked, awaiting Hannah's answer.

Hannah nodded, eyes still wide, heart still racing. She eased back into her seat a few seconds later, though her pulse ran rampant. They were still in the taxi. They were still driving. She was safe.

"Bad dreams?" Dee asked, her voice low.

Hannah tilted her head in a hesitant nod, still unsettled by what she'd seen.

"Use your bag as a pillow," Dee instructed, "You'll sleep better."

Hannah shook her head. "I don't want to. I don't know how I wound up asleep."

"You're exhausted," Ara supplied. She was sitting in the third row with Jax. "You need rest."

"I rested. I think I'll be fine." Hannah offered a tiny, reassuring smile. The muscles in her face refused to cooperate, so it ended up more of a grimace. She turned forward again, exhaling lowly.

They had been driving for a few hours now, the actual time unknown to her. Ara probably did, though. And so did Dee if she kept asking her every few minutes.

They faced almost no difficulty when sneaking to the cab. Sure, the driver had a couple of questions, like:

"Where's the reporter who booked this cab?"

And

"What are you kids doing here? Isn't this city shut off?"

And

"Where are your parents?"

Ara made him shut up real quick with an extravagant tip.

So far, their journey had been going smoothly, except for the reason they left. It all still felt like a giant lie, and Hannah was having a hard time believing everything that was happening.

"Ara, how much–"

"It's been three hours and fifty-four minutes, Dee. Please shut your mouth."

Dee grinned, flashing a mischievous smirk toward Hannah. "I already have a watch," She whispered, brandishing her wrist. "I just like annoying her."

Despite herself, Hannah's lips tilted up– a quiet, reluctant smile. It was awkward with her unused facial muscles, but the numbness inside her slightly thawed. Just a little.

***

Ara and Dee were arguing, as per usual.

Dee was facing backward, flipping through the stacks of money while Ara counted another pile. Both of them were taking jabs at each other and thus messing up the calculations, though that last part was mostly Dee's doing.

Jax tapped Hannah's shoulder and whispered. "Can we switch seats after we stop? Make them sit behind while we sit in the front?"

Hannah let out a dry imitation of a laugh. "Sure."

Minutes later, they were pulling into a gas station. The driver parked the car beside a petrol pump, turned around, and said:

"I'll fill up the car with fuel. You guys wanna step out and stretch your feet?"

Dee practically flew out the door.

Hannah, Ara, and Jax followed with less enthusiasm. As promised, the driver stepped out to put gas in the car, while Hannah stretched her legs with a relieved sigh.

She loved road trips, but being immobile for long periods wasn't her favorite aspect.

"There's a coffee shop nearby!" Dee bounced on the balls of her feet, eyes gleaming. "Let's go get frappes!"

Ara watched her, eyes narrowing. "Do you really need the caffeine?"

But Dee was already bounding in the direction of it, her duffle bag bouncing on her shoulder.

Hannah turned to Ara, shrugged, and began to follow suit, adjusting her bag and holster straps to fit together better.

"Get one for me!" Jax yelled from his post beside the driver.

Hannah frowned, turning around. "Aren't you coming?"

"Nah, I'll stay here and make sure–" He darted a subtle glance to the cabbie, "Nobody tries to leave."

Hannah rolled her eyes, knowing how paranoid Jax could be. "Fine. Which flavor do you want?"

"Actually, on second thought, don't get anything for me," Jax told her, checking his watch.

Hannah was tempted to question his indecisiveness, but Dee had already disappeared inside the cafe, and Ara was not too far behind her. Jax wasn't necessarily in danger of crystallizing because he wasn't alone. If she urged him to come, *she* would seem paranoid.

So without another word, Hannah followed her friends.

The atmosphere inside the cafe was lively and smelled strongly of caffeine. They purchased one chocolatey frappe for Dee, a latte for Hannah, and an espresso for Ara.

Hannah bought a small blueberry muffin for Jax, too. He'd appreciate the gesture and was extremely fond of blueberries.

While they were traversing back to the taxi, Dee and Ara entered into another squabble– this time on the topic of their drink options. Hannah paid them no mind, her mood improving from the coffee she was sipping. The warmth from it was comforting, the sweetness pleasing. She was eager to hand Jax his muffin.

But to her surprise, the car wasn't at the gas station. The area was abandoned.

Erie, silent, and devoid of life.

"Where's the taxi?" Dee asked, unlocking her lips from the straw.

"Where's *everybody*?" Ara frowned, scanning their surroundings.

Panic flared up within her, and Hannah clutched her latte tightly. "Was there another crystallization?" She said, a skittish edge to her voice. "Did all the statues disappear before we even got back?"

Ara shook her head, sensing Hannah's unraveling, and spoke with a softened edge to her voice. "That's unlikely."

"But there's a chance." She pressed. Her nerves were unwinding rapidly. "Where's Jax–?"

"Hey, what was that monocle thingy? Maybe Ara can try it now." Dee prompted.

Ara scoffed but extracted the monocle. She set her espresso down, then raised her glasses to accommodate the tiny lens. She blinked, and her eyes widened.

"There's... some sort of haze around here. It's purple... and... a very dark blue." She murmured, "I think it represents the magic here."

"But what do the colors mean?" Dee inquired, her brows raised.

"Maybe different types of magic?" Ara paused, looking at Hannah through the monocle, "The blue one is thickening rapidly."

Hannah's stomach churned. "What does that mea–?"

Huge thumping cut off her words, and a shadow fell over them. Very slowly, Hannah dared to turn around.

A massive lobster glared down at them, easily taller than the gas station roof. Its armor was a combination of gray and blue, and it shone metallically when the rays of the sun collided. Two beady eyes were fixed on them, underneath a pair of whip-like antennae. Its spindly legs propped it up, so it was standing upright as it snapped together its pincers, displaying razor-sharp edges.

Hannah's latte ended up spilled on the asphalt.

"What is that?" Someone choked out. Maybe it was her.

A glint erupted in her periphery– Dee had whipped out her sword, and Hannah had never been more grateful. But she'd also never been more terrified.

"Don't move." Ara murmured to them, "Lobsters don't have very good eyesight."

"It's out of water, though," Dee shot back, "And it's clearly not a regular sea creature."

As though it was proving its point, the monster let out a screech, something between a roar and a scream, and advanced.

"Run!"

Hannah broke into a sprint, letting her survival instincts possess her as she ran and ducked behind a petrol pump. The monster approached the station, ignoring Dee, and barreled straight for Ara, who was making a beeline for the gas station store.

Dee darted toward the massive ice cooler outside the store and leaped atop it, using a construction ladder she'd found to scale the roof. Ara had shoved her way into the store by now, returning the monster's attention to Dee.

"Do something!" Hannah hissed at Ozzie, pulse thundering as Dee disappeared above the gas station roof.

To avoid being crushed and to watch what was happening, Hannah scrambled to the end of the gas pumps and craned her neck to see Dee's progress.

Her friend raised her sword, posture surprisingly skilled as she charged toward the monster. In one leap, she'd used one antenna to drop herself onto its head. There, she searched for openings in its armor for her to drive her sword into.

Through her shock, Hannah couldn't help but be impressed.

The lobster screeched again and clamped its pincers down on the canopy. In one clean stroke, the roof of the gas station was ripped off and tossed behind it.

Now completely exposed, Hannah stared up at the pincer flying toward her. Pure desperation fueling her, she grabbed the closest thing near her: the petrol pump.

Dee locked eyes with her, and a silent understanding passed between them. Dee slid down its head as the crustacean bent down and sprang off.

In one expert move, she jammed her sword into the machine.

Gas erupted out of the nozzle, which Hannah aimed right at its eyes. The creature whined, stumbling back, just as Ara sprinted out, shouting:

"Pierce it's underbelly! The armor cannot protect it there!"

Dee wrenched her blade out of the crippled machine and did as told, driving the blade to its hilt. Considering the size, the sword shouldn't have done the amount of damage it did, but perhaps Dee nailed an important artery. The monster let out a wounded scream, and colorless liquid spewed forth from the wound, which tore open further as more blood poured out. The lobster cried again, slipping through the sludge on its tiny grey legs. It spun around, bellowed, and then slumped atop the store, crushing it under its weight. It didn't move again.

Stunned quietness hung in the air, interrupted when Dee let out a nervous laugh, which abruptly melted into a cheer. She was covered in the gross liquid but didn't seem to mind. A dimple appeared on her cheek as she retrieved her sword and turned it back into her ring.

As for Hannah, her vision swam. Nausea threatened to overtake her. Flecks of petrol covered her shoes, but other than that, she was clean.

She focused on breathing until the overpowering impulse of throwing up faded into a little nag, and she jogged forth, ignoring the corpse and searching for Ara.

She found the blonde on the ground, a giant pipe covering her foot.

"It fell from the store," Ara explained, her teeth gritted.

"Okay," Hannah crouched beside her, her stomach swirling unpleasantly again, "I'll help you."

It took a couple of tries, but Hannah managed to liberate Ara from the pipe. Her friend attempted to stand, clutching Hannah's shoulder for support, then hissed in pain.

"It's sprained." She muttered, seemingly angry at her own foot. Hannah could sympathize.

"Um, okay." She glanced back. "Dee?"

Dee jogged forward. "What's up?" She took note of the situation. "Crap– what now?"

"This store has collapsed, but there should be another one nearby." Ara supplied.

Hannah nodded. "Could you go get medical stuff?"

Dee frowned. "But we spent almost all our cash."

"Use whatever you have. Make something up, I don't know." Hannah thrust the remaining money into her hands.

"You mean I get to steal?"

Hannah was suddenly worried about how eager Dee looked.

Ara scowled. "No. Well, yes. Just go get it."

Dee gave a mock salute and bounded off. Hannah refocused on Ara and supported her to limp to the edge of a still-intact machine. She made Ara sit leaning against it and retrieved her and Dee's bags, which were lying near the ice cooler, a short distance away from the rest of the crushed structure.

"Dee will get the medical supplies, don't worry about your ankle," Hannah reassured, trying to feel an ounce of the comfort she was offering.

Ara fixed her a look. "It's not my injury I'm worried about. It's Dee. She's alone now."

Warnings flashed in Hannah's already reeling head, and she had to force herself to ignore them. It was unsafe to be alone when crystallizations were occurring throughout the world.

Something nagged at Hannah's memory, but it was overtaken by the unspoken wishes for Dee's safety.

CHAPTER 9

DIANA

It wasn't difficult to locate another convenience store, and when Dee did, a sense of accomplishment rippled through her.

She jogged inside, the caffeine from her frappe fueling her racing adrenaline. Dee was hyperaware of the sounds, smells, and sights, and she knew she couldn't stay still for the life of her.

She managed to grab some gauze, bandages, a splint, and an ice pack. They could just freeze it in the hopefully intact cooler outside the destroyed station. Pride bloomed through her, knowing that her mother's lecturing came in useful for once.

Dee waited in line, her foot tapping restlessly upon the floor as she waited for her turn in line.

Even though she would never admit it, Dee herself was surprised by how naturally her battle reflexes had found her. When brawling with the lobster/crustacean/*thing*, she morphed into a whole other person. Impulses and energy controlled her, and it was terribly exciting to submit to pure instinct.

Dee supposed all the training she'd been put through as a young girl had paid off, and for the first time, she was proud of her hidden heritage.

Her gaze snagged on the end of the store, where a flashy cartoon bandage exclaimed: *I got you covered!*

Snorting, Dee tore her gaze away and fixated it on something shiny.

It was partially obscured behind a shelf, and light refracted off of it, sending beams at the end of the aisle. Nobody had yet noticed it, but something about it dragged chills down Dee's spine.

"Could you hold my place?" She asked the lady behind her.

The woman huffed, but Dee had already moved on.

She padded toward the end of the store, nerves humming with anticipation. She rounded the corner, shock winding up her senses at the sight.

There was a crystal statue standing before her, arms slightly outstretched, fake eyes staring at nothing. She sucked in a breath as she took in the cold, ice-like material. The crystalline threads of hair.

She hadn't been able to take a glimpse from this close before, not even when Mrs. Thorne had been a statue. She and

Ara had just watched from the porch as Jax had hurried toward a broken Hannah and wrapped her in his arms. Dee hadn't been as well acquainted with Hannah then, but her heart had still itched to comfort her too.

But now, she was able to gawk at the statue as Dee waited for it to disappear.

It hadn't yet, which dragged another shudder through her body, accompanied by the realization: if this statue was fresh, that meant...

There was a scream from the front of the store, followed by incoherent shouts, and the sounds of people running. Dee scrambled back, squeezing her eyes shut.

It was here. The crystallizing-Orb-thingy was here and working. She had to get out.

Dee felt herself stumble back into a shelf, eyes still pressed shut, and her head stung with pain. She ducked down and risked opening her eyes.

A crack of violet light split the air, cold and humming like it was alive. Dee shrank back, heart pounding, legs itching to run as the light ceased.

After it had dispersed fully, she wobbled to her feet, mind woozy with pain and whatever she'd witnessed. Dee headed to the front, still stunned, eyes scanning over all the crystal statues scattered around the shop. The only noise was her feet padding along the aisle and her sharp intakes of breath whenever she neared a statue.

The cops would arrive soon to assess the latest crystal outbreak, and they'd catch her here, too. Dee couldn't afford to let that happen.

Without paying, she snatched out another ice pack and departed.

As she walked back, the sound of police sirens wailed after her. Dee assumed they'd ignore her.

Of course, assumptions were just as dangerous as hope.

An officer got out of his car and gestured towards her, asking her to stop. Instead of listening, Dee broke out into a sprint.

"Hey! Stop, we need to talk to you!"

She didn't reply. She just forced herself to keep running, her feet pounding across the asphalt as she spent her remaining caffeine-induced energy.

"Stop!"

Dee risked a glance behind and groaned at the sight of another officer.

Great.

Just what I needed.

She urged her legs faster and skidded around the corner, ignoring the stitch forming in her side as she inhaled bursts of air.

She spotted the half-destroyed gas station and lobster in the distance, relief and desperation warring together. Her pursuers were far off, but now they had assembled into a band of four officers.

Dee screeched to a halt in front of her friends. "Guys! *Getupweneedtorun!*" She got out, wheezing.

Hannah frowned, looking up at her. "What?"

"Officers... chasing me... need to move," Dee said in short gasps.

"Ara can't run!" Hannah shot to her feet, eyes flashing in distress.

"I'll be fine!" Ara intruded, craning her neck to see the cops, "Let's go."

Hannah hauled her up and moved to support her. Dee collected their bags, shoved the medical supplies in one, and moved to support Ara's other side.

And so they stumbled into an awkward, four-legged race. Dee's adrenaline was nearly over, pure desperation fueling her now. They ran past the dead lobster and away from the demolished store. Dee was hoping the carcass would distract the cops long enough for them to hide.

Before them was a thick forest. That would have to do.

Dee tugged Hannah and Ara toward the forest, and they turned without complaint. All three of them barreled into the wood, not daring to look behind.

At first, it was just a blur of logs, trees, sticks, and brambles. As Dee's energy faded, she was suddenly being tugged at by itchy bushes, stumbling over loose stones. The light dimmed drastically, blocked out by the dome-like trees.

But still, she was running. Her mind had tuned out everything else. Dee probably would've kept sprinting if it wasn't for Hannah abruptly stopping, tugging Ara back, whom Dee was holding. Dee tripped backward, sprawling on the pine-filled ground.

"Are you... Okay?" Hannah wheezed, standing over Dee, offering a hand. Dee shut her eyes, unable to accept, as exhaustion fully claimed her.

She managed a tiny nod, still breathing heavily.

The shadow that was Hannah stepped away. After a few minutes, Dee sat up sluggishly, hauling herself up to lean against a random stump.

A sudden drowsiness settled over her, turning her exhaustion into weariness she could hardly stay conscious through.

On top of her physical exertion, she'd sugar-crashed.

Dee barely managed to mutter: "The bandages are in the bag."

Then sleep dragged her under.

HANNAH

The forest was thick, the tree branches weaving into one another to block out sunlight. They were sprawled in a small clearing, roots under them, leaves above.

Hannah's legs wobbled and her shoulders ached, but it would be nothing compared to what Dee would awake to. Right now, she was passed out against a stump, her duffle bag serving as a pillow.

Hannah dug into the bags to find the gauze, splint, and what were supposed to be ice packs. Now they were just warm bags of gel.

Ara looked up from the stump she was sitting on, taking off her shoe. "Just give me the gauze and splint. I can do it."

Hannah was doubtful. "You're sure?"

"Just give it to me."

Hannah complied. Ara proved to be more resourceful than she expected, expertly aligning the splint and wrapping the gauze. She tied it off, then stretched her foot out, wincing slightly.

"Here. This will help you, Ara." Hannah propped up Ara's foot with a bag, then handed her a water bottle. To her relief, Ara accepted it without complaint; however, her eyes offered heavy scrutiny.

For a while, she didn't say anything, then quietly: "My real name is Amara."

Hannah lifted her head, eyelids heavy. "What?"

Ara shrugged. "Just thought you ought to know."

Perplexed, Hannah shook her head to chase away any weariness. "Why?"

"Because you kept calling me Ara," She said, her tone cool, "And because you helped me."

"Well... don't you want to be called Ara?" Hannah spluttered, unnerved by her calm demeanor.

The blonde made a face. "Gosh, yes. To be honest, I can't stand my actual name."

Hannah's voice softened. She could imagine why Ara hated her name, but wanted to confirm.

"Is it because your dad named you that?" She asked quietly.

Ara's eyebrows arched slightly, but her tone was flat when she said. "Perhaps."

The atmosphere had turned sullen, weighing unspoken words. Hannah wanted to grimace, but schooled her features into neutrality. "So, are you like, a rich heiress?"

Ara frowned at her. "You read too many books. I am wealthy– moneywise."

"But..." Hannah prompted.

Ara blinked at her, silently refusing to complete her thought. Hannah exhaled, dragging a hand down her face. A tiny smile pricked at her lips– Jax did that. A lot.

Cold dread seeped through her skin, rendering her frozen. Horror climbed through her nerves, silencing any emotion.

"Where's Jax?" She breathed, her voice drowned in the hammering of her heart.

Ara glanced up. "Hm?"

Hannah stood up abruptly, the world tilting beneath her. For a second, her lungs didn't function.

"Where's Jax?" She repeated, her voice alien-like and far away.

Realization claimed Ara. She inhaled sharply, features hardening. "I didn't see him."

The world spun, and Hannah lurched over to where Dee was sleeping. She shook her hard.

"Did you see Jax anywhere?" Hope and dread clashed.

Dee shook her head groggily. "No."

Hannah stepped back, squeezing her eyes shut. A few tears leaked out.

She wouldn't be able to handle this. Her father's crystallization broke her. Her mother's tore those flimsy shards further. Jax's...

No. She refused to think that way. Jax was not crystallized, dead, or missing. He'd simply escaped, though why or when Hannah had no idea.

What if he is waiting for me at the gas station?

A gasp brought her to reality. She dug into her shoulder bag, frantically retrieving her phone.

She powered it on with trembling hands and dialed his number. Pressed it to her ear. Squeezed it with one hand cupped to her mouth.

Please. She begged every star, every galaxy. *Please, don't let him be dead.*

Phones were wonderful inventions, but sometimes they were utterly infuriating.

Her call refused to connect due to the lack of service.

A frustrated growl tore in her throat as she shoved her phone back into her bag. Still standing, she glanced behind, silently contemplating finding him. Or at the very least, backtracking until she received enough service to call him.

Ara watched her as though reading her mind. "What if the cops find you?" She furrowed her brows. "You will jeopardize this entire mission."

"It's worth it." Hannah pressed. A headache flared from the downpour of emotions. "I'll be fine–"

"And what if he went back? What if he lost his nerve?" Ara challenged. "It's more risky to go than to stay. Besides, Jax was with the driver. Maybe he asked him to drive him back. Maybe he's safe."

"Maybe he was kidnapped!" Theories whirled around. Her heart rate didn't settle.

Dee lifted her head, blinking groggily. "Who was kidnapped?"

"Jax is missing," Ara informed her.

Dee's eyes widened, and she sat up. "Where'd he go?"

"I just said he was missing." Ara snapped.

"Oh... why does Hannah think he was kidnapped?"

"I don't know! I don't know if he was, or if he's safe, or even alive!" Hannah said, her voice suddenly shrill.

"He's probably safe. Maybe he just left? We didn't see him when we came back from the cafe," Dee told her.

Ara nodded. "See? Two against one, so our theory is more reasonable. He just left, mostly with the taxi."

Hannah's panic dimmed slightly. "You sure?" She croaked, dread still heavy in her heart.

Ara nodded, and Dee said: "Positive."

Uncertainly, Hannah lowered herself back on the stump.

He's not dead. She reminded herself, feeling her pulse return to normal. *He's safe.*

She wasn't entirely convinced, but it was easier to think he was out of harm's way. Sure, it was selfish, but Hannah had no choice.

But the memory of the now-squashed muffin in her bag still brought tears to her eyes.

CHAPTER 10

HANNAH

Dee had fallen asleep again, and Ara had her book propped open. Hannah alternated between looking at them and her phone, hoping even an ounce of service would meet it.

No luck.

Ara looked up at Dee for a moment, then returned to the book.

"Did it work?" She questioned without looking up.

"No," Hannah sighed, shutting it off.

"How did you become friends with Diana?" Ara asked suddenly.

Hannah frowned but told Ara how she'd been walking down the street, and was met with an unfortunately fast tennis ball. She narrated up to the point when Ara had entered the story.

"Ah, I see. You met her the same day I did." Ara said when Hannah had finished.

"Yeah. Why do you ask?"

"Just curious."

Hannah waited for her to elaborate.

She didn't.

"You know what? There's something I don't really understand." Ara told her, scowling at the book. She turned it so Hannah could see the pages about Yin and continued: "It has a holder and a guard. We know what the guard is– the Beast– but we have no idea about the holder, or whatever it has been bonded to."

Hannah pressed her knuckle to her lip, brows drawn. "Maybe it's another human?"

Ara tilted her head, pondering. "Could be, since Ozzie so rapidly began its attachment to you. Maybe another human accidentally– or purposefully– bonded itself to the Yin Orb."

"And since they are bonded, that person has access to all of Yin's powers, including teleportation. That's how they have been traveling and crystallizing-slash-draining people." Hannah supplied, dread coating her words.

"Yeah. I wonder why draining the soul from a flesh-made body turns it into crystal." Ara said, biting the inside of her cheek. Her gaze was sharp and cutting through the book.

"It is a mystery," Hannah agreed.

"Y'know what's not a mystery?" Dee mumbled from her spot, lifting her head. "My hunger. Does anyone have food?"

"I have granola bars... and... and a muffin. Though it's slightly squished." Hannah offered with difficulty. She knew she wasn't going to eat it, and she didn't want it to be wasted.

Dee didn't seem to realize the significance tied to the pastry and accepted it gratefully. "What's the plan now?" She asked through a mouthful.

"To make sure everyone has prepared for the next step of the journey, both physically," Ara glanced at Hannah, "And emotionally."

Hannah pretended not to see that.

"Nice job with the Lobster-thing," She said to Dee.

Dee's ears turned a little red. "Thanks. It was nothing."

"You say that as if you didn't kill a crustacean that was over twenty times bigger than you," Hannah remarked, grateful to feel something positive for once.

"Someday I'll write a book about it." Dee joked, "*Fighting Lobster-Monster.* Actually, no. I'd get too bored writing that. Ara can do it for me."

"You'd make me translate your idiocy for something readable on the page? No, thank you." Ara told her.

Hannah eyed her pointedly.

Ara rolled her eyes. "But great job with the creature," she said begrudgingly.

Dee beamed.

The bush behind them rustled suddenly. All three of their gazes snapped to it.

Hannah eyed it warily, half expecting another monster to jump out.

Instead, a crystal dog padded out. Its body was clear and colorless, yet it shone bright, even in the partial absence of sun.

Somehow, its crystal limbs moved like normal ones would, making it walk over to them innocently.

A strangled cry sounded from Ara. "Goldie?" Disbelief colored her voice.

Goldie, Ara's crystal dog, ventured toward them. For a moment, she looked calm. Gentle, even.

Then she lunged forward and pounced on Hannah.

Hannah screamed, falling flat on the ground. The dog turned around, clamped her teeth onto Hannah's ankle, and began to run.

Bits of grass and leaves crawled into Hannah's mouth as she was dragged somewhere, her pulse climbing. She scrambled to claw onto something, but couldn't get enough purchase on the forest ground.

Dee chased after them. Ara followed with some difficulty. Hannah lost sight of both of them as she was tugged into a small clearing.

The trees parted here, leaving a gap, allowing the sunlight to momentarily blind her. Hannah felt the dog let her go, and she frantically rolled to the side.

Something came down, hard, where she was a mere second ago.

Heart pounding and mouth agape, Hannah stared at the crystal dagger embedded into the grass. The owner of the blade was heartbreakingly familiar.

Hannah gasped, scrambling to her feet. "Mom?"

The crystal statue stared at her blankly, then returned her attention to the weapon. It was difficult to tell, but Hannah recognized those chiseled lines and numb eyes from the previous day.

The statue yanked the dagger out of the ground and raised it again.

Hannah watched in horrified fascination as the tip of the blade aimed at her heart. At the last second, she managed to dodge, and the blade narrowly missed her shoulder.

The statue paused, turned to Hannah, and aimed again.

This time, Dee's blade intercepted it. Her friend glared at the statue as she parried the next thrust.

"Take her dagger," She gritted out, twisting the hilt so that the statue lost its grip on the blade. It clattered to the ground, and numbly, Hannah snatched it up.

Now unarmed, her mother's statue sought the dog. They both melted in a pool of green.

Stricken, Hannah stared at the spot where they'd vanished, light still flashing in her periphery. She was still clutching the dagger, her knuckles white.

Dee kicked at the ground, grumbling under her breath. Ara inched towards them, her eyes flicking between them.

Hannah breathed deeply, turning to both of them..

They stared at her as though waiting for her to talk.

"Let's get out of this forest," Hannah mumbled, hating how meek her voice sounded.

She trudged back to their temporary camp and gathered supplies. A few minutes later, Dee and Ara arrived to assist her, too.

Hannah angled her face away, reluctant to let them see. Her thoughts were spiraling. Loathing bubbled up.

Within an hour, they'd already faced numerous threats, injuries, and inconveniences. Their entire plan had been turned askew, and Hannah was purely in survival mode, battling unstable emotions and maniacal creatures.

And now, she'd received a crystal souvenir too.

***

The sun had inched over the sky, lazing at a comfortable place now, preparing to make its descent in a few hours. Not that they could tell. It was humid and scruffy and itchy in the forest, and for the millionth time, Hannah was wishing they hadn't run in here on impulse.

After what seemed like days, they emerged on the other side of the wood, where Dee promptly threw down her bag and flopped into the grass. Ara tested her ankle strength, and it looked significantly better; barely swollen and able to bear weight.

Hannah sat down too, gulping down some water. She handed another bottle to Dee, who drained it quickly.

"Sorry," She wiped her mouth, "Was that our last one?"

"Yes." Ara scowled.

"It's okay," Hannah reassured her, giving Ara a pointed look, "We'll find a way to get more."

"And what are you going to do with that?" Ara pointed at the crystal dagger. Hannah winced at the sight.

"I don't know. Maybe I'll keep it. If that lobster was the first to come, it would be smart to have a weapon." Hannah tightened her fingers around the crystalline hilt, surprised at how perfectly it fit in her palm. It was exquisitely beautiful in a lethal way.

"But do you know how to use it?" Dee asked, beating Ara to the question.

"I don't know, how hard can it be?" Hannah said, pointing it at Dee.

Dee raised an eyebrow. "Is that a challenge?"

She pressed her ring with her thumb and hoisted her sword.

"Now I won't try to kill you, I just wanna see..." She didn't even bother to finish her sentence and swung her sword down.

Hannah ducked, flinching, to protect herself. Her dagger arm shot out and used the blade to block Dee's.

Hannah pried her eyes open. "What–?"

Dee gritted her teeth, blinked away her surprise, and pushed down forcefully. Hannah's arm shook under the strain before she twisted it, thrusting Dee's blade to the side.

Dee cocked her head, her eyes taking on a dark, amused glint. Hannah swallowed. She had seen that look once before, and it had been directed toward the lobster.

Hannah poised her dagger weakly at Dee's chest.

Dee smirked.

She leveled her blade before swinging toward Hannah's side. Hannah yelped, trying to dodge, but her dagger had a mind of its own. She jabbed forward, parrying the strike and twisting it, sending the sword flying out of Dee's hand. It nailed a tree, vibrating slightly at the impact.

Dee stared at Hannah, looking surprised and slightly offended.

Ara peeked through her fingers, alarmed.

Hannah watched them both, mouth agape, as she tried to wrap her mind around what had just happened.

"How did you just do that?" Ara said, cutting through the awkward silence.

"I... don't know?" Hannah glanced down at her hand, then at the dagger. Though the evening sky had started to dim, the jagged edges of crystal seemed to shine brighter, oblivious to the darkening atmosphere.

Dee turned and wrenched her sword out of the tree. She watched it melt back into the ring before saying. "Maybe Hannah just has skills we don't know of."

"No, it feels more like the blade is controlling *me*, rather than the opposite." Hannah hesitated, contemplating, then slid the dagger into Ozzie's holster. Instantly, the muscles in her arm screamed, heavy and unused to fighting. She sucked in a sharp breath and reached for the dagger. The pain died off.

"The dagger is giving me the fighting powers," Hannah concluded, letting go with a wince. "And thank you," She told Ozzie begrudgingly, now realizing why the holster had been gifted to her.

"Hannah, stop talking to magical objects. Take a look at where we are." Ara told her, brushing past.

Hannah plopped Ozzie back into the pouch and looked around. They were on the edge of what appeared to be a line of closed stores. As Hannah attempted to make out what the shops were called, flashing lights illuminated a tall building.

"Dragoncake Grocery?" Dee asked skeptically, reading the sign again just to confirm. Hannah's eyes fell on the sign right underneath it, which read:

24/7 Grocery Store! All you need! Free food samples!

Her stomach lurched in desperation, and hunger took over before the rational side of her brain calmed down. Instead, she focused on the tiny cartoon fire surrounding a glowing green jewel. The logo was an odd choice, but flashy, and good for attracting customers.

Dee spoke first. "Can we go there?"

She and Hannah both shared twin looks of hunger before glancing at Ara for approval. She frowned and shook her head.

"But *whyyyy?*" Dee whined, gesturing to the building.

"No money? Is that why?" Hannah said, reading Ara's expression.

"We don't need money for FREE samples," Dee looked at the sign again, desperately.

"And?" Ara said sternly, "What if they ask us to check out to leave the store? Then what will you do?"

Dee ran her thumb over her ring, not even bothering to wait before the sword materialized in her hand before brandishing it. "We are three teenagers with weapons. *Weapons.*"

"We want to eat their food, not disembowel them," Hannah interjected, casting a cautionary glance toward Ara before shooting a pointed one at Dee. Dee pretended like she didn't see that.

Ara turned it over in her head, pondering it. Hannah's heart flared, triumphant. If the seed had been planted, surely it would grow.

Ara could tell she was fighting a losing battle as both her friends looked at her, giving her their best *We promise we'll behave* faces. Ara sniffed, unconvinced.

"I'll take that as a yes!" Dee reached for Ara's hand and started to drag her across the street. Hannah quickly grabbed their packs and ran up to her friends, who, by now, had started to snap at each other again.

At least they'd lasted twenty seconds, Hannah thought, sighing.

***

After the dimming sky, the bright fluorescent lights of Dragoncake Grocery burned into their faces, blinding them momentarily. As their vision cleared, Dee gasped, darting over to a small stall that appeared to have tiny cheesecake samples in it. Dee grabbed one sitting in a small plate of waxy paper and popped it into her mouth, euphoria shining on her face immediately.

"Welcome to Dragoncake Grocery, ma'am," An oily voice said. Hannah and Ara jumped. To their side was a dwarf man leaning against the rows of grocery store carts.

"Thank you," Ara said, reaching over and grabbing a basket hesitantly. He nodded.

"This is the bakery section of the store, but if you go that way–" He pointed to a distant row of shelves to the left, "–you will see the rest of the grocery."

"Oh... thanks," Ara said, her expression still doubtful. Hannah tried for a friendly smile, relieved when the man nodded and trudged off. Ara watched him leave before shoving the basket back and grabbing her phone out of her pocket much more violently than necessary.

"Where's Dee?" She asked, not bothering to look up as she tapped something on her phone.

"Um . . ." Hannah looked around, spotting her friend at some other sample stall. As much as she wanted to join her, Hannah was also curious as to what Ara was doing. Her stomach growled in protest.

"Dee's eating something else," Hannah said, watching her friend grab something off a counter.

Dee walked back, beaming. "The samples in this place are delicious," she remarked, stuffing a small tortilla covered in nacho sauce into her mouth. Hannah felt her lips twitch with a smile, but the feeling was too short-lived. Ara examined her phone, frowning at the screen. In the bright lights that washed the store, her face seemed to take on a paler tinge, or it might've been the lack of food they'd consumed.

"What's wrong?" Hannah's throat felt dry.

"There's something up with this place, and I don't know what," Ara insisted, redirecting her attention to her phone screen. They all fell silent, the only noise was the day-to-day bustle from the people and the occasional tapping of Ara's fingers against the keyboard. Hannah wandered over to the aisle where Dee was, pulling Ara with her.

"I think I found something," Ara started.

"Oh, this ought to be good," Dee scoffed. She grabbed two more samples from a counter and handed one to Hannah, who accepted the treat gratefully. Dee popped hers in her mouth and rolled her eyes. "Now what? The store is run by magical crab monsters or something?"

Ara didn't reply. Instead, if possible, her skin turned even paler. Hannah paused, lowering the sample from her dry lips.

"What happened?"

Ara looked like she was going to be sick. "This is... not a real shop," She murmured, her eyes scanning whatever text on her phone. She glanced up, her frown deepening.

"It does not show on any pages, and when I searched for the logo, nothing showed up," Ara moistened her lips. Hannah's heart thumped.

Dee still looked oddly at ease. "So? Maybe this store is new, or its website is still being made. You can't judge by not being able to find it online."

Hannah stilled. "The monocle,"

"What?"

"Ara, get the monocle!"

Ara reached for the lens dangling down from its golden chain. Frowning, Ara peered through the glass, spinning around in a slow circle. Horror appeared on her features, and she let the monocle swing back down, looking stunned.

"There's poison," She whispered, wary of any employees nearby.

Dee's smug smirk disappeared into a frown. "What?"

"They're trying to poison everyone," Ara murmured.

"What? That's crazy. How could they even poison everyone?" A tense laugh came from Dee.

There was a beat of silence before Ara whispered, "The samples,"

Hannah's grip loosened on the waxy paper in shock, and the little treat tumbled to the floor. She hadn't eaten any, right? Neither had Ara and–

Dee

She whirled around to meet Dee's eyes, whose expression remained still with the ghost of her smile, as horror crept on, inching and twisting her features. Her eyes widened. Her face went slack.

She looked sick.

DIANA

Dee felt her insides turning to jelly as arguments crawled into her mouth, but she swallowed them down. Something cold swirled up in her stomach, and she felt like retching. Again, she gulped the overwhelming feelings down.

Just keep calm... Just keep steady... Everything is fine...

Her vision started to flicker in and out sporadically. She felt her brain fogging up. Her heart beat before her vision dimmed completely, and she felt herself fall to the floor.

Then nothing.

CHAPTER 11

HANNAH

A strangled scream exited Hannah's throat before Ara clamped a hand on her mouth. Hannah fell silent, gasping, at the sight of Dee's rigid, comatose state. Or that's what she assumed. When Ara released her, she kneeled, pressing her ear against Dee's chest. Her heart was still beating. Hannah released a sigh of relief before Ara pulled her back.

"We have to pretend everything is fine," She hissed, sending scattered, furtive glances nearby, "So that we can escape safely and get an antidote."

Hannah nodded, in a daze, peering down at Dee again. She snapped her focus back on Ara.

"What do we do first?" She asked.

"We need to find a way to find out about an antidote, but we can't tip them off." Ara's gaze softened as she slipped into thought.

"We can't let them find out about Dee, though," Hannah said. She glanced down at Dee again, her heart squeezing. How long had it been already? How long would Dee last?

"Yeah... but how would we do that...?" Ara blanched. Hannah followed her gaze, fear clambering in her throat. The dwarf man was making his way over to the aisle they were in, a friendly smile plastered on his pale face. His black hair shone in the dizzying lights, matching the ominous glint in his eyes. It was hard to feel threatened by a man shorter than them, but something about him gave Hannah the heebie-jeebies.

"Quick, we need to pretend everything's fine," Ara said. Hannah could practically see the clockwork turning in her head.

"We can't hide Dee anywhere soon enough," she said, ducking her head into the other aisle to peer from side to side.

Hannah bit her lip. "Then we have to pretend like she's not, y'know," She gestured to Dee's pathetic form.

"But *how?*" Ara said, hysteria tinting her voice.

Hannah turned it over in her head furiously, glancing at the man who had stopped to assist someone. That would buy them a few minutes at least.

A sudden, stupid thought came to her.

"No, ugh, that's so cliche," Hannah muttered, stooping to prop her friend up on the side of the shelf. Dee's head lolled to the side almost comically.

"What are you doing?" Ara asked, kneeling to assist her, although, for the first time, Hannah saw her look bewildered.

"I know this is really, really dumb," Hannah dug through her bag furiously, discarding whatever useless items she found behind her, "But we have no other choice."

"What should I do?" Ara asked, pausing to glance at the dwarf man.

Hannah faced her, fear clear upon her features. "He's walking here again, isn't he?"

Ara swallowed. "Yeah, but no pressure though," She offered a weak smile that Hannah barely returned.

"I found it!" Hannah extracted a pair of sunglasses from her bag and tucked them into her pocket. "Okay, now make Dee stand up."

They stooped down and lifted her into a standing position. Her head slumped forward, and Hannah gritted her teeth.

"Now lean her against the shelf," Hannah slowly released Dee, Ara still gripping her shoulders while pressing her against the shelf so she wouldn't fall.

"Okay." In a swift motion, Hannah stuck the sunglasses on Dee's face. She stepped back to scrutinize her work. Dee's face tipped back slightly, propped up against the sharp edge of the shelf. Hannah quickly added a more comfortable support by placing a loaf of bread behind Dee's neck. Her body was tilted awkwardly, but hopefully, with Hannah and Ara flanking either side of her, it would hardly be noticeable.

The small pitter-patter of the dwarf man's sleek shoes jolted her out of her thoughts. She joined Dee's other side and pretended to scroll on her phone as the man peeked into the aisle.

"Hello, everything okay? I thought I heard a scream," He squinted at the three girls. ". . . Why is she wearing sunglasses?"

He gestured towards Dee.

Hannah bit her lip. "Um... the bright lights of the store hurt her eyes. She's kind of sensitive, you see," She added, hoping she wasn't sweating from keeping Dee up.

The man looked doubtful. "Oh dear . . . I'm sorry. I wish I could dim the lights, but I'm afraid I may not have clearance for that."

Dee, as expected, was silent.

He glanced at Ara and Hannah peculiarly.

"Uh, she's deaf," Hannah said.

"And mute," Ara added, attempting what was meant to be a friendly smile.

"And I'm pretty sure I heard the scream there," Hannah realized she couldn't point to any general direction while supporting Dee, so she jerked her head to the right, hoping he'd get the message.

He looked thoroughly baffled, which counted as an accomplishment in Hannah's world.

"I see... Bye then," He scurried off. Hannah forced a smile until he was completely out of sight. Then she let out a liberating breath of air and stepped forward. Dee's knees crumpled, and Ara grabbed her shoulders before she face-planted. Hannah sighed and lowered Dee to the ground before she sank to the floor, letting out another labored breath.

"That worked," Ara panted, leaning against the shelf, "That was probably the dumbest thing I've ever taken part in, but it worked."

Hannah wasn't sure whether to feel offended or proud.

Ara's breathing calmed down. "Next step: find an antidote."

***

Hannah's fingers ran across her phone, tapping furiously. Ara would glance down at Dee occasionally, scrolling on her phone, no doubt searching for symptoms. So far, Dee's skin had taken on a light blueish pallor. Hannah's stomach lurched unpleasantly. Her eyes scanned Dee up and down as her heart felt a tight squeeze.

We'll save you, Hannah vowed, *I can't lose anyone else.*

Ara let out a grunt of frustration. "There's nothing here!" She switched her phone off and dragged a hand through her hair. Hannah fisted her pendant, racking her brain.

Save Dee.

She racked her brain. "What if... we snuck into the staff room?"

Ara pondered it. "We'd need to be out of there in half an hour then, lest a security team spots us on the cameras,"

Hannah wrinkled her nose. "Did you just say 'lest'?"

Ara rolled her eyes. "Is that really what you should be focusing on?"

"Right, carry on,"

Ara rolled her eyes again before continuing. "One of us needs to stay with Dee to keep her safe. Seeing as you're, *surprisingly*, the friendlier and–" She coughed, "the more charismatic out of the two of us, you should stay in case someone finds you,"

Hannah blinked. "Was that your form of a compliment?"

"Maybe." Ara shrugged, but her eyes twinkled sincerely. Hannah grinned. She'd take it.

Ara's expression shifted into seriousness again. "I should take up to fifteen minutes. If I take longer... well, it's safe to assume something went wrong."

The words resonated in Hannah's head for a second before they clicked together.

"Wait... you're sacrificing yourself?" Hannah grimaced at the same time Ara flinched at her words.

"No... I'll be fine," Ara seemed to be convincing herself as well as Hannah.

"Wait. Hold on. Backtrack," Hannah blurted, holding out her hands as if her three statements weren't enough, "How do we even know there is real danger besides the police catching you?"

"Hm, good point," Ara grabbed the monocle, took a deep breath, and stepped out of the aisle.

Hannah watched her go, a mix of dread and anticipation winding in her stomach.

AMARA

She pretended to browse the different types of bread while shooting glances through the monocle everywhere. Other than the small spots of poison in the samples, nothing odd happened. She whirled around, relief replacing her recent fear, when she gasped. Rooted to the spot, Ara peeked through the flimsy shard of glass, making sure she wasn't hallucinating.

Where there was originally an employee standing was a specimen that looked like a hybrid of a crocodile and a wolf. It seemed to be rearranging the muffins carefully, peering out of its eye slits. Its nails were jagged and sharp, making Ara wonder how it didn't pierce the plastic containers. Its teeth looked even more feral, sharp canine teeth jutting out of the sides of its mouth.

She gaped at the hideous creature before clearing her head and leaving.

As she made her way back to the aisle where her friends were, Ara ran into *him*.

The short man grinned at her, only now, he was neither short, nor a man.

Now he was much taller than Ara was, and more in touch with his wolf side than the other employees, but traces of crocodile parts still showed. He smiled.

"Can I help you?"

Her breath hitched as Ara realized she was still holding up the monocle. With a jolt, she let it dangle back down. His appearance returned to normal.

"No, thank you," She said through clenched teeth. She snaked around him and took off, walking briskly, purposefully going in the other direction before backtracking and sneaking back to Hannah.

"Well?" Hannah asked. Ara almost didn't want to tell her. She was still processing it herself.

She took in a gulp of air. "There's danger. The employees are these 'crocodile-wolf' hybrids in disguise." Ara shuddered.

Hannah dragged a hand down her face, her optimism clearly fading. She glanced at Dee's form, and her expression turned slightly more determined.

"Okay," She said, "We can do this. We've dealt with worse."

Hannah glanced at Ara. Her eyes were bright, containing all the unspoken hopes dropped on Amara's head, who wished she could resolve them all. Instead, Ara took a breath, already formulating a plan.

HANNAH

Ara inhaled, calming herself. "I'll go in and search for an antidote in the staff room for our Sleeping Beauty over there," She gestured toward Dee, and a hint of a smirk flickered over her lips. But it was short-lived.

Hannah felt her resolve. She inhaled deeply. "Okay," She said, proud of herself for not shaking. Fear clawed at her nerves, but it must've been nothing compared to the terror Ara was feeling, though she disguised it well.

Hannah pulled her into a short hug.

"I'll see you again," Ara murmured against her shoulder.

"Yeah, you sure will," Hannah promised.

Ara offered a small, confident smile before turning away.

Hannah watched her put up her hair and put on the sunglasses, trying to mask her identity. Smart. Ara hoped she'd get the antidote safely.

She also hoped it wasn't too much to ask.

CHAPTER 12

AMARA

Ara's hands itched with discomfort. She mentally reprimanded herself. Even though she wouldn't have the stomach to harm anyone, a weapon would be useful against the hybrids.

Ara had watched countless of her dad's action movies, and she was sure that if given the chance, she'd be able to figure out how to work a gun. Unfortunately, at the moment, there was no chance of getting one.

She dodged around the shelves, ignoring the increasing stack of nerves in her stomach. Ara kept her eyes peeled for any form of threat, but the employees minded their own business, and the dwarf man was nowhere to be seen. Her eyes latched onto the hygiene area, debating for a few minutes before grabbing dental supplies, just in case they'd need them. She crept along the side wall, pretending to examine the different kinds of dairy products, when Ara spotted two gray double doors labeled Staff Room.

She scanned the aisle for any employees. It was empty. She stood on her tiptoes and peered through the small glass windows into the Staff Room. Nothing but crates of boxes were there.

Ara clenched her teeth, taking a small, sharp breath of air before she entered the room.

Immediately, her gaze fell upon the small security cameras in the corners of the room. She straightened her posture and her erratic behavior, pretending like she belonged. Acting wasn't Ara's strong suit, but she'd have to make do.

Somehow.

She strutted past the large boxes, occasionally peering into a few. Just crates of produce met her eyes.

Puffing out an irritated breath, Ara slunk to the back of the room. How much time had passed?

She peered into a box. Nothing. She sighed, blowing out a loose strand of hair from her face, and went to lean on the wall, discouraged.

Her back hit a flimsy material. Startled, she spun around, surprised to see a thick silicon slab nailed to the panel. Ara felt the material, examining the edges. She crouched to the bottom, peeling some of the slab upwards, revealing another room.

Ara ducked underneath, crawled inside, and then sprang up again. Frigid air swirled around her, and she crossed her arms in hopes of staying warm.

This must be where they stock the dairy products.

She felt a pained laugh bubbling up, but smothered it. Ara couldn't believe she was thinking of the Dragoncake Grocery as a normal store.

The thought of the crocodile-wolves immediately sobered her up. Ara tucked the sunglasses away and reached for her monocle, ignoring the cold, and held it up to her eye. Magical gray haze was thickening. She followed it tentatively at first, then quickened her pace. Ara was met with another silicon slab, which she hastily ducked underneath.

After the cold of the dairy room, Ara almost felt blasted away by the heat in this one. As she got back up to her feet, Ara's breath caught in her throat.

Almost as though he was waiting for her, the originally short man was in his *other* form, even though Ara wasn't looking through her monocle. His smile widened as he spotted Ara, his canines glinting in the dim light of the generator room. Next to him posed a giant, coiled snake-lady. A forked tongue slid out of her lips. She bared her fangs, which were almost as big as Ara's arms.

Ara forced herself to look away from the menacing glint in the snake lady's eyes and scanned the room for anything useful since these monsters clearly wanted more than a chat.

Out of the corner of her eyes, Ara saw little corked vials stacked into a box, labeled *antidote*. She swallowed. She'd have to talk her way out of this since Hannah wasn't there to do it for her.

Hannah. She'd be very worried by now. Ara tried not to let that distract her.

"Hello, Ara," The man said.

She swallowed again. "Hi," Then after a beat, "What are you?"

The snake lady reared up higher. "Come on, Troy," Her forked tongue slid out of her mouth, "Get to the point. I'm not waiting forever."

The man, Troy, cast an irritated glance at the snake-lady. "She just got here." His voice had gone from oily to deep and menacing, but the snake lady barely glanced at him.

"If you're busy, I could come later. I just need to grab something, then I'll be off." Ara interjected, proud of her voice for not shaking.

Troy snapped his focus back to Ara, and he grinned. "You're not going anywhere."

"And you're gonna make for a *tasssty* meal once we're done with you," hissed the Snake.

Ara furrowed her brows, feeling a ridiculous amount of indignation flare up. She stiffened. "Okay. Well, since I'm here, enlighten me," She glared at both monsters, "What are you, and what is your dumb plan of poisoning people?"

Troy raised an eyebrow. "Dumb plan? But it worked perfectly, well, almost."

He smirked. "If only you and Hannah had eaten the samples too." He drawled, stepping closer.

"It would have made everything so much easier, right, Filisea?"

"It would," Filisea agreed, slithering forward.

"Answer me," Ara snapped.

Troy rolled his eyes. "Maybe ask your friend– Dee, was it?" He smirked. "She'll tell you all about Melumora. Our home.

"For the next part of your question, here's the answer: the people who faint from the poison are sent to be turned into crystal statues. Any more queries, Miss Interviewer?"

Ara's eyebrows shot up. "No giant speech?"

Troy looked her up and down with distaste. "No?"

"Okay, then," Ara muttered. She'd been counting on him monologuing– like most villains were supposed to do– about all the deeds he did, hoping it would buy her some time.

Now what?

Ara glanced at the antidotes again, inspecting her chances. She could dart over and grab one vial, but Filisea would be able to catch her. There were large crates stacked on the sides of the walls and in the corners. They looked sealed shut, so there was no hope of finding a weapon inside; however, packaging peanuts and stuffing littered the floor. She could duck back behind the silicon tarp, but it was unlikely she'd make it far before Troy or Filisea caught up with her.

The heat from the room was starting to make her sweat, her glasses slipping on her nose. She glared at the vents for distributing the painfully warm air.

The heat.

Her brain quickly dissolved into a frenzy, trying to gather facts. The maximum heat for reptiles was around a hundred degrees, or above. Filisea appeared to be a crystalback rattlesnake. An enlarged, intelligent one, but still a reptile. Troy was also part reptile, part wolf. The maximum heat for them would also vary around one hundred degrees Fahrenheit. She could work with that.

There were five vents around the room, each positioned in a consecutive line above the monsters, near the ceiling. It was much too high for Ara to reach, but with the crates...

She refocused on the monsters, who were watching her with grins on their faces.

"Finally realized the sssssituation?" Filisea cackled.

Ara ignored her and spurred herself into a run. Troy tilted his head from side to side, receiving satisfying cracks before turning to Ara's running figure with a malevolent glint in his eyes. "What are you trying to do now...?"

He grinned and took off behind her, Filisea at his side.

Ara didn't dare to look back. She sprinted over to the box of antidotes and grabbed one corked vial, tucking it into her pocket before she rushed over to the stacked crates. Ara clambered over them, one by one, making her way to the vents. She knelt, scooping up packing peanuts and stuffing as much as she could fit.

The monsters paused, intrigued, as they stared up at her. Ara ignored them and started to stuff the vents. When she finished, Ara glanced back, feeling her heart race. The monsters stared up at her, confused.

"And what was that supposed to do?" Troy grumbled. The temperature in the room had started to drop slightly. Ara felt a surge of confidence and haste warring with each other.

Filisea rounded on Troy. "I'm not waiting any longer," She sneered, stealing a hungry look at Ara, "I'm going up there,"

She started to bend her long body into a U-shape, about to crawl onto the crates, before Troy grabbed her tail and swung her back.

She hissed, displaying her foot-long fangs, ready to sink them into Troy's shoulder. Ara flinched.

"Hold on, now," Troy spread his fingers in hopes of halting his snake friend. "She has nowhere to go. She'll come down soon enough,"

Filisea still had a murderous glint in her eyes, but she paused and hissed at Ara.

Despite her fear, Ara sneered right back, her stomach twisting with uncontrolled indignance and anxiety. Was her plan working? By now, the temperature had dropped much more, and she could see the vents struggling to keep the heavy loads of packaging stuff she'd blocked in.

Troy stared at her, smirking. "What are you gonna do now? Fight us?"

Ara knew there was no way she could fight them, especially without a weapon, but maybe she could feign confidence. "Sure, why not? All I have to do is beat a leather rope and a puppy," She taunted, pleased when anger twisted their horrible features.

But then Troy's voice turned eerily calm, and he laughed off his anger in a single sharp bark. "You miscalculated," His eyes narrowed, "You didn't consider the Dragon."

Ara's stomach dropped, and a swarm of confusion clouded her brain. "What?"

Before Troy could answer, the vents exploded, shooting out the packaging and blasts of hot air. Something registered in Ara's brain: this was the part where she was supposed to run out and duck into the dairy room, but her feet refused to move. She could only watch, praying that the air would be too hot for them to handle.

The temperature shot up, and sweat started to bead up on her forehead. At first, the monsters looked around in annoyance, but then Troy's chest started to sag and Filisea uncoiled in a desperate attempt to get cooler. Sweat soaked the back of Ara's shirt. Her heart shot up...

Then plunged right back down in disappointment. The heat had been enough to halt the monsters, but it hadn't been hot enough to kill them.

However, she was still alive too, so that was a plus point.

Troy glared up, gritting his teeth. He snapped his fingers, and the sound resounded in the large room, which began to rumble. Ara gulped and crouched down on the crate, ready to spring off to the next one if necessary.

Something green started to glow in the corner of the room. It levitated off the crate it was on and flew to the center of the room. It wasn't Ozzie, which caused another wave of disappointment, and when Ara peered closer, it looked to be a giant gemstone, the side of a softball.

Thick green smoke started to pour from the gem, filling the room. When it had dispersed, a gasp caught in Ara's throat.

Where there was the jewel, there was now a creature with the build of a lizard, except it was so tall that its head reached the ceiling. Two leathery wings remained folded at its sides, and as it puffed out a breath of air, smoke plumed from its nostrils.

Ara couldn't believe her eyes.

She was staring at a dragon.

Its back was to her, but it slowly stomped around, fury in its beady eyes. Ara's gut sank, wonder replaced by realization. She was going to die, right here and now. One breath of fire from the dragon, and she'd burn.

Tears surfaced, but she blinked them back. No point in crying, although the heat had caused her hair to plaster to her scalp and brought moisture to her face. In the corner of her eyes, she saw Filisea and Troy smirking, though the heat had gotten to them too. They looked deranged and slightly withered.

The dragon's jaw unlocked, and Ara could see fire churning in its throat, ready to be blasted. She squeezed her eyes shut, bracing herself for the impact.

"Why. Are. You. So. Dang. Heavy?!"

Ara peeled one eye open. She knew that voice. The dragon paused, turning back to see the intruder.

Hannah fell through the silicon door, Dee's unconscious body rolling beside her. Hannah pulled Dee in, pausing when the heat reached her. She glanced up, and her expression melted away into pure terror.

"What in the–?" She spotted Ara above on the crates, and her face contorted into confusion, then horror as the realization hit her.

"Ara!" She screamed, dropping Dee's arm and springing to her feet.

"Hannah!" Ara pointed below, indicating Troy and Filisea, who looked taken aback. Hannah paled, beads of sweat dotting her forehead. Her gaze flickered to the side, spotting the antidote crate, before snapping back at the scene.

"Liu, you take care of the blonde girl. We'll take care of the newcomers," Troy grinned, stepping forward, Filisea beside him. Liu, the dragon, huffed and turned back to face Ara, only she wasn't there.

Ara jumped down the stack of crates, one by one, ignoring the way the heat stung her face. She sprinted toward Hannah, gritting her teeth as her wounded ankle smarted.

Liu paused and glared at Ara with renewed fury. Troy and Filisea flanked him on either side.

"Well, looksss like it'll be two on three," Filisea cooed, coiling up. Ara turned to Hannah, who glared at Filisea with surprising confidence.

"No, it won't," Hannah said, "You missed our friend there!" She whipped her finger in a random direction. The monsters turned around hastily. Hannah, looking grateful that another one of her dumb ideas had worked, took off toward the antidotes. She grabbed one— before Ara could tell her about the one in her pocket— and ran back just as the monsters whipped back around.

"That'ssss enough sssstalling!" Filisea reared up and struck. Hannah narrowly deflected one of her fangs with her blade after tossing her vial of antidote toward Ara. She took off running, hoping to distract the monsters from her friends. Troy and Filisea followed her. Liu still glared at Ara and bent down, ready to incinerate her.

"Come on, come on!" Ara uncorked the vial with shaky fingers and shoved the magic blue liquid down Dee's throat.

Nothing happened.

"Ugh! The one time I need you!" She shouted, glaring at Dee. She glanced up again, the heat sending her damp hair into her eyes before she brushed it away. The ball of fire in Liu's throat expanded.

Dee's eyes flickered open. She blinked and gasped, shooting up to her feet and grabbing Ara, pushing both of them out of the way right before fire shot at the back wall, burning the area where they were a second ago.

Ara and Dee tumbled away, scrambling to a stop. Liu blinked, standing up again and turning.

"What just happened?!" Dee shrieked, jumping to her feet. Ara copied her, though she didn't know how much longer she'd last. Her adrenaline was fading.

"Guys!" Hannah warned. She sprinted toward them, Troy and Filisea still following close behind. They understood and made a beeline for the exit.

Liu unlocked his jaws again, fire emitting from the depths, burning the entire storeroom. The heat had probably gone well above a hundred degrees. Ara dared to look behind, seeing that Filisea had collapsed, too weak to continue. Troy still pursued Hannah, but they both had slowed down.

The heat was unbearable. Dee and Ara ducked under the silicon tarp. Ara stuck her head back in to watch for Hannah. Her friend had stowed her dagger back in its sheath and reached her hand out, her fingers almost grazing the silicon. Ara reached to grab Hannah's palm just as she prepared to jump through . . .

In one final, desperate lunge, Troy reached forward and sank his canines into Hannah's shoulder, right where it met her neck.

The scream that escaped Hannah's lips could've broken glass. Even Troy ducked away, blood coating his mouth, to cover his ears, though the damage had been done. He collapsed, a triumphant smile on his bloody face.

Ara pulled her friend desperately through the door and screamed, "Orb, *Advance!*".

H. D. GIDWANI

Ozzie's smoke crackled from Hannah's pouch.
Blinding white light swirled, washing them away.

CHAPTER 13

DIANA

"**D**ee!"

"Mmm,"

"Dee, wake up!"

"What-?" Dee shot up with a gasp, and her eyes focused on her surroundings. They were surrounded by trees. The sky was black, with no stars twinkling. No moon shining down on them either. A shiver ran up her spine.

"Are you awake?"

Ara's face looked ghostly in her pale phone light, her blue eyes watery. She was cradling Hannah's head, murmuring soft words of encouragement.

And Hannah...

Panic jutted through Dee's bones, electrifying her heart. The junction of Hannah's shoulder and neck was covered by Ara's hands as she attempted to staunch the bleeding. But redness still oozed out of her fingers, bathing them while she kept the phone propped up awkwardly. Ozzie's light was flickering unevenly.

Hannah's face was slack and pale. Beads of perspiration and dirt were streaked over her face. Her eyes seemed far away, her breathing ragged.

She was on the verge of death.

"No, no, no–" Dee launched to her feet, pulse thundering.

"Diana," Ara's voice trembled, as unsteady as her hands, "There's a little shack behind those trees. Help me take Hannah there."

Without a question, Dee stooped to help hoist Hannah. Together, she and Ara half-dragged, half-carried the dying girl.

Tears swam in Dee's eyes as she rapped against the rotting door. She waited exactly two seconds before desperation urged her to shove the door open and pull them inside.

They laid Hannah down on the couch. Panic was soaring through Dee's nerves by the time they'd stopped moving.

"Hannah, hold on. Just hold on a moment." Dee felt flimsy words slip her mouth, dulling once meeting open air. Violent sobs threatened to rack through her body as she and Ara switched places. Fingers against Hannah's wound, Dee craned her neck to see Ara.

"Hurry!" She screeched, turning back. Hannah took a shuddering, ragged breath. Her eyes momentarily flicked to Dee's, and tears pooled in her hazel eyes.

"My parents," She whimpered, imploring Dee to understand. "Tell them."

"You will tell them yourself," Dee promised, her vision blurring through tears, "When we save them."

Hannah's eyes were glassy, but she nodded, staring off into the distance again. "Tell them..."

Ara had started to take warbling, small breaths in as she dug into her pocket and fumbled for the original antidote vial. Dee's hopes shot up, combining with loosely tied logic.

It was magic, right?

It would work on Hannah, *right?*

Ara's hands were trembling violently as she uncorked the shimmering vial. Despite the shuddering, she managed to part Hannah's lips and tip the blue liquid in her mouth gently.

Hannah swallowed it obediently, and for a moment, her vision cleared.

A full breath entered her lungs.

But Dee's imagination must've rewritten what she'd seen because, in the next moment, Hannah's eyes drifted shut.

She exhaled.

Ozzie's light blinked out.

Ara dropped the empty vial. It hit the ground with a dull clink. She stared for a moment longer, frozen in place. Ara sank to the ground, legs crossed, eyes hollow and empty, staring at a corpse.

She didn't move.

Neither did Dee.

Her vision swam with futile tears. Her throat burned.

She watched her fingers return to her body, drenched in blood. She couldn't bring herself to do anything other than stare at it.

Tears slipped down her cheeks, hot and silent, as something tight and awful ballooned in her chest.

It was her fault.

She'd eaten the stupid samples.

She was the idiot who got poisoned.

She wrapped her arms around herself, knees pulled up to her chest, trying to fold into something smaller than this moment.

In movies, this was the part where the hero clenched their fists, screamed to the sky, and vowed revenge. Rose from the ashes, or whatever.

Dee just... sat there.

Heavy. Useless. Empty.

Her chest ached, but her brain was too loud. Playing it over and over: the way Hannah's breath left her body. The way the light in her eyes had died.

She'd never forget it.

Not in a thousand years.

Dee had killed her friend.

Ara suddenly gasped. "Look!"

Dee's head jolted up, tears pausing to register her shock.

Blue light shone through Hannah's veins and injuries, healing them. It swarmed through her skin, alighting her body. Ozzie's smoke reappeared along with it.

Dee glanced down at her fingers, noticing all the blood was gone.

The light engulfed Hannah, momentarily concealing her before it faded.

Her eyes fluttered open.

Pure, unfiltered shock seized Dee, leaving her powerless. She just watched, dumbfounded, as the life poured back into those familiar hazel eyes.

"What–?" Hannah blinked a few times and turned her head to the side, staring at a stunned Dee and Ara. She raised an eyebrow.

"Why are you guys staring at me?"

Dee felt a billion words swirling on her tongue, but none came forth. She felt petrified, afraid that if she moved, this would all be a ruse. That Hannah would drop dead again. Ara, for the first time, looked speechless.

Hannah sat up and poked each of them in turn. "You guys are starting to creep me out now. Are you okay?"

"Are we *okay*?" Ara asked hoarsely.

"We're spec-spectacular," Dee stammered. They glanced at each other in disbelief.

Hannah swung her feet off the couch. "What happened?"

Simultaneously, Ara and Dee wrapped their arms around Hannah, crushing her into a hug. Hannah flailed underneath them at first, then returned it gingerly, as if afraid to trigger them.

"There, there, easy," She slowly backed out from their embrace. Dee used the time to scrub the remaining tears off her face, noting how heavy her eyes felt.

"You..." Ara grasped Hannah's wrist and felt for a pulse, letting it fall back down after she'd found it.

"You had... You had..." Ara grimaced as if she couldn't bring herself to say it.

Hannah raised an eyebrow. "If you don't want to tell me right now, you don't have to."

Ara sank, nodding gratefully, wiping her face free from tears and grime.

Dee staggered to her feet, swaying slightly as the blood rushed to her head. Following shock-induced instinct, she grabbed the moth-eaten couch for support, turning around to survey their surroundings.

The living room had a couch, a small, sooty, brick cavity where there used to be a fireplace, and worn photo frames, the pictures inside them long withered. A small lamp hung so low that Dee nearly walked into it. When she tried the switch, the light barely flickered on before sputtering out.

Stupid lamp.

She fumbled for her watch, turning on the flashlight as she padded down the corridor. She opened a wooden door, grateful to see a tiny bathroom.

"Hey, Ara! I found a bathroom!" Dee called, surveying the old tiles and rusted shower. She studied her reflection in the smudged, slightly cracked mirror. Her eyes were rimmed red, and her hair was tangled. A tentative, haunted smile turned up the corners of her lips. She couldn't tell what was worse– how she looked or how she felt.

"Really? Gimme a second!" Ara shouted back.

Dee heard some scuffling and a thud against metal before Ara's triumphant voice called back, "There's still some water in this old tank! Try the sink!"

Dee twisted the knob. A few clunks echoed, and a distant sound of water swished around before sputtering out in the sink.

"It works!" Dee shouted.

"Turn it off!" Ara yelled back.

Dee rolled her eyes but did as told. She trudged down the corridor again, finding herself inside a bedroom with an old, slightly dusty bed. No doubt there were bugs, but they could easily be brushed off.

A sudden realization crept upon her. She gasped, bursting into the living room. Ara turned to her, furrowing her eyebrows.

"What?"

"We- the bedroom- it's nighttime- what?" Dee spluttered.

Hannah cocked her head to the side. "Huh?"

Dee groaned. "Don't tell me we have to sleep here tonight?"

Ara raised an eyebrow. "What do you suggest we do then?"

"I don't know, get an Uber or something? Why do we have to stay here?" Dee scratched her arms uncomfortably, wondering how many species of insects were currently staring at them.

"Look, I don't like it either, but wouldn't it be easier to rest tonight than continue our journey tomorrow?" Ara slapped Dee's hand back to its side. "Just find a bed. Or the ground, if that's easier,"

Dee bristled, opening her mouth to retort.

"I'm tired," Hannah interjected with a meaningful glance at them.

Ara shot one last glare at Dee before turning away.
Dee made a face before gingerly creeping away to the
bedroom.

She studied the bed before pulling off the covers. She
groaned and used her sword to scrape off the dead– and alive–
bugs. After deeming it somewhat insect-free, Dee crawled into
the bed.

A sigh of contentment escaped her, and relief crept in.
All thoughts of insects faded away into nothingness as her eyes
drooped close...

And much-needed sleep snatched her away.

***

BANG!

Dee flinched and promptly faceplanted on the floor.
She stayed there a second, sprawled on her stomach, blinking
into the dark. Her neck craned toward the hallway as she
strained to hear.

Silence.

Then—scuttling. And a series of shrill, unholy shrieks.
She held her breath.

More scuttling.

Okay. Time to investigate.

Dee pushed herself to her feet and checked her watch.
1:47 AM.

Seriously?

Who was even awake right now? Hannah and Ara had
knocked out around eleven. So had she.

She tapped her thumb against her ring, and the
familiar weight of her sword shimmered into place in her

hand. With a quiet breath, she crept down the hallway, ears tuned to the weird noises echoing through the house.

She peeked into the living room, then padded toward the kitchen. Something rustled under the tablecloth.

Correction: something large.

Dee flipped on the flashlight embedded in her watch and crouched down, lifting the table cover.

It wasn't a dragon, which was a plus.

But it wasn't better.

The stench hit first, like fish guts and rotten bananas had decided to throw a party in a dumpster.

Then the culprit came into view: a raccoon, blinking up at her with the dazed look of someone who had absolutely no regrets.

"Seriously?" she muttered.

He hissed at her, clearly offended by the intrusion. Dee straightened and grabbed a rusted metal poker by the fireplace. With it, she corralled the creature out. Dee opened the door for him. (Not out of kindness — mostly because she didn't want to deal with the smell.)

"Scram," she said, flapping her hand at the creature.

The raccoon screeched but turned tail and waddled out.

Dee slammed the door, throwing down the poker. "And stay out!"

A croaky voice behind her mumbled, "What happened?"

She turned and found Hannah squinting from the couch. Dee quickly switched off her flashlight.

"There was a raccoon. Don't ask." She crossed the room and sat beside her. "Why are you sleeping out here?"

"I didn't want to get up," Hannah muttered, burrowing back into her makeshift pillow.

"Right," Dee said, though her eyes lingered on her for a beat too long.

Ara appeared in the hallway, her hair a mess, glasses absent. "What was that?"

"Raccoon," Dee said, scowling. She didn't necessarily have anything against the creature, but it woke her up and reeked.

Ara rolled her eyes and padded back to her room without comment.

Hannah yawned, curling deeper into the couch cushions. Dee watched her, something heavy tugging at her ribs.

"Hannah?"

"Mmm?"

"I'm sorry."

One of Hannah's eyes cracked open. "What?"

"I'm sorry," Dee repeated, quieter.

"No, I heard you. But... why?" Hannah sat up slowly.

Dee looked down at her hands, twisting the ring around her finger.

"You... you died," she whispered.

Hannah blinked. "What? Okay—pause. I heard you, but what do you mean?"

Dee didn't look up. "I think you died. The antidote brought you back. But you wouldn't have even needed it if I hadn't—if I hadn't eaten the samples. And—"

"Don't." Hannah placed her hand over Dee's, warm and solid. "It's not your fault. You didn't know. And if you spend all your time staring at the past, you'll miss the future walking right by."

Dee blinked. "That's suspiciously wise for someone who still has to ask which way to hold a map."

Hannah smiled and laid back down. "What can I say? I have a gift with words."

CHAPTER 14

AMARA

The sunlight poured through the window, the half-broken shades useless. Distant noises in the forest echoed: the sounds of birds, insects, and the breeze of wind tousling leaves.

Ara swung herself off the bed and stretched, ignoring the twinge of pain in her ankle. She slipped into her jacket and buttoned it up to her collar, then twisted her hair into a high ponytail. She slid her glasses on her nose, brushed her teeth, and padded down the corridor, euphoria floating through her.

The simplicity of the routine pleased her. No disappointed fathers or reprimanding agents. No snobby tutors or gawking reporters. Just a clean, steady flow of movements.

Ara rounded the corner, expecting to see her friend. "Hannah, you awake– Hannah?"

Ara stopped short. The couch was empty.

"Hannah?" Ara squished the alarm down and headed into Dee's room. The musty, worn area contained Dee only.

Muttering under her breath, Ara backtracked to the main living room. Splinters from the rotted wood bit into her skin as she swung the main door open.

But then her heart relaxed– Hannah was outside, perfectly alive and safe. She was sitting in a patch of grass, offering a clover to a toad, wildflowers in her hair. Ara's lips twitched. Hannah looked peaceful, even a little whimsical.

Ara smiled, not even bothering to mask it. To her face, it felt strange.

She shook her head and marched back to Diana's room, throwing open the moth-eaten curtains.

"Wake up," Ara told her.

Dee grumbled under her breath, glaring through one eye.

"Good morning, Dalila."

"Ugh," Dee sat up and rubbed her eyes. "Morning." She yawned. "How's Hannah?"

Ara lowered herself onto the bed. "She's okay. She's outside, looking much better than... last night."

Silence fell. Both Dee and Ara watched each other, a mutual understanding passing between them.

Hannah was too precious to have dealt with something like this. Ara could still smell the blood that had collected on her hands. The way her eyes flickered shut, sealing out the rest of the world.

If Ara hadn't possessed that second antidote, Hannah wouldn't be with them now.

Dee's lips twitched in a small smile, trying to lighten the mood. "Can I join her outside?"

"No," Ara cleared her head, "Not until you get ready and eat something. Also, don't leave your ring on the side like that. What if you lost it? Keep it with you."

"Okay, *Mom*," Dee mocked, lying down again.

Ara rolled her eyes and yanked the covers off. "Get up," She said, thrusting a spare toothbrush at her.

Dee squinted at it. "Why do *you* have a toothbrush?"

"'Cause I came prepared, and also because I grabbed them at the Dragoncake Grocery," Ara grumbled, "Just hurry up,"

Dee made a face but obeyed. Ara waited outside impatiently, counting down the minutes. Time was scarce, and Ara refused to waste any of it.

When she'd finished, the two of them strolled outside. This time, Hannah was crouched beside a rabbit and petting it.

"Morning, guys!" Hannah exclaimed.

"Where did you find the bunny?" Dee asked, eyeing it suspiciously.

"In the woods. He– or she– put up a tough fight, but I found a way to bring it to me,"

The rabbit chittered in agreement. Dee squinted. It glowered at her and twitched its nose.

"It doesn't like me," Dee decided.

"Hey, you guys," Ara intruded, eyebrows furrowed as she pulled out her phone, "Anyone remember what state the Dragoncake Grocery was in?"

"Ohio," Hannah murmured. She stood up, and the rabbit scampered away.

Ara nodded. "Exactly. But look at what my phone says. Right now we're in... Tennessee?"

"What did Tennes-see?" Hannah asked, a humorous glint in her eyes, "The same thing as Arkansas!"

Ara tore her gaze away to stare at Hannah incredulously. Of all times to crack a joke, she'd chosen now.

"Right. Sorry," Hannah developed a sudden interest in her shoes.

"What do you think, Dora?"

"I think we should stop blabbering about this and find a way to get to Florida," Dee announced, spinning the ring on her finger.

"You're right," Ara said, tucking her phone away. Ara's words were followed closely with regret when Dee brightened.

"Ooh! You just said that I was right," She taunted.

"Ugh," Ara stomped inside the little log cabin, not bothering to check if she was followed.

Ara padded into the main bedroom and set to work, rapping the walls with her knuckles and pressing her ear against them, searching for any hollow spots.

"Watcha doing?" Hannah asked, perplexed.

"I assumed," Ara said suddenly, still repeating the process, "Since someone had lived here before, and all their possessions are still here, they must have had money."

She knocked on the wall, then shook her head and continued to the next spot.

"Now this is a place where the security is not great, so they must have hidden it in a safe and hid the safe in the wall . . ." Ara knocked on the wall, and her face broke into a grin. She slid her fingernails in a small groove and pried a secret panel off the wall. Behind it was a rusty combination safe.

Ara turned back, a little smug once she saw her friends' awestruck faces.

"Dee, get rid of the lock."

"Okay," Dee complied, slicing it off easily with her sword. Inside the safe were stacks of old hundred-dollar bills.

Ara folded it and carefully put it in her pocket.

"That's cool," Hannah remarked, "Although that means whoever lived here needed a better security system."

"Yeah, 'cause imagine a random raccoon came in and found the safe," Dee chuckled.

"Imagine they got their money stolen by a *raccoon*," Hannah giggled.

"That raccoon would be hella rich then,"

"Imagine it pulls up in a limo and Gucci clothes,"

"With a golden chain–"

They doubled over, wheezing.

Ara rubbed her temples, sighing.

Why do I even bother?

She rolled her eyes, which only made them laugh harder, and double-checked she'd grabbed everything. Hannah attempted to place a steadying hand on Dee's shoulder, but the sudden pressure knocked Dee to the ground.

"Okay, that's enough," Ara pressed her lips together— ignoring any impulse of a smile— and hoisted Dee up.

"Okay, okay," Hannah steadied herself, smiling so much it looked like it hurt her face. "Time to go."

CHAPTER 15

HANNAH

Hannah gritted her teeth, her foot falling dangerously close to a loose root. Her feet were throbbing with blisters in her shoes as they stumbled through the weeds and brambles of the massive forest.

She grumbled, biting back the pain. How hard could it have been? They had two phones, both capable of calling an Uber. Only, it is difficult to call for a ride in the middle dense forest. Their only sense of navigation was Ara's phone's GPS because they wanted to save Hannah's phone's battery, which was also barely working without cellular service.

Without warning, guilt started to gnaw on Hannah's insides. She squashed it down, but her mind had already begun to unravel.

Even though the rational part of her knew their situation was Yin's fault, Hannah couldn't help blaming herself. She was putting all their lives at stake and might've even risked one.

Jax. She missed him. More than she'd even admit out loud.

Hannah paused, straightening. The realization struck her before she could process it.

Hannah fumbled for her phone, praying it would work. She dialed his number and held it to her ear.

She counted the rings, chewing her lower lip.

One.

Two.

Three.

Four.

Then–

"Hello?"

Hannah let out a cry of relief. "*Jax!* Are you okay? I'm sorry I couldn't check in before, I was busy. Where are you? Are you safe?" She bit her tongue, letting him speak.

"Hannah? This... isn't Jax. It's me, his father. I arrived from my business trip yesterday." The voice, which Hannah just realized, was much deeper than Jax's.

Her stomach plummeted.

"What– where's Jax?" She held her fingers up and crossed them.

"You haven't heard the news?" He fell silent for a moment, taking a deep breath, "Jax was killed yesterday near a gas station in Ohio."

Hannah's arm fell limp at her side. Her mouth turned dry, as opposed to her eyes, which collected shocked tears. Jax's father mumbled about the details of his son's death, but Hannah barely heard them.

Jax was killed...

Her head ached with the bitter emotions swirling inside. Within a second, Ara and Dee were at her side, asking her what was wrong.

But she could hardly think— hardly breathe— as the words echoed around her head.

She heard Jax's father disconnect the call, and she let her other arm fall limp, too.

Jax was dead.

And it was her fault.

"Snap out of it!" Dee pinched Hannah's arm. Hannah looked at her, noticing the way stress clouded her features.

Another thing that was her fault.

"Hannah, what happened? Please tell us," Ara said, her eyebrows furrowed.

Hannah's voice was hoarse when she whispered, "Jax was killed yesterday."

Their jaws dropped, and shock replaced their confusion. They exchanged sorrowful glances at each other and then looked down at their shoes.

The silence felt suffocating but appropriate. Hannah blinked, surprised to find the tears had disappeared. She felt her face, which was dry. The tears had subsided without falling.

She shook her head, clearing her thoughts. "Let's keep moving,"

She traversed forward, not meeting her friends' eyes.

No point in crying, Hannah reminded herself. She imagined gathering all her thoughts in a giant box and shoving it corner of her mind.

But her momentarily empty brain quickly replaced the absence with a memory.

A memory she had long tried to forget.

It was around dawn. Hannah had been sleeping peacefully in her room. The air was still. Quiet.

She remembered the way the soft glow of her nightlight flickered against the walls — until her door creaked open and light from the hallway spilled in.

Her mother stood there, tense, flicking on the switch. "Hannah, baby, are you okay?" she asked, voice tight.

Hannah could still picture the worry carved into her mother's face, the way her hair was mussed and shoved to one side, like she'd gotten out of bed in a rush.

"Yes," little Hannah had murmured, blinking the sleep from her eyes. "What's wrong? Where's Daddy?"

Her mother hesitated. "Oh, sweetie... Daddy had to go to work early." She frowned, glancing toward the clock. Then, without another word, she crossed to the window and peeked through the blinds. Her eyebrows drew together.

"Why is his car still there?" she whispered.

Hannah slid out of bed and padded after her mother down the stairs. They stepped out into the cool air of the driveway.

She saw it before her mother did — the silhouette of something still. Too still.

It would've been better if they hadn't seen anything at all.

Mrs. Thorne froze. A shaky hand rose to cover her mouth.

Hannah followed her gaze. Her breath caught.

There — standing in the driveway — was her father. Or what was left of him.

A crystal figure, perfectly frozen in place. His face twisted in panic, mouth slightly open, eyes wide in fear. He must've made a sound. Must've called out. And then—

He was gone.

Not dead. Not asleep. Just... stopped.

Her young mind hadn't been able to comprehend it. People turning into crystal was the kind of thing she'd heard about in rumors. In whispers. In internet stories. None of it had ever felt real.

Until now. She reached for his statue-hand, trying to shake it. It didn't move.

"Mommy?" she whispered, voice cracking. "What happened to Daddy?"

Her mother didn't speak. She just pulled Hannah into her arms, tightly, like she was trying to keep her from disappearing too.

"But... Daddy—" Hannah turned back, twisting in her mother's grasp.

That's when she saw it.

The statue—her father—was glowing. A sickly, neon green light oozed across his surface, curling into the cracks like acid. It pulsed, shimmered.

The light clashed almost beautifully when it reflected in her hazel eyes.

And then, slowly, he began to vanish.

Crystal fragments peeled away into the air like ash, crumbling until there was nothing left but empty space.

"He's... gone," Hannah whispered. Her voice was small, but her heart was suddenly so heavy she thought it might break.

Her mother just squeezed her tighter.

When Hannah first realized what had happened to her father, she couldn't accept that he was *'gone'* gone—and yet, she was powerless to do anything about it besides talk. Endlessly, helplessly.

She hardly remembered the first day of first grade—only that when school ended, she bolted outside, looking for her mom. And then it hit her.

So abruptly. So sharply.

A memory.

Her father's arms had wrapped around her after kindergarten. He and her mom had taken her out for ice cream to celebrate. It wasn't anything grand, but it had become one of her fondest memories. Thinking of it sent a digging ache into her ribs, sharp enough to take her breath. She remembered gasping, trying to force the emotion down, but the tears broke through anyway.

She didn't even notice the boy at first.

"Hey, are you okay?" a voice asked gently.

She looked up, sniffling. A tall third grader with dark brown hair stood over her, concern softening his face.

"I'm fine," she squeaked.

"No, you're not," he said simply. "What happened?"

She shuddered. Her neck hurt from snapping her head up too fast. He seemed to realize and lowered himself on the steps so she wouldn't have to look up anymore.

Most kids wouldn't share something so personal with a stranger. But Hannah had been a dumb, naive, lonely six-year-old.

So she told him.

And she remembered, even now, the way his face twisted into a frown. How his brown eyes softened—not just with sympathy, but with something else.

Curiosity.

And... a growing determination.

"What if," he said slowly, "there was a way to bring your dad back?"

She paused, wiping her cheeks. She'd thought about it before—of course she had—but never knew where to start.

"We'll figure it out," he promised. "It'll be like a mystery!"

And somehow, she believed him. She warmed to his voice, to his calm, to the strange spark of purpose behind his words.

"Yeah... we could do that." She hesitated. "I'll see you tomorrow, um—"

"Jax," he said sheepishly, realizing he hadn't introduced himself.

"I'm Hannah."

She smiled as she stepped away. Her mom spotted her and swooped her into a hug.

"Who was that boy you were talking to?" she asked, setting Hannah down and taking her backpack.

"That was Jax. My new friend."

Hannah turned to wave at him. He waved back with a wide grin before walking home alone.

Hannah felt her head ache from all the suppressed emotions and thoughts. She hadn't even realized when her friends had caught up with her, walking silently, their faces solemn. Hannah fought down the painful lump in her throat, sealing the heated emotions into an unwanted, depressing box. She labeled it *For Later*, then shoved it away somewhere deep into her mind.

Hannah listed her head. "Ara, do you want to tell Dee what happened in the Dragoncake Grocery?"

She cringed when she heard her voice so painfully hoarse, but luckily neither of them seemed to notice.

Ara smirked. "Oh, Dave, you have no idea how dumb you looked."

"What the– *Dave*? Also: why? What happened? What did you guys do to me?" Dee glared at both of them, alarmed, while Ara tossed her ponytail onto her other shoulder.

"Well, for starters, you became deaf and mute, and a literal rag doll, which we had to lug around everywhere," Ara laughed when Dee's face contorted into confusion. Hannah felt the sliver of a smile approaching, but the feeling left all too soon. She listened in silence as Ara filled Dee in, brushing aside unwanted brambles and leaves that would drift down to her head lazily.

While walking, Dee stumbled over a root, careening forward while grabbing the collar of Ara's shirt and letting out an alarmed shout. They tumbled to the ground, landing in front of Hannah, who momentarily stopped walking.

Ara growled and lifted herself to her feet. Dee continued to lie on the ground, letting out a drawn-out groan. Ara grabbed her phone, making sure it was okay before traipsing forward. Hannah sighed and hoisted Dee up before continuing along the wild path.

"We're almost there!" Ara called, "Even though there's no service on my phone, I can hear the road up ahead!"

Hannah wanted to speed up, but her knees shook with exhaustion. She glanced at Dee, who trudged on beside her with a rocky expression. Hannah noticed a leaf caught in her black hair and quickly brushed it out. Dee turned to her, questioning at first, then grateful, then somber.

"You're okay, right? Not gonna quit on us now?" She asked softly, her eyes uncertain and searching.

Hannah's stomach twisted. She had prepared herself to sacrifice everything for her parents, but thinking about it made her feel colder and emptier than ever.

"No," Hannah whispered, casting her eyes to her shoes. She was afraid that Dee would see the guilt and lies etched on her face if she looked up.

"If y'all don't get over here in the next five seconds, I'm leaving without you!" Ara screeched from ahead. Hannah stumbled forward, grateful for the excuse. Dee grumbled but copied her.

They emerged on the side of the highway. What few cars they had heard had sped away, barely dots in the distance.

"Okay, genius. What now?" Dee asked, squinting against the bright sunlight.

"I'm barely getting service here, but it's still working. I'm calling a taxi," Ara said, punching a few buttons on her phone and then setting it down."It's gonna take a while, y'know, considering we are in the middle of nowhere."

"That's okay," Hannah said. She pulled out the dagger from the gifted hilt and stared at it. The noon sun beat down on it, sending small shimmering dots reflecting on the trees and grass. Hannah tilted the blade, watching them shiver.

"Please tell me you have something useful with you, like, I don't know, sunglasses?" Dee grumbled, using her sword to shield her eyes.

Hannah opened her mouth suddenly, then shut it again, disappointed. They had lost their bags in the Dragoncake Grocery, and the remainder of their supplies included their phones, Ozzie, the dagger, Dee's sword/ring, the clothes on their bodies, and wads of money. Everything else was gone or burned, including the Yin book, the note, and–

Hannah released a strangled cry. "The map!"

Ara turned to her, her face twisting in confusion. She paled, then flushed in relief again.

"Geez, Hannah, you scared me. I took a picture of the map when we were in the cab,"

"You sure?" Dee asked unhelpfully.

"Yes," Ara said firmly. Hannah released a breath she didn't know she was holding.

Overcome with relief, she slumped against the tree, ignoring the spots of pain that danced between her eyes as the sun beat down. A stray breeze tousled her now-messy light brown hair, whipping it across her face. The top of her spine tingled, filling her with barely noticeable buzzing. Hannah reached for Ozzie and tossed it between both hands. The sliver of cold from the glass made her hands feel less sweaty. She closed her eyes, relishing the feel.

There was a giant blockade holding all her emotions lumped together, but Hannah didn't dare prod it, lest the feelings overcome her. Instead, she let it sit, a frothing storm as heavy as an anvil weighing her down.

"Ozzie doesn't break, does he?" Hannah heard Dee ask.

"Nope, knock yourself out."

Without opening her eyes, Hannah held Ozzie out and felt it leave her palm.

"What are you doing?" Ara grumbled.

Hannah sighed and cracked one eye open. Dee was bouncing Ozzie on her knees and head, a childlike excitement in her eyes.

"Ara, catch!" Dee flung the Orb at her, and Ara caught it in her hands, scowling.

"This is a mystical artifact, and you're playing with it like it's a tennis ball?" She chided, handing it to Hannah. Dee snatched it back just as fast, her face twisting with untold glumness.

She dropped to the ground and crossed her feet in her lap, rolling Ozzie on the ground, her original joy gone.

Hannah glanced at Ara, who looked mystified. Ara shrugged and leaned into the shade, her shrewd features softening. Hannah leaned back and closed her eyes again, a drawn-out sigh escaping her lips.

DIANA

Guilt was pressing down on Dee.

So.

Much.

Guilt.

It felt like clawed hands were gripping her throat, slowly suffocating her. Slowly burning her away.

Because she knew what she was doing was wrong.

Not the *helping-Hannah* part, no. The *not-being-able-to-accept-what-is-happening* part. She'd instantly resort to denial, and it was the reason she couldn't admit her family was gone.

In other words, she was deceiving herself.

Especially when they had tried so hard to blend in like a normal family in the suburbs. Enrolling in a normal school, living in a normal kingdom– er, country.

She should've felt happy.

Instead, Dee only felt a ghost of her past whispering in her head, the intriguing, deceptive kingdom where she'd lived for the first few years of her life.

She hardly remembered Melumora other than peering down at the vast, underwater, mystical city, diluted with haze from her five-year-old brain's memory. She watched the swirling spires disappear into sea bubbles and foam as she and her family were carted away, stepping through the fabric of reality, then entering a new one.

Dee wasn't sure how much Adrian or her mother remembered. They never talked about it. It was a secret. One she'd also been forced to keep.

And it was killing her not to tell someone, or just, one day, use her powers.

Because Dee was not normal.

She was a siren.

The so-called "magical" spirits were known to lure sailors to their deaths.

But the sirens of Melumora had all sorts of different powers. Dee, for instance, could use her voice to make anyone do anything for a short time. But eight years without use may have disturbed her powers, making them weaker. She wasn't sure, though. Dee hadn't tried in all that time.

Dee was sick of being stuck at home. The moment Hannah stumbled into her life, she'd been swept into the whole crystal mess — like it or not. But truthfully, it wasn't just that. There wasn't much left for her at home anyway.

Thinking about Hannah sent another pang of guilt through her chest. She wanted to tell her — wanted to tell someone — the truth. But she couldn't. Disrupting the fragile balance her family had managed to hold onto felt too dangerous, and besides, she doubted any sane person would believe her.

Sirens were supposed to be these majestic, deadly, cunning creatures. Dee was far from all those things.

Well, apart from deadly. Her sword skills had already proved that.

Her sword.

She remembered training with smaller replicas– mere, foggy glimpses of learning how to wrap her hand around the hilt, how to balance it. Before she'd left Melumora, someone had given her the sword. She didn't remember who, but the blade had been stored away in her basement for a long while now. Dee was pleased with its condition, however, and admired the shimmering blade.

It was minuscule, almost invisible unless you thoroughly inspected the sword, but a small line of initials had been etched into the side of the hilt.

Dee stopped rolling Ozzie around— which flew up towards Hannah, she assumed— and activated her sword. In a burst of azure blue light, it materialized in before her, sending a glare into her eyes before she blinked it out furiously. Dee inspected the hilt, finding the initials.

A.A.

N.A.

H.A.

B.A.

L.A.

No doubt, those people were the previous sword owners. Dee wondered if she was related to them since it was possible that once her mother relocated them to America, she'd made new identities for all of them.

Still, the name Diana had remained the same. She suspected it was because her mother loved it very much.

Absently, Dee pricked the tip of her finger. She glared at the midnight blue liquid that trickled out.

Siren blood.

Before either Hannah or Ara could see, she wiped her finger on her dark jeans and let the sword transform back.

AMARA

The time spent waiting felt mind-numbing, and Ara stopped checking the taxi's ETA every two minutes after resigning to the fact that it would be pointless to berate her situation silently. She sank to the ground, her fingers itching to pull a book from the bag that, unfortunately, was probably reduced to ashes by now.

Angry at herself for losing it, she sought to distract her mind. Ara pulled out the wad of old dollar bills and counted them silently, her mind spiraling elsewhere.

Goldie, her poor, sweet, loveable dog.

One hundred.
Two hundred.
Three hundred.

It was so blatantly cruel, the way life kept testing her. She recalled, not memories, but feelings when her life was perfectly normal.

Her mother was alive back then.

Her father was attentive and kind back then.

She was joyful back then.

And then it came.

Heart disease.

Ara didn't know all the details about it, and she didn't want to know.

All she remembered was the sickening feeling of heartbreak when she walked in on her father in the hospital, his face in his hands, his body shaking with barely concealed sobs.

And her mother was gone.

Four hundred.
Five hundred.
Six hundred.

Since then, Ara had barely remembered anything other than falling into a state of depression. Her father was also low-spirited. That was when he had started to draw back. To forget how to feel. To numb himself.

Soon, the media noticed, and Ara was forced to undergo several interviews where she'd just sobbed for them to leave her alone. She never wanted to be part of her dad's acting career, and always supported her wishes.

But this time, it was like he didn't care. Let her go through the interviews and press. It wasn't his place to speak against.

Her father had built acting empires but could never spare a second for Ara. She hadn't lost him to crystal now—she lost him to ambition then.

Eventually, someone suggested getting Ara a dog.

Then it was like sunlight had finally melted a patch of ice that had lasted for far too long.

The first time Ara met Goldie was when she was a puppy, and Ara was ten years old. The small golden retriever had trotted towards her and prodded her shoes, sniffing Ara up and down. Goldie then deemed her interesting and nuzzled into her palm.

For the first time in a long time, Ara had given a real smile.

And since then, Ara had loved and cherished Goldie as her best friend, even if she was an animal.

And now, her dog was crystal.

At this point, she would do everything in her power to bring Goldie back or die trying.

She'd rather perish with faith in knowing she had at least tried to save her than live knowing she'd done nothing.

And it wouldn't matter anyway. The crystal pandemic had increased exponentially in the last few weeks. Seven more days, and soon, no one would remain human.

Six hundred and twenty.
Six hundred and forty.
Six hundred and sixty.
Six hundred and sixty-five.
Six hundred and sixty-seven.

She gathered all the money and aligned the bills so they landed in a neat pile. Then she folded it carefully and tucked it away. Ara pulled out her phone and checked the taxi status.

Canceled

Glaring, she tapped it furiously. Canceled? She hadn't *canceled* anything.

Your taxi has been canceled due to an unexpected issue with your location. We apologize for any inconvenience.

Ara glared. "They should apologize," She muttered to herself, standing up. She sighed, her eyes sweeping over Dee momentarily before stationing them on Hannah. Her head was tipped back, leaning on an oak tree, her eyes shut. She looked awful, with dark spots underneath her eyes that looked like bruises, but strangely calm too. Like she'd accepted everything life had thrown at her and knew what to do with it. Ara admired that about her, how resilient she was.

Ara sighed and tapped Hannah's shoulder. Hannah pulled open her eyes and peered at her groggily.

"Taxi's here?"

"No," Ara said regretfully, "It's not coming."

Hannah rolled her eyes and then glanced at her. "Sorry, I'm not trying to be disrespectful to *you*, I'm just rolling my eyes at life in general."

Okay, scratch the part about Hannah knowing what to do with her situation. She clearly didn't. Ara suppressed a pained laugh and pulled up a GPS on her phone.

"The nearest rest area is only a couple of miles away. We can walk there,"

"Ugh, more walking," Dee groaned, rubbing her index finger on her ring.

Ara frowned but didn't comment.

Hannah used her arms to push herself off the tree, like the mere action of standing fatigued her.

"Okay," She murmured, grabbing Ara's shoulder to steady herself, "Lead the way."

CHAPTER 16

DIANA

Dee could feel her endurance being tested with every step on the side of the highway. She was tempted to finally try her powers to convince a random car to stop and give them a ride, although Dee wasn't sure she'd be able to tell the driver in time before they sped away. Her powers only worked when she could speak clearly, and other people could hear clearly.

So she pressed her lips into a line and didn't complain, although Dee really, really wanted to.

"How much further?" Hannah asked, wiping sweat off her brow.

"I can see it!" Ara said excitedly.

Dee whipped her head up and could make out a small, boring building in the distance. With newfound vigor, she brushed past Hannah and Ara, already tasting the cold water in her mouth.

HANNAH

Ozzie stayed immobile the entire time, which was good because seeing it gave Hannah the heebie-jeebies, even now. She released a relieved breath once they stepped into the rest area, where Ara left to use the restroom immediately, and Dee stared at a vending machine. Hannah traipsed over to her, and her dry mouth begged for a sip of *anything* as she stared at the drink options. They both salivated there until Ara came back, already holding their money out.

"I've never appreciated water this much," Dee murmured between gulps.

Hannah couldn't disagree; her eyes closed in satisfaction as she savored the coolness.

"I'm going to get a bag for these bottles. And food." Ara added.

"I'll come with you," Dee exclaimed, draining the rest of her bottle. "You coming, Hannah?"

"Yeah," Hannah finished off the rest of the water, "You guys go without me, I have to go to the bathroom first."

"Okay,"

Hannah watched them round the corner and leave. Sighing, she tossed her empty bottle into a trash bin and started to walk to the ladies' washroom.

A sudden shadow fell over her, and she turned around, frowning. In the entryway of the rest area stood a tall man in a knee-length brown coat, his face hidden underneath a bowler hat.

Hannah's nerves tingled, but she remained silent. Her fingers curled around the hilt of her dagger by themselves.

The man lifted his head, and she caught a glimpse of his face. He had copper-colored skin and dark hair. His eyes widened once he saw Hannah.

Hannah wanted to shrink under his gaze, but she forced herself to remain calm.

"Are... are you...?" He whispered, "You're that girl from Grand Rapids. The one who wasn't crystallized."

Hannah's brain screamed, and all that was left was a faint buzzing in her spine again, growing louder, so she said nothing.

"Don't you have friends who weren't crystallized either?" He asked, watching her cautiously.

"How do you know that?" Hannah asked, suddenly defensive.

The man shrugged. "I'm a reporter. My wife is a cop. We were all tasked with looking over specific individuals' files. I got yours, and before the city powered down, we caught CCTV footage of you and three other accomplices leaving the city." he frowned at her, "You shouldn't be here. "

Hannah turned his words over in her head, letting them digest. She was tempted to explain herself, but another question weighed in.

"Wait, you said you're a reporter, right?" She asked suddenly.

The man raised an eyebrow. "Yes,"

"What topics do you cover?" Hannah asked, chewing her lower lip.

"Mostly crime," He said slowly, "Why?"

Hannah paused, inhaling to steady herself. "Do you cover the crystal disappearances?"

The man fell silent for a moment. "Yes, I do,"

She wrapped her fingers around Ozzie. "Has anything changed in the past few days?"

The man hesitated. "I'm sorry, but that's confidential."

Hannah stalked up to him and unsheathed her dagger, pointing it at him threateningly. She had no actual intention of harming him—Hannah just needed to scare him.

"You *have* to tell me. Our lives depend on it."

The man shrank slightly, thinking.

Finally, he said, "The 'crystal disappearances' are now being called 'the crystal abductions' due to the recently increased aggression towards the victims."

Hannah's mouth went dry. "Describe,"

"The victim's homes are being found torn apart, their wealth stolen. More people are being crystallized day by day. There have been photographs and videos of the statues before they melted away. The presidents haven't yet ordered a lockdown, but there have been rumors." He listed, in a monotone, unfeeling voice.

Hannah squeezed her eyes shut, cursing under her breath.

"And the people? What are they thinking?" She breathed, afraid to hear his response.

"What few people who were considered crackpot conspiracy theorists have now turned into over sixty percent of the remaining population. The remaining, however, believe they're delusional," his lips quirked, "Or they're trying to. These statistics are only from the U.S., of course,"

Hannah glared. "What about the rest of the world? This is also affecting them."

"I have not gathered data outside of America."

Hannah shoved her blade back and let out a frustrated grunt, tearing her hands through her hair. More people were being crystallized.

People who, although they were unaware, were counting on *them*.

On Hannah.

She turned back to the man, whose face had become an emotionless mask, and grimaced.

"Listen to me," She hissed under her breath, her eyes scanning for any security cameras around them, "You will not speak of this meeting, understand?

His gaze hardened. "I'm afraid that is not possible. This would be excellent news for my article,"

"I don't think you understand," Hannah growled, "I know you don't believe it, but this is a matter of international safety. And, if you must, publish whatever you want about me, but wait a couple of days until I'm gone,"

"And how do I know that you're not some psycho? For all I know, *you* could be behind the crystal abductions," He argued.

Hannah turned away, massaging her temples. "If you care for humanity's well-being, I suggest you listen to me," she faced him, eyes blazing, "I'm going to leave. This never happened."

He gritted his teeth. "It did happen, but I'll talk about it later."

Hannah tilted her head in a curt nod. "Fine."

She stalked away, her heart thundering, her mind spinning in countless directions.

Hannah nearly crashed into Dee as she rounded a corner. Ara thrust an arm between them, keeping them from thudding into each other.

Her face fell once she saw Hannah. "What's wrong?"

Realizing she probably looked frustrated, Hannah quickly schooled her features. "Nothing. Well, I got some more information about the whole..."

She twirled a finger around as if it could signify the situation. Luckily, they seemed to understand and nodded gravely.

Hannah cleared her throat. "I'll explain later. First, we need to decide how to get to Florida. Ara, the map?"

Ara thrust her hand into her pocket and extracted her phone. She tapped it a few times before handing it to Hannah, the screen displaying the map.

Dee frowned and leaned over Hannah's shoulder. "Have you guys actually seen *where* in Florida our destination is?"

Hannah's eye twitched, realizing the line just led to the center of Florida, not necessarily a specific location inside. She wanted to yell and bang her head against a wall, frustrated with her stupidity. They should've decoded that a long time ago before frolicking off.

A painful silence stretched on before Ara said, "It's okay. Let's just focus on getting to Florida without dying first."

"Good plan," Hannah muttered, "Ara?"

"I already booked the taxi," She reached for her phone and Hannah handed it to her obediently, "Let's eat before it gets here,"

"On it!" Dee called from behind them. They whirled around to see her sitting on a chair, her feet propped on another one, while the bag of snacks lay on the table beside her. She had already started munching on a hamburger.

Hannah followed suit, sinking into a chair, pulling out her burger, and eating. Through the satisfaction, she barely noticed when Ara joined them.

Dee prodded the bag of tater tots. "What are those?"

Ara quirked an eyebrow. "You don't know what tater tots are? What rock have you been living under?"

Dee suddenly froze, looking like she had been caught committing a crime. Watching her, Hannah tensed, before Dee sank into her chair again, an uncomfortable smile on her face.

"Ha, tater tots. I know what they are... I just haven't eaten them... in a long... time," Her voice faded as she focused on the food. She picked one up, pushed it in her mouth, and chewed carefully.

"Yeah, I remember them." She swallowed, "My mom's a bit of a health freak, so she doesn't let us eat this kind of food."

Ara and Hannah traded skeptical looks.

"Well, at least she won't find out about this," Ara said, gesturing to the abundance of fast food before them.

"Yeah, we won't tell her," Hannah nodded, sipping her Sprite, savoring how the carbonated drink bubbled across her tongue.

Ara's phone beeped. She swiped it up and unlocked it.

"The taxi is here. It's gonna drop us in Georgia, where we will take a train to Orlando. Seeing how it will be busy with people there, we can easily blend in and figure out what to do next."

Hannah frowned. "When did you plan all that?"

"While you two were busy stuffing your faces," Ara slid out of her seat and strutted outside. Dee rolled her eyes, grabbed their rubbish, and tossed it in the trash can before she and Hannah joined Ara.

They clambered into the back of the cab, Ara on one end, Dee on the other, while Hannah squeezed into the middle, mostly to keep them from fighting.

"You girls got money to pay?" The driver asked, giving them a toothy grin. Hannah squirmed uncomfortably.

"It's prepaid," Ara glowered at him, "Now stop trying to rip us off and do your job, unless you'd rather we find another taxi?"

The man shrank in his seat. "Alright, alright, I'm sorry,"

"You should be," Dee muttered, staring out the window, digging her thumb nail into the flesh of her pointer finger absently.

Hannah raised an eyebrow at the small cut mark on her skin, looking like it had only recently healed. Knowing Dee, it was probably some other wound she'd attained.

Still, the dried blood around it didn't look dark red, like normal scabs. Instead, it was dark, much darker than regular blood. Her eyebrows creased as she reached for Dee's finger.

Dee flinched and wrenched her hand out of Hannah's grip. "What are you doing?"

"Shh, give me your hand," Hannah held open her hand to hold Dee's.

Instead, Dee shrank away even more, looking strangely panicked. "Why do you need it?"

Hannah felt a flare of annoyance in her chest. "I need to check something,"

Dee kept her hand curled tight, but Hannah grabbed it and forced it open. Ara looked over, frowning slightly.

Hannah inspected the finger and felt Dee shudder.

"It's fine, I accidentally cut myself with my sword."

"Yeah, but your blood looks strange," Hannah pinched it, hardly eliciting a grumble from Dee, and gasped when she saw midnight blue blood trickle out slowly.

"Dee?" Hannah let go of her hand and backed away subconsciously. Hurt and panic flickered on Dee's face.

"What in the..." Ara leaned forward hesitantly but remained beside Hannah, whose brain was hurtling in every direction as it scrambled to justify what she was seeing.

"Dee," she asked quietly, "Why is your blood... blue?"

The driver tossed them a concerned look that no one noticed, but kept on driving. Dee locked her jaw and pulled her hand away, finger curling into a fist, smearing some of the blood onto her palm. Hannah grimaced.

"Is that from an infection?" She asked, darting a worried glance at Ara, whose eyes were wide. She shook her head. Hannah whipped her head back, just as a low, forcing voice spoke, molding Hannah's will.

"*It's nothing, you don't notice it, now leave it alone.*"

Hannah's brain struggled against the words, but felt the fight drain out of her. Everything was fine. Nothing was out of the ordinary. Just leave it all alone.

She sank into the leather seat obediently, staring ahead, dazed. Her thoughts were muddled and confused, but she could barely feel it as it was wrapped in a tight blanket and tossed into a corner of her mind, still buzzing hyperly, but trapped.

Her cervical spine was also buzzing, but that annoyance seemed minor to her foggy head.

Her eyes gazed at the road speeding away underneath the vehicle, but not really watching.

DIANA

Dee leaned against the seat, mentally exhausted, barely glancing at Ara and Hannah's unnaturally silent forms.

She felt guilty for using her powers on them, but it had slipped out of her throat and latched onto her words before she could think. Her throat itched with discomfort. Ignoring her powers for over eight years was like pulling a barely used muscle.

It *hurt*.

Immediately, her throat had started burning like she had the flu, and Dee had lunged for the bottle of water and downed it rapidly, feeling the burn dull into an irritating ache.

Dee's fingers ventured up and pressed against the hollow of her throat. That did little to ease the pain.

She turned, biting the inside of her cheek, as Hannah and Ara stared outside dazedly, blinking slowly. Glancing in the rearview mirror, she saw the driver also looking outside groggily, his eyes scanning the mirrors routinely.

She knew the power's effects would fade in half an hour, but considering it was so weak now, it would only last a few more minutes.

Dee tried to tell herself it was good that it wouldn't last longer, but some part of her felt withered and disappointed. Like she had lost a piece of her identity.

She leaned against the window, pressing her cheek against the glass, watching the trees and road race away.

What would her mother think of her now, if she could?

Would she be disappointed?

Her thoughts were interrupted by a gurgle in her stomach.

Dee turned around and dove into the plastic bag where they'd saved leftovers. She reached in and pulled out a small, greasy cardboard box that held little potato cylinders.

Tater tots, she reminded herself as she popped one into her mouth. Crunchy on the outside but softer on the inside. Her tongue begged for more.

Hannah and Ara blinked more rapidly. The spell must've been fading.

Dee leaned against the glass again, schooling her face into nonchalance as she ate the tater tots.

CHAPTER 17

DIANA

The station was in a dull, brick building with boring glass entryways. Dee almost groaned in exasperation when she saw it, but too occupied with stepping out, she pressed her lips into a tight line and stepped out of the taxi.

Hannah stumbled out after her, and Ara followed suit, already shuffling through their money.

"I'm gonna go get tickets," Ara placed a steadying hand on the wall and bent her knees once.

"Okay," Hannah rubbed her eyes drowsily and set her eyes on Ara, grabbing the sleeve of her shirt and closing her eyes to let Ara lead her.

Dee mumbled something about going to the bathroom and trudged off.

It wasn't difficult to find. The ladies' restroom was incredibly noisy and populated. Bustling mothers urged their children to wash their hands. All the teens were either touching up their makeup or fixing their hair. Small kids were scooping up water from the faucets and flinging it toward their siblings. Dee padded toward the floor-length mirror as she waited for her turn.

Her reflection in the mirror looked unlike the robust, bored girl she remembered, but it felt strangely suited for her. She looked paler, her short black hair was in messy strands slightly past her chin. Alert gray eyes blinked back at her. The blue jade ring rested snugly on her pointer finger.

Dee coiled her fingers around it. What would these people think if a random girl pulled out a sword and started waving it maniacally? Dee was almost tempted to find out.

A familiar brown-haired girl placed a hand on her shoulder, wrenching her out of her impulsive thoughts..

Dee whirled around. "Hannah!"

There was no one there. Startled, Dee turned back to her reflection, where a stone-faced Hannah stared at her, one hand still on Dee's shoulder.

Dee turned around again, but it was only her. She looked back into the mirror and tried to duck from under Hannah's grip.

Only she couldn't move.

"Hannah?" Dee let out an uncertain laugh, placing her fingers on Hannah's. Hannah bristled and her reflection shoved Dee aside, making *real* Dee stumble.

"What...?" Dee lifted her hand, ready to swipe at her ring and activate her sword. She froze when Hannah's reflection's hazel eyes melted into glowing pink light.

Along with her eyes, her arm veins also began to glow with pink light. Dee whipped her head around, stunned that no one was noticing.

Hannah lifted one arm, smiled, and the floor started to quake.

Dee backed against the wall, her eyes darting furiously to the people around her, who started to frown.

Hannah's reflection cocked her head to the side, grinning. Her smile fell, and her arm reached outwards...

It penetrated through the surface of the mirror and latched around Dee's throat, holding her against the back wall, her feet dangling down. The ceiling began to collapse.

"Run!" She choked, clawing at Hannah's fingers uselessly. Everyone stared at her, stunned.

"*Run!*" She screeched, pouring magic into her words.

Everyone straightened and bustled out hurriedly.

Dee's throat screamed with agony, and she would've doubled over if she hadn't been pinned to the wall. She activated her sword, but it hung limply in her grasp. Her vision dimmed.

So this is how Dee would die: strangled by a reflection of her own friend. She'd laugh at the idea of it if she could.

Hannah's reflection cocked her head, but her expression remained stony and scrutinizing, her eyes still glowing light pink. She opened her mouth, but no words came out.

"*Hi, Dee,*" A sinister, more high-pitched voice rang in Dee's head.

"H-Hannah?" Dee's skin was burning hot, her body dissolving into pain.

"*That's me...*" Instantly, the pressure lifted off of Dee's neck, and she collapsed to the ground, wheezing. She shrank her sword and leaned on the back wall.

"*Hannah,*" The reflection was a mere reflection again. Dee took lungfuls of air while Hannah's reflection stared at her, unsmiling.

"What are you?" Dee gasped, pouncing to her feet again, though she wasn't sure what good that would do; she could get attacked again.

"*I know your secret,*" The reflection taunted, ignoring Dee's question.

Through Dee's muddled brain, a single thought formed: *Rude.*

"*I* know *you, Dee,*" She whispered, the curves of her lips tilting up.

But just *barely.*

Dee barked out a laugh. "You don't know anything about me, you weird, phantom thing— why am I even talking to you? I need to get my friends,"

Dee turned on her heel.

"*You're from a different dimension, aren't you?*"

Dee froze, heat rushing through her spine. Even though her back was facing the mirror, she could tell the reflection was smiling now.

"*You don't belong, do you?*"

Dee's strong heart began to splinter, as though the reflection was unraveling her, piece by piece.

"I do belong," She heard her unsteady voice say. It was an overused lie.

"*Look at me, Dee,*"

Dee bit her lip, every ounce of her begging to just *leave*. Find the real Hannah and Ara. Forget this ever happened.

But then again, good decisions weren't her strong suit.

She turned around with what she hoped was a frosty glare. Hannah's reflection stared back at her with such intensity, Dee thought it would burn a hole through her head.

"*You're a little siren right now, but someday, your blood will turn valuable, and then... be careful.*" Her gaze softened slightly, "*All of you,*"

"But no one knows I'm a siren," Dee crossed her arms, suddenly defensive.

Hannah's reflection loomed closer to the surface of the mirror, angry. "*You must learn to control your power before it controls you. This is a secret you shouldn't keep.*"

Dee let out a laugh. "You just told me to be careful about letting people know I'm a siren, then you told me to tell everyone? Are you crazy?"

Hannah's eyes glowed brighter, but she didn't look angry. "*I might be crazy. But that just comes with having great power.*"

Dee laughed again, but it sounded fake.

"*You won't remember this.*" Her reflection reached out of the mirror, but for some reason, Dee didn't flinch as her cold skin pressed against her forehead. "*But when the time comes, you will find me,*"

Dee's vision dimmed black, transforming everything into a meaningless blur. Her brain felt like it was running back, an endless backward marathon.

Then suddenly the floor tilted towards her, and her palms met the gross, white tiles.

**

Something cold and wet trickled down her face. Dee's eyes shot open, and she gasped. Her hand instinctively went to her throat. She wasn't sure why.

Hannah kneeled over her, her face etched with guilt and concern.

"I'm sorry I splashed water on you. Are you okay?" She placed a hand on Dee's shoulder and stared at her, waiting for a response.

A flash of panic ripped through Dee's brain so alarmingly that she nearly flinched out of Hannah's grasp. Dee bit her lip as her vision spun, and she squeezed her eyes shut, trying to fight the wave of pain that crashed into her.

Why?

Why was she agitated upon seeing Hannah?

Why was her throat hurting as if she'd used her power?

Why was her neck throbbing?

Why was her head pounding with a headache?

Whywhywhywhywhywhywhy?

"Dee, you're starting to worry me," Hannah said, retracting her hand.

Dee's attention snapped to Hannah's face. She had sparkling meadow eyes, which Dee now realized were much brighter than usual.

"What's wrong?" Dee stumbled to her feet hastily, the blood rushing to her head. She leaned against the wall and breathed in deeply, trying to reorient herself. It felt like whatever strength she had drained out of her just before she passed out from–

What was it she'd passed out from?

Hannah bit her lip and stood up, wiping her palms on her jeans. She looked like she was going to throw up.

"There's something wrong," She whispered, her fingers traversing to the hilt of her dagger instinctively, "I think it's a monster."

Dee wanted to groan, to shout, to find whoever was dragging them on this journey and use her power to make them heed her every word. The one moment where she was weakened? That wasn't fair.

She leaned against the wall and inhaled a few rejuvenating deep breaths. Hannah fell silent too, and a vague, low humming filled the air outside.

They exchanged uncertain glances.

Hannah pulled her dagger out of her belt, and Dee activated her sword and cleared her throat a few times to shake off the dulling ache. They nodded to each other and then sprinted at top speed to the exit.

The humming grew louder, but this time, it rattled the ground and sent a shock to their nerves. Screams pierced their ears, followed by gunshots.

Dee was practically flying to get to the exit.

They burst outside and–

Dee turned away, pressing her lips together in horror, lunch threatening to make a reappearance.

Bees the size of rhinos hovered around them. Their mouths frothed with acidic yellow liquid, and their black stingers pulverized the ground.

Dee felt the tater tots coming up in her stomach. She inhaled deeply, trying to keep herself from emptying her lunch onto the cement.

Ara.

Dee's eyes scanned around, then latched onto the blonde.

She had something black and silver clutched in her hands and pointed at the bee monsters. Her fingers shifted nimbly across the contraption, and small bullets punctured the bees on the sides, each one slumping to the ground in a dying buzz after enough damage had been inflicted.

Ara had learned how to work a gun.

A gun.

It was hard to squish down the awe Dee felt, especially as more and more bees died with anguished cries. But where one died, two more would take its place. Ara wouldn't be able to kill them all with a small gun.

Dee banned any more thoughts of puking and flicked her ring, activating her sword. She raised it and plunged it into the nearest bee.

There was a dying buzz, but Dee had already ripped her sword back, and she was running.

It was times like these when she felt true power coursing through her veins.

The world had disappeared into a storm of yellow and black. Gray and blue. Sharp winds. Maddening adrenaline. The smell of rotting bananas.

She might've even laughed.

Acid dripped around her, melting the ground inch by inch. Melting fabric in an instant. Melting skin...

She sucked in a quick breath through her teeth every time she felt the liquid splatter across her skin. But Dee was too adrenaline-driven to attend to the wounds.

Sometimes she'd hear a bullet embed itself in her next target, and then Dee would turn on her heel and search for another. Ara was doing surprisingly well for her first time with a gun. And Hannah–

"Hannah!" Dee shouted, lopping off one bee's stinger. "Kill that– Hannah?"

Her friend's face was pale white, a look of unspeakable terror etched on her face. Dee wrenched her sword out of a bee, staring at Hannah. She'd never looked like this before– never looked at anything with such horror before.

In the split second, the bees took advantage of Dee's distraction and closed in for the kill.

"Dee!" Ara screamed. She threw her pistol at the bees, which knocked one fairly in the eye, and darted toward Dee, barely grabbing her hand before dragging her forward. She reached for Hannah.

Her fingers closed more firmly around Dee's as they sprinted forward. Dee willed her legs to become more stable to push her forward as they ducked into the station. She didn't dare look behind as the bees crashed through the walls, their eyes flashing murder.

Ara jumped onto the train, pulling Dee and Hannah with her. She let go of their hands and sprinted towards the conductor. Dee heard some shouting, a little screaming, maybe even a slap, but in the next second, they heard a sharp whine as the train groaned and began to haul itself out of the station. Dee and Hannah stumbled backward at the sudden propulsion and thudded onto the floor. Dee made zero attempt to stand back up again. The adrenaline drained out of her, and suddenly her head was a bowling ball.

Out of the corner of her eye, she saw Hannah sit up and press her back against the padded corridor side. She tucked her head into her knees and didn't move. Dee's own eyes drifted shut.

"Get up," Dee felt something hard tap her shoulder. She opened her eyes to see a scowling, panting Ara hovering above her, prodding Dee's shoulder with her shoe.

Dee groaned and stretched a hand up comically, which Ara promptly slapped back down. She dragged herself up to a sitting position and let out a very drawn-out breath, which morphed into a small, tired grin.

They were beaten up, bruised, bloody, and in a little more than pain.

But they were alive.

CHAPTER 18

HANNAH

Hannah's eyes felt warm as she pressed her palms against her eyelids. Warmer than usual. She sighed and let her hands fall back into her lap as her gaze swiveled around, eventually latching onto Ara, who was fiddling with her new weapon. Hannah grimaced as the light reflected off the steel when Ara tilted it to check how many bullets were left in the magazine.

She turned away to stare at Dee, who was leeching out any remaining traces of acid off her skin by wiping it away with a piece of cloth.

Here they all were, sprawled in the entrance of the train hallway— aside from Ara, who was leaning against the side— completely ignoring the dozen, silent, traumatized passengers who had managed to cram into the back seats before the train had been rushed out of the station, courtesy of Ara.

Dee threw the rag onto the floor, sighing, as she met Hannah's eyes. "Bees?" she asked, rubbing her neck with a groan, "You're afraid of bees?"

She did not say it unkindly, but Hannah's insides still clenched with a feeling she did not know. Perhaps it was more than one. A whole smoothie of feelings.

"I'll go find us some seats," Hannah said flatly, feeling her body stand up on its own accord and stalk off. Her stomach sank even further when she saw Ara give a pointed kick at Dee's shin.

Hannah trudged on further, her feet landing in soft thuds against the padded floor of the nearly empty train. She emerged in another empty car and sighed, feeling the weight of emotions press against the thinning barrier of denial.

She was miserably failing at... well, everything. In fighting, Dee was the one who slayed every beast, who saved them every time, and who actually did something impressive. Even Ara, who, despite not having something to fight with until an hour ago, was able to use her wits to destroy any monsters. All Hannah had was a lethal dagger that somehow gave her natural fighting instincts, but only when she held it. There was no point in the stupid blade when Hannah's apiphobia came in the way.

And that's another thing; Hannah was afraid. Her nerves were so frayed, she was worried they'd wither away. How come Dee was never scared? How come Ara knew how to hide her fear? She was all filter, while Hannah was none.

She longed for her parents, but as of now, they were of the same material as the dagger strapped to her.

The unraveling emotions swirled inside her, her wounds ached and stung from being untreated, and her breathing grew unsteadier until she was practically gasping for air. She slumped against the car wall and closed her eyes until she felt her breathing come to normal, and that's when she realized what she was feeling.

Guilt.

Guilt for dragging along her so-called "friends" on this suicide mission. How could she even dare to say out loud that they were her best friends if she was stringing them along with a false purpose? If she might have to leave them for dead?

Just when things couldn't get worse–

More guilt.

Guilt for letting her parents turn into mindless, crystal slaves. Guilt for breaking the promise she had made to herself. This wasn't going to work. Hannah was just a thirteen-year-old girl. What sort of *child* could defeat a *monster?*

Ara could. Her mind whispered *Dee will.*

Or will they?

Hannah inhaled sharply, straightening. Dee had to. Ara had to. Because Hannah was too afraid. Because Hannah couldn't get over a simple fear of bees, much less a monster known to incapacitate with a single glance. But Dee and Ara could. They had to.

It was little comfort, but Hannah gripped onto it with iron fists. She buried her nails into it until the thought bled, soaking her brain with its essence.

She chanted it in her head like a mantra, sinking onto a chair shakily. She branded like with ink, stamping it to her consciousness, as she started to feel herself get lost in a sea of broken promises and flimsy words.

***

"No, Dee, you may not wake her up."

"I'm not waking her up, I just want to tell her something, then she can sleep again."

"Oh my god, you're like a child. Let her sleep,"

"I am a child."

"By child, I meant toddler."

"Should've said it—"

"Can you guys, like, shut up?" Hannah mumbled, trying to pry her eyes open. She heard a *thwack*, followed by an enraged growl, and Ara's voice saying, "Great job, genius."

"Hannah, wake up," Dee urged, waving a hand in front of Hannah's face. Hannah managed to peel her eyes open all the way to see an excited Dee waving Ara's phone under her nose. Hannah hauled herself up as Dee hit play on the video, which depicted a hawkish-looking lady staring at the screen.

"—*Recent footage from an attack in a Georgia train station shows some sort of bee species noted to be around six feet tall. Researchers are baffled at the sight of these winged contraptions; are they mutants? Having monsters like these, along with the 'crystal disappearances', poses a threat to the safety of individuals. We urge you all to stay inside and stay safe.*

"*Furthermore, in the footage, there is a girl who, upon further inspection, has been identified as Hannah Thorne. She lived in Grand Rapids, the city that had recently been shut off due to the* disappearance of the entire population. One of our reporters has been able to converse with her already. Let's see what he has to say."

The screen changed, and suddenly there was the man from earlier; the one Hannah had threatened in the rest area.

"Thank you, Margaret. Yes, I did have the chance to speak with Hannah. So far, she seemed troubled, not mentally, but emotionally. She kept insisting I had to remain quiet enough for her to leave, saying, 'It is for the safety of the people', or something along those lines. She also asked for more information about the 'crystal abductions', and seeing as she was a citizen, I gave it to her."

His expression darkened, and he seemed to be fighting something on the inside, then–

"There is something terribly wrong. Right now, she may seem troubled and mentally ill, but I can guarantee you: Hannah, wherever she is and whatever she is doing, is trying to help the crystal situation, much like a hero. And so should you.

"Shelter your families. Stay safe in the early hours. To the people who think this is fake: Stop neglecting the situation simply because you are afraid. To those who are already trying: Keep up the good work.

"This is likely just a mysterious, dark time in the timeline of humanity as the number of disappearances gets higher, but we will try as hard as we can to recover the crystal people and find a way to reverse the effects. Thank you for your support."

He nodded at the screen, and it flipped back to the lady, but Dee switched it off entirely.

"Hannah?" Ara asked softly, studying her closely, "Are you okay?"

Hannah couldn't bring herself to answer. The overload of information kept bouncing off the corners of her brain, multiplying into so many thoughts she could hardly keep up. Out of all the thoughts, one was highlighted.

"Why didn't they include you?" Hannah blurted.

Dee scoffed. "I know! Like, we are helping you, too!"

Despite the utter shock, Hannah's lips still twisted into a smile. "They called me a hero?" Her grin fell, "But I haven't done anything other than blow stuff up."

"And yet they're calling you a hero," Ara nodded, her lips twitching with a faint smile, "Funny how that works, doesn't it?"

"Yeah," Hannah mumbled as the moments before she'd fallen asleep rushed towards her, "But it isn't me that is the hero. It's you guys."

Dee blinked at her. "We're a team,"

Hannah laughed, though it sounded hollow, "Yeah. A team."

"We're serious. Dooble and I agree on something for the first time. We're a team, no matter how much we want to throw each other out the window," Ara then smiled. A full, wide smile. Seeing her warmed something inside Hannah's heart. Especially when Dee nodded triumphantly and then turned her head in Ara's direction so rapidly that a violent *crick* could be heard from her neck. Dee winced, but her expression of outrage didn't fade.

"*Dooble?*" She repeated incredulously.

"Something wrong, Dalia?" Ara asked sweetly, laughing when Dee gave her a less-than-friendly hand gesture. Hannah felt herself grin. At the same moment, the back of her mind whispered her doubts, insecurities, everything she was scared of, everything bad she'd ever done.

But for the first time, she ignored it.

AMARA

Ara studied the map splayed across her phone screen, frowning. It told them their destination was somewhere in the middle of Florida, but they couldn't cover every inch of the state before their deadline.

A pulsing ache in her head made her groan and reach up to massage it. She switched off both phones and set them aside. There would be plenty of time to figure it out later.

Hannah and Dee walked in carrying a few trays of what was supposed to resemble regular food. Still beats plane food, though.

Ara supposed she was slightly spoiled, having grown up with a celebrity as a father, although she was anything but spoiled emotionally. So she accepted the tray without complaint and began biting into the cold, hard sandwich. Dee, however, seemed perfectly content *to* complain.

"Bleh, what is this vegetable?" She asked, lifting a shriveled green.

Hannah turned to her with little interest. "I actually don't know. Just eat it anyway."

"It's edamame. It's a type of soft-cooked soybean." Ara said blandly.

Dee stared at her. "Soft-cooked? This is as hard as a stone."

Ara rolled her eyes, feeling a ghost of annoyance flare into her. It felt relieving after acting so nice with Dee lately. "Eat it or don't. I'm not your mother."

"Thankfully," Dee muttered, placing the edamame in the corner of her tray. Hannah sighed, which Ara had come to determine was reserved for her and Dee's squabbles.

"So," Dee said, pushing another green away, "What's the *new* plan?"

Again, Ara's eyes landed on Hannah, like an instinct. Hannah's skin took on a paler sheen this time, and her eyes flicked down into her lap, where her fingers fiddled with the sandwich crust. Her lips were pressed together so tightly they nearly turned white. This was odd, even for her, but seeing as they were much closer to reaching their destination, she must've been feeling anxious. Her fingers left the shredded crust and wrapped around the hilt of her dagger mindlessly.

Ara tore her eyes away, not wanting Hannah to feel any more nervous under her scrutiny. "Once we reach Orlando, we have to find a way to get closer to Yin. I think if we use my monocle, we can try to find the source."

"Great plan. Then, when we find it, we fight?"

Ara suppressed a resigned growl. "No, we have to outsmart it. Or, at the very least, try to lay low until it's time to spring the attack. We have to keep the element of surprise."

"You're talking about all of this stuff like you are ready for it," Hannah said quietly, "Do we even know what we're up against other than the giant body I described to you the other day?"

An uneasy silence stretched out as Ara fought to come up with a response.

"No," Ara said finally, "We don't know."

And that's when she felt it.

Pure, bone-shattering fear erupted inside her. They had no idea what, where, when, or how to deal with this. They were running into it blind, head-first, with nothing more to protect them than a gun, a sword, and a dagger, all of which could easily be disarmed.

Something akin to panic swiped through her brain, and suddenly, breathing became difficult. Her lungs felt constricted, denying vital airflow, but she bit it down. Ara only had a panic attack twice before this one: Once when her mother died, the second when Goldie was gone.

Ara would not go through this indignifying process in front of them, so she bit down on her lip until her breathing slowed to normal, and her mind cleared.

Hannah, it seemed, wasn't feeling too well either. She staggered to her feet and mumbled something about taking a walk, and Ara hated the obvious relief she felt. They'd have to find some other time to talk about this, but it was liberating not to have this conversation now.

Dee stared at Hannah's withdrawing form, then she reached for her sword. She began cleaning it with a tissue meticulously, trying to bring it back to its former shine.

Defeated but relieved, Ara sank back into her seat and tilted her head up, letting her eyes flicker shut. She beat away the swirling, negative thoughts and calibrated her mind to filter out all traces of emotion.

Only then, it seemed, could she actually rest.

CHAPTER 19

HANNAH

Hannah could feel something tear inside her, letting all the words she'd so desperately contained come pouring out.

I will be killed.

I want to go home.

I want–

Something near her hip sent a jolt of ice into her body, so cold she cried out in pain. Her hand shot into her pockets and retrieved a freezing Ozzie.

"Ow, ow, ow," She tipped it onto a nearby shelf, hissing as the cold seeped into her skin. She rubbed her hands together rapidly, trying to generate some warmth. The car lights suddenly dimmed, and Hannah's face was bathed in alarming violet light. The smoke inside Ozzie rumbled violently, both from the shaking of the train and as a warning.

Yin, its twin, was nearby.

And it was at work.

"Oh no," Hannah muttered, grabbing a sprawled nearby blanket and cupping Ozzie into it, "Oh no, no, no, no, no,"

She sprinted toward Ara and Dee's car, dumping Ozzie onto a seat. Dee's head snapped up when she entered.

Ara sprang up, alarmed. "Hannah? What–?"

"No time," Hannah tossed the blanket away and curled her fingers around the hilt of her dagger, but didn't pull it out. "I think it's here."

"It's here?" Dee got to her feet, looking the most level-headed Hannah had seen her. Hannah nodded, her heart pounding against her ribcage.

"But why would it be here? And why would Ozzie be so bright? And–?"

"I don't know!" Hannah gripped Ara's shoulders, knowing she probably looked crazed and out of her mind and terribly desperate. But her mind was running with so many words and instructions that Hannah could barely decipher them before they flashed out of space.

"Okay, Hannah, calm down." Dee placed a hand on Hannah's arm, and Hannah inhaled deeply and let go of Ara, already feeling her mind race again.

Dee whirled a startled Hannah around and tightened her hold on her shoulders. "Okay, let's think. Did you see it?"

"N-no, but–"

"Did you hear it?" Dee cut her off, her intense gray eyes boring into Hannah's hazel ones.

"No, but Ozzie clearly–"

"Okay..." Dee let go of Hannah to pace, "Ara? We're toward the back of the train, right?"

Ara nodded, her face set into a stern determination.

"Hannah? How close were you to our car when you left?" She paused her pacing to glance at Hannah.

Hannah swallowed, already feeling stupid at how she reacted when Ara and Dee were supposedly so calm. "I just went a couple of cars ahead."

Abruptly, the dim lights of the train started fading in and out, and the train began to shudder on the tracks. They were all thrown to the floor.

More violent shaking.

Ara swore under her breath. "It's in the cab."

Hannah and Dee gave her nonplussed looks.

"The area where the conductor drives," Ara simplified.

"But why...?" Hannah felt her fists clench to grip something as realization hit her as fast as the train they were on, "The conductors. It's going to crystallize the conductors,"

Without thinking, Hannah staggered to her feet, grabbed Ozzie, and bolted down the cars, ignoring the few terrified, perplexed passengers who stared at her as she darted past. Her thoughts raced, realizing too late that she would be crystallized.

But Hannah brushed the thought aside as she rammed into the cab, vaguely realizing Ara and Dee had caught up with her to see the horrifying spectacle.

Ozzie's smoke had morphed into a cool green again, as its twin had seemingly disappeared. But two men at the front were now transformed into cool, crystal sculptures.

Hannah felt her grip loosen on the orb and dagger, and they both landed on the padded ground in soft thuds. She stared, feeling as though she, herself, had turned into crystal. Stunned tears had pooled in her eyes, blurring her vision as memories flooded her brain.

Her father, beside their car, a horrified expression encased in crystal.

Her mother, beside their car, a terrified expression set in crystal.

It felt like déjà vu, a cruel trick played on her by the universe. But this time, there was no one beside her when it happened– apart from Jax.

And then he was gone, too.

"Hannah," Someone shook her hard, "Hannah, please, we're going to *die*,"

Hannah snapped her head back to the person. Dee stared at her, imploring her with her pleading eyes to listen.

Even though she was still in shock, Hannah was listening.

"Ara is trying to figure out how to stop the train, but we will likely crash," Dee swallowed, "We need to get everyone to safety at the back of the train."

Hannah nodded, scooping up her dagger and Ozzie. She tucked them safely in their holding places and then sprinted down the train.

Dee followed and cupped her hands around her mouth. "Get to the back of the train! We're going to crash!"

Hannah directed people towards the back, while the non-crystallized train assistants staggered to the front.

When they were sure everyone was at the back, Hannah and Dee made their way to the front of the still-speeding train.

"Any luck?" Dee asked, breathless.

Lights flashed, attendants stumbled, and Ara was hugging the wall, trying to inch her way to the corner of the cab. Her fingers fumbled on the side of the wall and latched onto something big and red.

She wrenched it down.

Everyone was thrown to the front as the train squealed and hissed. Red emergency lights flashed, bathing their faces in panic. Hannah crumpled to her knees, dimly recognizing Ara and Dee dragging themselves to where she was sitting.

Hannah clutched her pendant to her chest, desperate to hold on to something. She squeezed her eyes so tightly, small tears leaking out of the corners. Hannah held her breath as the momentum of the train came to a rapid decline, and she drew into herself, retreating, away from the pain, the panic, the peril.

It all came rushing back to her as the train came to an abrupt, squealing stop. After a few gasping breaths, Hannah's heart started beating in its normal pattern again. She pried her eyes open, still alarmed to see the crystal statues still there.

It was like she'd fanned the flames. One minute, the realization comes, and the next, the statues are melting into an acidic green puddle on the floor. Then, there was no trace of them, no puddle either. They were gone. They were never there.

Hannah took another deep breath, then tore her eyes away from the spot that once held two people and instead latched onto her friends. Dee and Ara groaned, rubbing their heads, and slowly sat up, staring at Hannah with obvious relief.

Despite her internal turmoil, Hannah offered them a victorious, pained smile.

CHAPTER 20

DIANA

Ara was such a pain.

That's what Dee would've said if the blonde wasn't pressing an ice pack to the back of Dee's skull, easing the headache that had erupted once she banged her head against the control panel when the train had come to its abrupt stop.

So Dee tried to show she was grateful for her help because she was occupied trying to figure out where they would have to continue their trek. Even though no one voiced it, she knew none of them wanted to hop off the train and hike the rest of the way to Orlando.

She gritted her teeth as Ara shifted the icepack so it dug into her skull harder.

"It's bad enough that you've given up strategizing–"

"Not given up," Ara corrected, "Giving you a chance to try to put that brain of yours to use,"

Dee rolled her eyes. "Right. And the head injury I got *might* be getting worse by how hard you're pressing that ice pack on my head."

"Guys, not right now." Someone sighed, padding into the room. Dee craned her neck to see an exasperated Hannah drop down into the seat across from her and take a few gulps of water from a bottle, leaning back leisurely.

"I have a *head injury*–"

"Actually," Ara said, lifting the ice pack and prodding at Dee's head with her fingers, "You just have a bump. Hopefully, you got some sense knocked into you."

"I'll knock some sense into–"

"Okay, enough!" Hannah straightened, setting the almost-empty bottle down. "What are we going to do now?"

Dee shrugged as the freezing weight of the ice pack descended on her head again, courtesy of a now-smirking Ara.

Hannah leaned closer, lowering her voice. "How are we going to get out of here and to Orlando? We're not too far from the station, but I don't know, or think, anyone here knows how to drive a train, considering Yin–"

She shuddered, continuing, "–took out both conductors and the locomotive engineer."

Dee's head shot up, suddenly eager. "Drive a train? Just find a YouTube video to help. How hard can it be?"

***

Turns out, learning how to conduct a train *is* hard. Dee's head spun with the diverse options of blinking lights and bamboozling switches, and her gaze steered clear of Ara's smug grin.

She turned to one of the train attendants. "You're saying there were only three people here on this train who could conduct it, and all of them are gone?"

The lady peered down at her, adjusting her collar haughtily. Even though her expression told Dee exactly how irritated she was, her voice was all sunshine when she said, "That would be correct. Unfortunately, there is not much we can do at the moment, as it is quite a unique situation. We urge all passengers to please remain seated as we try to sort through this inconvenience."

Dee bit back a few unique and colorful words.

Hannah cleared her throat. "We don't mean to pry, especially as young girls who naturally have no business looking into these matters. However..."

Hannah's face went stony as her mouth pressed in a grim line.

Ara glanced at her. "However, we are traveling to meet my grandmother. She is quite ill and we need to check on her soon, so you understand the haste."

"Yeah. That." Hannah agreed, still uncomfortable.

Dee frowned, but her attention had already flicked away. It was bright in here. Arrays of buttons winked back at her. The smell was metallic.

The lady stared, clearly baffled, but she didn't question them further. "I see. I hope she gets better..."

"Who?" Dee asked absently, tearing her gaze away from one blinking light.

The lady's expression turned even more peculiar. "The grandma?"

Ara elbowed Dee sharply in the ribs. "Thank you for your concern."

The lady offered her a single, polite nod, obviously singling Ara out as the responsible one.

"Anyway," Hannah interjected, redirecting this mindless conversation, "We were hoping to understand what exactly the issue you are trying to fix and how you are going to do that. For curiosity purposes, of course. And we've never been in this situation, and we have to call our parents and let them know."

Hannah's voice cracked on the last few words, and suddenly her confidence was warped. Dee felt a twinge of sympathy for her, but didn't linger on it as the lady said–

"Of course. Currently, we've let the rest of the trains know this track has been shut down, and we're waiting for a new conductor to come here to drive the train."

"And how long will that take?" Ara asked, her tone urgent, as though she needed to be proved wrong.

"At least half the day," The lady coughed, "We apologize for the inconvenience."

Half a day?

They didn't have free hours to spend away like that; they had to leave. And soon.

Dee sighed, already feeling the ache in her throat return. The thought in her head was so bizarre and very unlikely to work, but they were out of all good options. "Hannah, Ara, go, I'll handle this."

Ara blanched. "No, absolutely not–"

"Listen, I know you probably don't believe me, but I think I can try to get this train moving. In the meantime, why don't you try to find a way to get to–" Dee bit her tongue, "–grandma."

A muscle ticked in Hannah's jaw, but she nodded and tugged Ara away. Ara threw one last disbelieving look Dee's way, then allowed herself to be dragged off.

Dee closed her eyes, exhaling. She could hear the attendant's feet retreating down the narrow aisle, and immediate words drew themselves on her tongue, outlined by the sharpness of magic.

"Come here." Instant pain erupted in her throat, turning her already weary voice into a rasp, but Dee refused to stop.

She opened her eyes to see the attendant still in front of her, her eyes unfocused, her mouth a whitened line.

"Follow me," She bit her tongue to dilute the agony and stepped into the cab, shutting her eyes again, blocking out the hundreds of switching and flashing lights. Her mouth filled with the taste of blood. Her teeth released their iron grip on her tongue to prepare for the next words:

"Hands on the throttle,"

Vaguely, she could hear the attendant's hands curling around the metal.

"The nearest station is not too far from here. Get us there fast."

A beat, before a low whine, and suddenly Dee was tipping backward, her eyes finally ripping open to fling herself onto the nearest wall as the train accelerated.

She clutched the edge of the entryway, her knuckles white as she watched the attendant transfixed on her singular order. Dee's order.

Trees were soon flying past them, the ground tumbling beneath them. Only the sky was unaltered, a vast painting of brilliant blue, streaked with thinning gray that were clouds. Dee chose to focus on that as her stomach heaved and her eyes watered. Her head pounded, begging for a release she couldn't offer. Her throat burned, begging for a rest she couldn't afford. Her power trembled, confused and unused. Reality felt like a mindless, eternal game for fools. Only those who were insane and hopeful could traverse on. Those who were sane, who knew better, could liberate themselves from the clawing grips of life.

What was wrong with her?

Her chest was twenty pounds heavier. She was ten times more nauseous. This felt like guilt, but what for?

Her gaze landed on the stiff attendant, mindless and silent. How would Dee like it if she were stripped of her mental wishes? How would she feel if her thoughts had been muffled by the orders of a random *stranger*?

Dee had never once thought how terrible this power was, turning her tongue into a knife. Her words into stones. It was so brutal, just like her.

Her fingers tightened around sharp metal, jolting her out of her agonized mental spiral. She uncoiled her tightened hand, surprised to see the ring had cut into the soft flesh of her hand, drawing midnight blue blood to stain her skin. She stared, the sudden boldness in her veins reduced to a trembling weakness.

She was a monster.

She was a manipulator.
She was a siren.

***

Ara had found her in the bathroom, staring at the mirror, her face gaunt with self-loathing. After emptying the contents of her stomach, every single fiber of her being burned with agony she both could and couldn't explain.

So when Ara had asked her how she got the train moving again, Dee gave her a terrible, mumbled response that Ara would definitely ask her to repeat, just in a less... terrible way.

Dee's loathing for her was rapidly increasing by the minute.

But for now, she lay sprawled over three seats, her arm over her eyes, soft breaths escaping her nose that could pass off for snores, hopefully convincing her friends.

She heard Hannah sigh. "Ara, now what do we do?"

A beat, before Ara murmured, "There's nothing else we can do. After we get off in Orlando, I'll use my monocle and we'll... we'll figure it out."

Uneasy, melancholy silence stretched out. Dee turned her breathing into shallower, quieter breaths.

"Hannah, don't yell at me for this, but don't you think there is something... up with Dee?" Ara whispered, her voice tinged with uncertainty.

Excuse me, what?

Dee almost jerked upwards, ready to start arguing, when she remembered she was supposed to be asleep.

Right.

Play it cool, play it quiet.

"What do you mean?" Hannah asked, her voice defensive. Dee mentally cheered her on.

"She has excellent sword skills as a *fourteen-year-old*, a sword that came from nowhere, and she's *really* good at convincing people, not to mention she has little experience with the outside world."

Dee was harnessing every ounce of willpower not to get up and bash Ara's face in.

Hannah puffed out a breath. "All of which is true, but maybe it's because she's homeschooled? And you are the daughter of an *actor*, Ara. You've always had experience with the outside world."

Ara's father was an actor? Dee, despite her annoyance, felt shame creep into her ears. Every day was proving she knew less and less about her companions, which was fitting because they knew next to nothing about her.

Ara exhaled slowly, with a tone that made Dee picture her pinching the bridge of her nose. "Fine. We'll talk about this later."

"Okay. How long until we reach the station?"

There was some rustling and a few taps until Ara said, "About an hour."

We're almost there, Dee traced out the words in her head, letting them fill out the expanse of her mind. They'd been on this dreary train for a full day now, and Dee was eager to feel her feet on solid ground again, to breathe in fresh air, even if it was only bringing them closer to their fate.

We're almost there.

CHAPTER 21

AMARA

Ara pushed her glasses higher up on her nose as sweat threatened to slip them down. Cursing the weather under her breath, she smoothed back her now frizzing blonde hair as they stepped outside the station.

Orlando was one of her favorite places to travel to when accompanying her father on one of his shoots, but in the summer, this place just screamed with the thickening heat and tropical vibes.

Not too far away, a tiny lizard scampered up the brick wall. Ara's eyes tracked it until its scaly tail disappeared around the corner.

"I'd forgotten how hot it gets here."

Ara turned to see Hannah folding up her sleeves to her forearms, already looking uncomfortable with the heat. Her dagger was on full display, but Hannah didn't seem to care. People would probably mistake it for a prop, anyway.

In Ara's case, however, a gun would be a very flashy threat, and despite the heat, she wished she still had her coat to tie around her waist– it would've concealed her weapon perfectly. Unfortunately for her, it was left on the train.

Dee shuffled behind Hannah, her gray eyes squinting in the harsh sunlight. The sleeves of her dark t-shirt were already short, but now she'd rolled up the ends of her jeans to accommodate the temperature. The smooth metal of her ring sent a glare into Ara's eyes. So she averted them, instead choosing to focus on their bleak, sun-stained surroundings.

She turned to see Hannah watching her expectantly. Ara sighed and reached for her monocle...

Before her fingers could plunge into her pocket, something cold and stiff curled around her wrist.

She whirled around and came face to face with a crystal statue.

A stunned gasp exited Hannah's mouth as they all glanced around to see a ring of crystal statues frozen around them. Their faces were expressionless, their stance simple.

Ara had seen statues such as these three times before– the first when everyone had crystallized, the next when Hannah's mother and Goldie had ambushed them in the forest, and the last on the train– and all three times Ara hadn't been able to see them properly. It was painfully inappropriate to examine it when Hannah's mom had crystallized, and the other two times, adrenaline and desperation had blinded her.

But now, bathed in the sunlight and frozen, she had all the time Ara needed to study the statues.

They looked as though they were made of ice; crystallized but opaque. Their faces were chiseled to the tiniest of details. Their eyes were soulless, unfeeling, like frozen soldiers. The sunlight made the statues infinitely brighter.

Ara shifted to examine the one in front of her, then remembered the unforgiving grip the statue had on her wrist.

Hannah's face was white, and Dee's showed she was alarmed. They both looked over at Ara.

Ara stared back. "What the heck?"

"Where did they come from?" Dee asked, her voice steely as she glared at one statue, already in a defensive stance.

"I don't–"

Abruptly, something shifted, and then so did the statues.

They all launched into a defensive position, drawing various blades and pointing them. The one holding Ara dragged her toward her friends, releasing its grip on her wrist so Ara could join Hannah and Dee. She immediately straightened, her hand flying to her gun with a sneer aimed at the soldiers.

They stood, back to back, all of them with their weapons drawn. There were around eight soldiers, forming an octagon around them.

"We can't kill them," Ara muttered, glowering at each soldier in turn, "Just disarm them. I'll take–"

The crystal soldiers surged forward, and Ara immediately leveled a gun toward one soldier's arm, her finger on the trigger, about to shoot, when–

Hannah stepped in front of her, her dagger thrust up to meet the soldier's. Upon impact with the bases of both daggers, she twisted her blade downwards, sending the soldier's knife clattering to the ground as she rounded her blade and pointed it at the statue's heart. The soldier's arm shot out to snatch Hannah's blade, which she deflected and thrust to a surprised Ara.

"Contain him," she gritted out, already turning to disarm another incoming soldier.

Ara tore her eyes away, astounded, and set to placing her gun to the soldier's head as she forced him to sit on the grass on his hands. The soulless monstrosity was satisfyingly compliant.

Just as she stepped behind him to monitor her friends' progress, three more statues were flung her way. She set to detain them as well, aiming the gun at each of their heads in a pattern. The method was weak, especially with her inexperience, but the effect was visible. The statues seemed to understand that if they moved, they'd receive a bullet to the head, and since they were crystal, they'd be blown to pieces.

It was kind of depressing to think about. That was all they knew and understood: violence.

Another soldier came careening towards Ara and tried to grab her shoulders. Ara jumped to the side and gave it an extra push. The soldier tried to scramble away, but with a glare and a gun pointed at it, the statue dropped beside the rest of its companions and stilled.

Dee let out a triumphant grunt, and Ara spun to see her pin one soldier to the ground, her foot on the sprawled statue's back. Hannah, on the other hand, jerked the crystal sword out of her attacker's hands, sending the soldier sprawling into the grass face first. She tossed the sword aside without a second glance and stalked over to the warrior, pinning its arms behind its back with dark malice in her eyes.

She clenched the soldier's wrists in one fist as she finally looked up, a look of approval flashing through her gaze when she saw Dee, and then her eyebrows raised at Ara in a question.

Ara gestured to the detained soldiers beside her with her gun. Hannah's eyes flicked to them, then back to Ara's face.

"Well, that was easy,"

"Easy?!" Dee shook her head, amazement upon her face, "How did you do that, Hannah?"

Hannah frowned, still atop her new prisoner. "Do what?"

"You better be joking." Dee laughed, now staring at the pile of crystal warriors, her eyes dark with humor, "You literally took down six soldiers with, what, a dagger?"

Hannah glanced at the blade in her hands with surprise. "Yeah, I guess so. Crazy, isn't it? There's that instinct–"

"Yes, very interesting, Hannah, but we have more pressing issues here." Ara interrupted, gesturing to the heap of crystal limbs. Hannah's lips pressed into a tight line.

Dee rolled her eyes. "Let the girl have her glory."

Ara frowned. "Shut up."

"For what?"

"I said shut up!" Ara glanced around, doing a quick mental count. With the soldiers she had, plus Hannah's and Dee's, there was a total of seven soldiers.

Seven.

So, where was number eight?

"Hannah look out!" Ara cried, forgetting all about the crystal warriors beside her and tackling Hannah off her soldier just as the eighth nearly drove its blade through her. They tumbled to the side as Dee quickly jumped up and wrenched the crystal sword out of its owner and gripped its wrist, shoving it down into the grass.

They all stared at each other, panting, wordlessly confirming they were all okay.

"The soldiers," Ara gasped, shooting to her feet, "They–"

Her words were cut off with a strangled choke as the freed soldiers faded away into neon green light. Hannah staggered to her feet too, her face gaunt with self-accusation. Dee stumbled to her feet, aghast, staring at the spot where the crystal soldiers once were.

Ara whirled to her. "Where's the last one?"

Dee stared down at the empty grass. Her head shot up, swiveling around to scan their surroundings. "There!"

The last soldier was already fading into green light, its head turned away in the direction of the high noon sun.

Ara was already running, willing her legs to pump faster, her glasses bouncing on her nose as she took off sprinting. Hannah and Dee darted beside her, all three of them racing towards their goal.

Their target.

The remnants of the soldier were fading into the light, ceasing to exist.

Ara refused to let that happen.

She fisted the evaporating crystal and felt Dee and Hannah latch on, too. Suddenly, they were being drawn in, green light enveloping them, clouding their eyesight. Ara felt herself being sucked into the light, squeezing her eyes shut as the world faded away, them dematerializing with it.

CHAPTER 22

HANNAH

Hannah felt herself as dust.

And light.

And teeny little molecules swirling in an inferno through time and space.

Hannah could only feel her consciousness amongst the chaos and found solace that it was still there.

Then, as quickly as it started, she felt her brain and heart materialize, followed by the rest of her body. The world was filled with blinding, green light. It was kind of pretty, a lot like the Northern Lights.

The lights then faded, and Hannah—as pleasing as they were—was relieved to see them go. She toppled face-first into swishy strands of grass, her body sprawling on the now soft ground.

The first thing she noticed: the smell. It wasn't stinky, but it wasn't exactly a candle scent either. It smelled of both greenery and desolation. It reminded her of how sometimes fire was a good thing; its flames drawing out a path through the world, consuming everything in its wake, including the corrupted plants. That removed unnecessary weeds and allowed new plants to grow. No matter how devastating the truth and reality could be, it was the purest thing nature offered.

The word flashed in Hannah's mind, and it seemed to fit the smell. Pure. It smelled pure.

When her eyes reopened, they met a wall of varying shades of green. Hannah rose to her feet, her eyes drinking in the sight around her.

She was in a lush, green meadow with waist-long grass and all sorts of exotic flowers. The sky was bright blue and cloudless, the sun amplifying the beauty of it all and beaming down on her. Hannah inhaled, feeling the pure air fill her lungs as a sense of joy sparked within her.

Which was wrong.

Someone gasped behind her, and she spun around, her gaze first landing on her splayed friends beside her, then the extent of the meadow, which was endless. The meadow stretched for miles and miles, farther than her eye could see. Its beauty was stunning.

.

.

.

Except for the dome in the center of it all.

The giant rock formation was hundreds of feet tall and probably double its width. The stone was dark, even though the harsh sunlight was directed right at it. A small, sparkling river snaked around the side of it, perfectly innocent, combined with the cave as though its cheery accomplice. In the center of the cave was a comically small-scale opening, the inside filled with darkness shrouding its secrets, though Hannah had a pretty good feeling it was the home of the thing they had come to destroy.

Sure, they had almost died a lot of times, but now, staring at the giant cave, their adventure felt a whole lot real.

And a whole lot more treacherous.

Everything was quiet except for the pleasing swish of a cool breeze, and the small clinks of crystal in the cave, which slowly exited in the form of crystal soldiers. Their gazes were harsh and unforgiving, but also soulless and devoid of expression. They marched out in neat, concentrated formations, each carrying some form of a merciless blade. Hannah didn't know what to feel. Blobs of fear, dread, excitement, nervousness, terror, anger, hatred, and hope stacked together inside of her. Making her feel strong, but weak at the same time. Determined, but unsure. What if she couldn't do this? What if she'd come all this way just to serve as another crystal soldier?

Her thoughts were interrupted by a strangled gasp.

Dee's limbs were shaking, her gray eyes wide with horror, her jaw slack, her mouth open. Hannah followed her line of vision and felt a stab of shock, quickly replaced with sorrowful empathy.

Near the mouth of the cave were three crystal soldiers. One that was tall, thin, and feminine. The other was young, tall, and had messy hair. And the last was childlike, small, and girly.

Mrs. Adrane, Adrian, and Pelli.

Hannah turned back to Dee and placed a comforting palm on her shoulder, hating the way Dee looked suddenly sick.

"Dee?" Hannah asked gently, trying to get her to meet her eyes.

"They– they were safe," Dee whispered, her eyes pleading, asking Hannah to offer her some consolation that this was a fluke. As though she just realized the severity of the situation. "Nothing was going to happen to them."

Hannah's gaze lowered solemnly. "That's what we all thought."

Dee inhaled a shuddering breath, closing her eyes. The angles of her face hardened.

And then she took off running.

"Dee!" Hannah whispered-hissed as she bounded after her. They darted through the grass, weaving out a path that would surely get them all seen and killed. Hannah lunged after her, tackling Dee and sending them both skidding in the grass. Dee flailed under Hannah's grasp but only managed to shove her off before Ara grabbed Dee's arm and forced her to sit.

"Wait," Hannah panted, splaying out her fingers as though calming a rabid beast, "We're here to get them back."

She didn't add the *maybe* that was floating in her mind. The thought alone made her want to puke.

"You idiots!" Ara growled, shoving both of them down behind the grass, "They're looking in our direction now!"

"I didn't ask for Dee to sprint so we could play tag!" Hannah snapped, lying low on the grass.

Both of them turned to glare at Dee.

"Hey, I didn't ask for my family to be taken away!" she protested, her words stumbling over each other to get out.

"None of us did," Hannah mumbled, staring into the grass ahead.

They laid down, hardly breathing, ears strained to pick up on some sort of clue where the soldiers were.

Just then, a ground-rattling roar blasted from the cave. It was deafening, reverberating through the meadow as the sound waves bounced off the ground and cave. It was so thunderous that Hannah reached for her ears and squeezed her eyes shut, which had started to form tears from the pressure of being coiled so tight, of withstanding such a harsh, resounding noise. After several agonizing seconds, the roar ended, and she could breathe again.

"You guys okay?" Ara's voice asked, seemingly farther away, even though with a quick turn of her head, Hannah saw Ara still beside her. There was a faint ringing in Hannah's ears, but she swallowed the fuzziness down and responded with a weak, "Ouch."

"Only Hannah would answer to something with an 'ouch,'" Dee said, her tone sounding like an eye roll went with it.

"Oh, I'm sorry," Hannah retorted, "I just had my eardrums blasted by some formidable monster thingy. Want me to respond with a nice cup of coffee and cookies like an interview next time? Especially in the middle of a field, trying to go unnoticed by a few soldiers who would like nothing but to kill us?"

"*No*," Ara said firmly, "Just, *no*."

Hannah couldn't help but snicker. Dee snorted too, earning a scoff from Ara.

"Wait a minute," Ara tensed, pushing up to peer out of the grass, "Where was the soldier we teleported with?"

Hannah's stomach dropped. She crawled to her knees and glanced around, her brown hair flying into her eyes as the breeze tousled it even more. The weight of the orb felt much too heavy.

A cold, rigid hand closed on her shoulder.

Hannah gasped and spun around so rapidly that the grip of the statue twisted the skin on her arm. She immediately ripped her dagger out of its holster and swiped at the soldier's feet. The crystal soldier toppled to the ground, and Hannah wasted no time crawling on top of it, positioning her knees on either side as she lifted her dagger above the statue's face, angling the tip an inch away from its translucent nose.

She heard Ara suck in a startled breath. "If you even move an inch, I will put this knife in your face." She hissed, pressing its crystal arms into the ground with her knees, the stony consistency biting into her skin.

The statue froze underneath her.

"Um... is it okay?" Dee crept forward, prodding it in the arm with her sword. The soldier's hand shot out and wrapped around Dee's blade, a high-pitched sound emitting from it at the same time.

Hannah frowned, more annoyed than startled. "What? What's wrong with it?"

The air instantaneously turned bitter, and the small clinks of crystal statues moving near the caves suspended, all in the same moment. It was alarmingly noiseless.

Then the crystal sparked back to life and surged forward. Hannah glanced at Ara, soundlessly questioning. Ara peered above the grass and paled.

"We have to go. Now." She hissed, staring at both Hannah and Dee in turn.

"Why...?" Dee peeked through the green stalks, and the lines of her face changed, immediately giving way to terror.

"Crap,"

"What?" Hannah pressed, momentarily forgetting the soldier underneath her, "What's wrong?"

"Come on!" Ara tugged her to her feet, off the still-frozen soldier, "Run!"

Hannah staggered up just as a cold hand grasped her ankle. She turned and kicked the soldier, just as another grabbed her arm. After blinking and squinting in the painfully bright sunlight, she realized it was not the blazing threads of light blinding her. No, it was what was surrounding them reflecting the sunlight.

They were surrounded by crystal statues, all of them reaching for one thing: The Orb.

Hannah gasped as she felt one arm plunge into her pocket, and she spun around, swinging the handle of her dagger into the statue's head, which caused it to collapse to the ground. Another pulled her into a headlock, but its arm quickly retreated, giving her the chance to elbow the crystal warrior. Though they couldn't feel pain, she assumed, they could still fall over.

Through the mass of flailing crystal limbs, a fleshy one grabbed her and pulled her into a sprint.

Hannah's legs pumped underneath her, immediately carrying her out of the chaos and behind Dee and Ara.

"The cave!" Dee shouted against the wind, her black hair swinging into her eyes as she raced beside Hannah, "It's the only place where they aren't there right now!"

Ara swiftly pulled up on Hannah's other side, her glasses bobbing on the edge of her nose dangerously as she shoved them up higher.

Hannah snapped her focus back to the front, where the dark cave entrance loomed closer with every stride of her burning legs. It beckoned for them tauntingly, daring them to turn away.

Hannah was not going to.

Through the adrenaline feeding her desperation to distance herself from the crystal warriors, Hannah vaguely realized she was heading straight for the monster that stole away her father.

That crystallized her mother.

That was the reason why Jax is dead.

That snatched away more and more people every day.

But it was also the monster that brought her to Dee and Ara.

That brought her to The Orb.

So with Ozzie stowed in her pocket and her friends on either side, Hannah had never felt more ready.

This was either the end that would let them uphold the glory of saving the world.

Or the end that would kill them.

And it was that thought that accompanied her as they were swallowed into the darkness.

***

Hannah swallowed the recurring bile down again for the millionth time, tossing furtive glances over her shoulder every few minutes, though the effort was futile– there was nothing but eerie blackness cocooning them. Hannah could not shake off the feeling that something was following them, though there were no audible crystal clinks. Their phones were lost during the ambush, so there was no way to call for help.

Not that they'd be able to.

Hannah turned to stare forward again and padded delicately on the stone floor, cautious to avoid bumping into anything. The noiseless presence of her friends on either side comforted her, though Hannah suspected their silence was a disguise for the nerves sparking with anxiety. She could sympathize, barely hearing the sound of her own footsteps over the blood roaring in her ears.

And so they sank into a familiar rhythm, one foot in front of the other, sure of nothing but each other's presence and their footfalls. In her pocket, Hannah felt Ozzie's temperature drop steadily, soon a little colder than room temperature. Hannah still remembered the way the icy feel had stung her skin on the train, adding to the blockade of nerves confining her heart, which only served to make it thud against her ribcage harder. But she was in too deep to quit.

She lifted her head, staring dead ahead, cloaking herself with false hope and comforting thoughts, every sense heightened in this cave of darkness. She let them guide her forward, refusing to let the stubborn, relentless whispers in her head consume her.

DIANA

Every limb in Dee's body hummed with unspent adrenaline and energy, likely intensified by the buzzing nerves in her stomach. But she forced herself to walk at a tolerable pace, the same one Hannah and Ara were treading with, lest she get lost swimming in the inkiness. Desperate for a distraction, Dee plunged into her memories, sifting through something to think about.

Something akin to pain burst in her chest, making her currently stable emotions teeter dangerously into being, well, unstable.

Nevertheless, she followed the trail of emotions until an image popped into her mind.

Her mother, looking like a translucent ice sculpture, too bright for the eyes to see, reawakened the uproar of turmoil inside her, one she had to pause to deal with the more pressing situations of being attacked. But now, with only her dreary thoughts to keep her company, Dee could mull over every spike of emotion, every dip of surrender she'd felt– though she was proud there weren't many of the latter.

Her heart clenched at the thought of her brother, who, even though he was calm, responsible, and downright annoying because of those traits, made her smile and love his warranted nagging despite how much she wanted to punch him for it. The thought of him as an unfeeling crystal statue made her sick to the stomach.

While she was already in her mental spiral, Dee decided to tread into dangerous waters, coming to the one topic she knew would tear her apart on the inside: her sister.

Pelli could either be extremely sweet and precious or ignorant, sassy, and infuriating. Not a very good combination with Dee's easily sparked anger issues. Still, Dee would never wish anything ill upon her little sister and would gladly rip anyone apart for even laying a finger on her.

Seeing all three of them together as cold, unfeeling crystal soldiers changed Dee. Finally made her accept the reality of it. Now she wasn't just fighting for herself– she was fighting for her family too.

She held her chin up, casing herself with fiery hope and stubborn thoughts, every sense heightened in this pool of shadows. She let them urge her forward, refusing to let even an ounce of indecision consume her.

AMARA

Ara smoothed down her fraying nerves for the hundredth time, hating the way they split even more with every forced shutdown. She hated how easily a few stalks of fear could seep into her carefully crafted mask.

They were nearing their doom– she could feel it with every step. Every wave of anxiety left her doused and shuddering on the inside, making her wonder why she even bothered coming on this trip.

For Goldie? A small voice whispered in her head, but it felt uncertain. This wasn't for Goldie at all, Ara realized. This was for herself.

She was tired of constantly being downplayed by her father, by the nosy vultures that call themselves the press. She was tired of searching for a warm embrace, for friends who didn't care about her. For warmth in a dad who had long ago lost that title.

And if the world was going to go to crap, then so be it. At least she would perish knowing she'd at least tried to make a difference. And if she succeeded... even better.

She lowered her gaze, shrouding herself with plain, straight facts and repetitive thoughts, every sense heightened in this pit of nothingness. She let them ease her forward, refusing to let the spiraling emotions in her head consume her.

HANNAH

Every second felt like a million years smushed into every shallow breath Hannah released. Her feet had begun to ache with a dull pain, likely from all the recent sprinting they had to do. And still, nothing had begun to show. Not a single soldier. Not the Beast. Ozzie remained relatively the same, too.

What if there's nothing here? An uncertain voice slithered into her head, drawing out her fears to the front of her brain.

What if–

A speck of gold light emerged in the distance, blinking innocently and yet greedily hoarding all the brightness for itself, refusing to let even a drop spill into the dark cavern. Hannah blinked, her heart tripping over itself in the sudden twist her stomach did.

The entrance for their doom was steadily approaching, the dot growing wider as they neared the cavern room.

Hannah didn't know what she was thinking when she suddenly burst into a silent sprint. She just wanted to see light again, wanted to wrench herself out of this desolate, gloomy tunnel. She was tired of hiding, tired of waiting.

She slowed into a brisk walk the minute she set foot in through the opening. Gold light blinded her, and when Hannah's eyes adjusted, a gasp lodged in her throat, astonishment decorating her features.

The cave was covered floor to ceiling with wealth; gold bars were stacked into tiny pyramids, the rest lining the edges of the mountainous dome. Coins were splattered carelessly high and low, and all sorts of them: cents, euros, rupees, yen, pounds– every type of coin from the corners of the world were dumped here, enhancing the endless splendor. The ceiling stretched up, forming a dome at least a hundred feet above their heads. Small dark openings left little exits out of the enormous cavern, bearing untold secrets within their barely lit chambers. As for the current cave room, the expanse of it was overwhelming; it stretched much too far for the eye to see. It was so massive that tiny ledges were scattered arbitrarily along the stone formation, containing their own fair share of wealth.

Through her awe, Hannah could hear a pair of pounding footsteps behind her, signaling Dee and Ara had caught up with her, both of them huffing with indignance at being momentarily abandoned. Hannah turned her head in time to catch their twin expressions of amazement at the entire view.

They stepped beside her, eyes darting along the entire expanse as though they couldn't take it in fast enough. Hannah turned around again, drinking it in along with them. Apparently, when Yin turned a person into crystal, he took their wealth along with them. How many people had to turn into crystal for all of this? Hannah felt her stomach twist nauseatingly at the realization.

The Orb in her pocket was suddenly a hundred pounds, and Hannah was hyperaware of the reality of it. She was going to kill the Beast and destroy Yin. She was going to find a way to end it and its grip upon the now thousands of families missing a relative.

Missing someone who was turned into crystal and pulled into this insufferable dimension.

As the resolve took root in her mind, letting the waters of confidence assist its growth, a sharp, cutting voice sliced through the air.

It wasn't hers.

Nor Ara's.

Nor Dee's.

No, it was none of them.

And yet it was a voice Hannah knew perfectly, one that had been branded into her eardrums, one that she had listened to advise and support her, and one that she would continue to listen to if that voice hadn't been lost from the world.

Or so she had thought.

"I didn't actually think you'd make it all the way here. But then again, you never fail to surprise me, Hannah."

Hannah's chest constricted, a thousand elephants were stampeding over it as she turned, slowly, so very slowly, time having her in a chokehold as her eyes tracked the figure that stepped out of the shadows.

There, with a wide smile on his face and a crystal sword at his side, was Jax.

CHAPTER 23

HANNAH

Hannah's head was spinning, and her lungs thrashed, unable to intake air. A series of fleeting emotions flooded through her, each one barely registered before it was whisked away, replaced with something new. Shock, fear, denial, hesitance, acceptance, and relief swirled through her in turn, coming to land on confusion. She didn't know what was up or down, right or wrong, or why Jax was here— *here,* of all places.

He was dead. Her brain sputtered. *Wasn't he?*

But here he was, standing in front of her, very much alive, a cocky smile spread upon the face she'd seen a hundred times.

Hannah heard a sharp intake of breath on her right, sounding like Ara. That noise alone jolted her back to reality.

"Jax?" Hannah whispered, her voice timid and hushed, afraid everything would come crashing down with that single syllable.

But Jax's smile just widened. "Hello, Hannah. Good to see you."

The familiarity of his voice sent a sharp shudder through Hannah's veins. Her body itched to run to him and throw her arms around him, tell him how much she'd cried over his death, be reassured her friend was still here, alive and well.

But something stopped her.

Perhaps it was the fact that Jax was here, holding a weapon, that kept her rooted to the ground. Maybe it was the victorious glint in his eyes that halted her thrumming pulse. It could be the entirety of the situation that left her breathless and nauseous all at the same time. And so she didn't move, hardly breathed as her eyes traced his face over and over again.

His grin grew wider at her, seemingly pleased with her reaction, and the absurdity of it felt like a truck slamming into her. She blinked, dumbfounded, as Jax extended a gloved hand toward her, offering her to take it as support. Hannah stared at it like it was the most surprising thing she'd seen all week. Dee shook her shoulder roughly, likely to shake Hannah out of her trance, though it did nothing to slow her racing mind.

The three girls fell silent, staring at Jax, until the blonde opened her mouth.

"What is this?" Ara asked, her voice visibly shaky. Hannah suspected it was Ara's concern for her that made her mouth tremble with barely concealed rage. Ara seething with the anger of *not knowing* was always unpleasant to watch.

"I'll tell you, but I need Hannah to snap out of her shock first." Jax's startling dark eyes snapped on Hannah again, which did nothing for her stupefaction.

Jax's gaze softened slightly. "I don't have all day, Han."

The nickname spread like ice through her skin, at least getting her tongue to attempt to form words.

"Are you the one bonded with Yin?" She asked stupidly, cringing at her own words.

Jax's eyes twinkled with barely contained hilarity as he burst into laughter. The sound of it both calmed and agitated Hannah.

After a good round of laughing, Jax wiped his eye with a painfully charming grin. "That was cute, Hannah, but no, I'm not bonded. That would be absurd."

"Oh," Hannah let out, heat climbing to her cheeks as well as the cooling sensation of relief painting her nerves before they unraveled again. "Then what are you doing– here of all places? I–" Hannah choked back the sudden emotion forming into an agonizing lump in her throat, "I thought you were dead. Your dad said you were dead. You— you were gone, Jax."

Hannah's voice had dropped again. "You were gone," She whispered, tears forming again.

Jax's expression allowed for sympathy that didn't quite reach his eyes. "I know, Han. I know. My death," He said, taking her hand gently and twining it with his, "was faked. Because I needed to throw you off my trail."

Hannah's focus on their clasped hands nearly caused her to miss his words. She whipped her head up, and her eyes clashed with his. "Faked?"

He nodded, his lips curling with amusement, as though he knew something she didn't. "I had never died, Hannah. I've been living, biding my time," He let go of her hand and stepped back, cocking his head to the side, "For longer than you think."

Hannah's mouth went dry, and she completely ignored Ara's warning glance when she asked: "Who faked your death, then?"

The corners of Jax's mouth tipped up, which gave Hannah's heart an involuntary flutter. "I did."

And just like that, whatever comfort she'd felt in the last minute was shredded to flimsy slivers, much like her sanity. When no sound escaped her lips, Dee took charge.

"Why? Do you know how worried Hannah was? How worried we were, even though we barely knew you?" She demanded.

Jax's eyes flicked from her to Hannah again. "And for that, alone, I am sorry."

Dee frowned. "For making us worry?"

"No. For making Hannah worry. Don't take this the wrong way, and I'm flattered you worried for my well-being, but I hardly know you two. Why should I worry about your worries?" He said simply, eyes scanning over the three girls.

Hannah felt a twinge of confusion replace the momentary gratitude. "Jax, please explain what... all this is? Why are you here? Why did you fake your death?" Hannah stepped forward, painfully aware of how desperate she sounded, hands itching with nothing to hold onto.

"Just... why?"

Jax's calm, amused composure melted as though he'd fixed a mask upon his face, leaving him callous and indifferent. Only a hint of a sparkle remained in his eyes when he said–

"Yin is bonded, but not to me. And I control the Beast."

Hannah felt her eyes roll up. Felt her body collapse. She heard two alarmed shouts before everything blacked out.

***

A feather-light touch swept over her cheek, followed by a few colorful words, and then suddenly someone was yanking it away. Hannah abruptly shot up, her eyes ungluing themselves as a golden chamber flickered into view, interrupted by a tall, brunet figure leaning over her, empty concern in his dark eyes.

Hannah's hazel ones widened, and she glanced around, only relaxing slightly when she saw Dee and Ara on either side of Jax, perfectly safe.

Her stomach tightened at the memory replaying in her mind, and she forced herself to look up at a kneeling, unconcerned Jax.

"You didn't faint when your mother had been crystallized," He said, cocking his head to the side, "What changed?"

The reminder didn't initiate her soul-crushing sorrows, but rather, red-hot rage flooding every sense. Hannah let out an angered cry, and suddenly she was leaping towards him, dagger in hand. He immediately jumped to his feet and dodged her stab, turning behind her simultaneously. He wrapped one arm around her waist and pulled her back flush against his chest as the other arm wrapped around her wrist, twisting it so Hannah's grip on her weapon faltered and Jax could send the weapon clattering to the ground.

Hannah yelled in protest as Jax twisted her around and– although she loathed him for it– gently pushed her into Dee and Ara, whose arms gripped Hannah's, preventing her from charging at Jax.

Tears were streaming down Hannah's face as she struggled against the rigid grips of her friends, who were also shouting, telling Hannah to stop this madness. They'd never seen Hannah this angry before. Hannah had never seen herself this angry before.

"I trusted you!" She screamed, aimlessly kicking her feet, "And you sent the monster after my parents! You're killing this world! You're–"

Jax bowed his head so that his and Hannah's faces were aligned. Her words cut off as he leaned close, devoid of expression.

"You trusting me was the best and most terrible thing you've ever done, Hannah," He said bluntly, the light from his eyes faded from the dark pools staring into hers. His calculating gaze searched her face, and for some reason, Hannah fell silent under his scrutiny, all her rage dimming into gut-wrenching pain...

He turned away, and the fury slammed back into her. Greedily, she relished it, grateful to mask her feelings behind anger, to let this hatred flood every nerve instead of mind-numbing distress. As Jax turned his back on her, all she imagined was driving her dagger through it, even though it had been forgotten on the ground. As though she had read

Hannah's thoughts, Ara hesitantly released Hannah and retrieved the dagger, sliding it back into Hannah's sheath wordlessly.

"I only sent the Beast after your mother, Hannah," Jax murmured. Hannah growled at the back of his head, straining against Dee's iron grip uselessly. She glared at Dee, who, for the first time, didn't look impulsively angry. Instead, her eyes pleaded for Hannah to stop resisting. Hannah glowered at her and directed her gaze at a still-calm Jax.

"You're cruel. You're terrible. Why would you do that?" She bit out, fighting every impulse to break into a fit of enraged screams again.

Jax whipped around, his lips tilted into a cruel, calculating grin. It was psychotic. "There are a lot of reasons why I would do something like that, and if I stay here telling you all of it..." He paused, considering, and a weak, stubborn part of her claimed it as a victory, even though it was nothing of the sort.

He smiled again. "Well, we'd be here forever if I started discussing that. But when I tell you this, keep it in mind."

Jax waited until Hannah was listening– really paying attention and not just cursing him under her breath– until he said:

"It *hurt* me to send the Beast after your mother. I doubt anything *I've* ever done has caused me the level of pain I felt when I saw you crying outside."

At that, the fire in Hannah's heart froze. She was unsure of what to do with that information.

"Anyway," Jax sighed, plowing on as though Hannah hadn't just been suspended in time with his confession, "It seems the effort was well worth it in the end. You were initiated into this adventure, which was exactly what I needed."

"Stop giving us your little backstory and tell us how– and why– you ditched us." Ara gritted out, fingers curling into fists so tight it must've been painful.

"No one ever wants to hear my stories," Jax mused, shaking his head bitterly even though a small smile graced his lips. "Fine, then. I'll tell you.

"When we had stopped at the gas station and you three had left, I was about to fade away–" He cocked his head. "Do you know what that is?"

"Yes, the teleportation thingy." Dee snapped. "Go on."

Jax nodded. "I was about to ditch the cab driver and fade away, only I realized there was another source of magic there. The one from the Lobster creature. It didn't take much to convince the cabbie to drive away, and by that time, I had called the Beast in front of us, turned the driver into crystal, and let him crash the car. By then, I had faded away, but not after ensuring that whoever found that car knew I was in there. I left my phone there– I didn't need it anyway– and let the news spread."

An uneasy silence stretched out, leaving Hannah appalled.

"Your parents are devastated, Jax. How could you do that to them?"

The lines of Jax's face hardened. "Don't pretend to understand things you don't, Hannah. It's idiotic."

Hannah flinched, unaccustomed to the sharpness of Jax's voice. The awareness of her flinch led to a whole other bout of mute rage bubbling up.

Jax inhaled, as though calming himself, and the rigid lines softened into an indifferent expression, which was to say, about no expression.

"You don't have *any* idea, Hannah, everything I have done for this. And I know you probably want to unalive me as of this moment, but maybe think from my perspective for once. I truly am your friend, and I never wanted to upset you. But I've also made a promise that I can't let go of now."

"Cut the sweet talk and keep explaining. Any more monsters you know?" Dee growled, her hands unconsciously tightening around Hannah's arm.

Ara gasped. "That's right. You were dealing with the Dragoncake Grocery, weren't you?"

Jax's eyebrows raised, and he opened his mouth, shut it again, pondered, and then said: "Yes, I was dealing with them. For efficiency."

"They tried to kill us!" Hannah bit out. Her neck throbbed with the reminder of the fatal wound that once punctured the junction between her shoulder and throat. "I nearly died! Wait– screw you! I did die! The antidote revived me... or something," She tossed a confirmation glance at Ara, who grimaced but nodded. Hannah turned to Jax with newfound vigor, but was cut off with–

"And that is why I stopped dealing with them. Well, that, and you guys exploded that entire portion of land with your Orb." His eyes brightened, "Speaking of which, now is the perfect time to hand it over to me."

His arm stretched forward, palm open and awaiting a familiar crystal sphere to be placed in it.

Hannah stared at it, her stomach winding into a knot as the weight of Ozzie pressed against her hip. She wouldn't hand it over, but then again, did she really have an option?

"You..." Hannah bit her lip, her mind unfurling with desperate ideas, "What about your parents?" She blurted, trying to reel the topic back.

Jax's eyes darkened, his outstretched arm sagging slightly. "What about them?"

"How did you get into this, Jax?" Hannah hoped he didn't hear the plea behind her words as she changed the subject again.

Jax's arm reeled back to hang by its side, and he forced a breath, rearranging his face so it was inscrutable.

"The Beast came after my parents." He delivered the words indifferently, "I managed to grab on before anyone was crystallized. As the Beast teleported away, I got sucked into the same vortex, and I teleported here, in this grassy meadow.

"I managed to get away and hide, but the Beast didn't even come for me. I think it was equally surprised and... scared. And then... I realized,"

Jax's lips tilted in a smile that would've been welcoming, pleasant, even, but it didn't harmonize with the unhinged glint in his eyes. "I realized the power, the *greatness* this creature had. This world is corrupted; it's steadily heading to its inevitable death. Someone had to change it. Wars are just the beginning."

He padded closer, his boots quiet against the stone as he advanced. "What if there was a way to change all of that? People are the problem... and I found the solution."

His absurd grin spread wider and directed right at her. At Hannah. She pressed her lips together, something akin to agony numbing her.

"So you were plotting against me all along?" Her voice cracked, and she loathed herself for it.

His grin faded. "No. I wasn't plotting against *you*, Han—"

"But you were, weren't you?" Hannah went rigid, and Dee immediately released her, sensing the sudden tension.

Every muscle in Hannah's face went taut. "That's why you showed me the secret library, and why you helped me with my research. You didn't want to *help* me, you wanted to hurt me!"

"What I want is something you don't even understand!" He snapped, allowing bare traces of anger to carve the lines of his face before they cooled, masking emotion.

Again.

"You don't understand," He murmured, his eyes clouding. A flimsy smirk appeared, and his eyes cleared. "I've been planning this for longer than you know. A whole lot of trying, failing, building, conquering...

"I'm also immune to its gaze. How, I won't tell you, for safety purposes. All you need to know is that I am incapable of turning into crystal, so you can't even turn my own monster against me."

Dee glowered. "You're the mons—"

"Why are you telling us all of this?" Ara interrupted. Her face had drained of all color, and the observation sent Hannah on edge. She tensed, her hand instinctively wrapping around the hilt of her dagger.

Jax offered a smug, slightly sympathetic grin. It was eerie how well he could manipulate Hannah's emotions, how skillfully he could manipulate his own. He spread his arms, eyes twinkling.

"I was just waiting for my army to get here. That way we can have a nice little chat without the risk of you threatening to unalive me."

Instantly, ominous crystal clinks echoed behind him, and Hannah only realized the severity of the situation once a cool, crystal sword was pressed against her throat.

They were trapped.

CHAPTER 24

AMARA

Ara's glasses were on the verge of falling off her nose, and to prevent the humiliation of it dropping, she was forced to tip her head back in hopes they would slide back into place.

No such luck.

She couldn't even push them up with her fingers because her wrists were currently shackled behind her back, a crystal soldier marching on either side of her as they treaded through the gold-lined cavern. At least they hadn't yet spotted the gun tucked in the waistband of her pants. It rested against her hip snugly, and the cool metal comforted her.

Risking a glance behind her shoulder, she spotted Dee, whose gaze was murderous and darting between her captors.

Her wrists were also bound behind her back, restricting access to her sword. Ara turned forward again, her eyes landing on Hannah ahead. Her arms weren't bound together, but the soldiers still had their hands on their swords in case she attacked, not that Hannah would attempt such a thing; her dagger had been confiscated.

Completely and utterly powerless, they were forced to march alongside the crystal soldiers, unaware and more than a little terrified of their fate. The monocle was clipped to her gun and dangling on her hip, the lens biting into her skin with the sudden absence of heat radiating from it.

If the glass itself was so cold, Ara couldn't imagine how frigid Ozzie had become inside Hannah's holster's pouch. But all of it just signaled their imminent encounter with the Beast.

On and on they were forced to march, until the soldiers abruptly stopped and corralled them together on the ground, them sitting back to back in a triangle. Ara could barely see either of her friends, and she hoped that Hannah would do *something*. Anything that could get them out of this situation. Jax seemed to care greatly about her well-being. She hoped Hannah could use that against him and get them out of here– hoped Hannah would have the heart to take any action against him at all.

Because if she failed, the consequences could have them dead before the Beast even got here.

HANNAH

Hannah should've felt scared. She even recognized the ideal sensation she was supposed to feel. But all she felt was... strange, still mulling over the last few minutes.

Strange because Jax was alive.

Because he still cared about her feelings.

Because he controlled the Beast.

Because he seemed sympathetic... even kind towards her.

Because he bound her friends.

But left Hannah unscathed.

And the whole reality of it all left her so befuddled that she nearly stumbled when the warriors forced them to sit. Hannah complied, carefully sinking onto the ground so as not to provoke the soldiers into tying her up as well. She couldn't imagine the discomfort that it caused her friends, but wasn't willing enough to find out, especially when they both got matching pieces of tape gluing their mouths shut. They both struggled against their bindings with futile efforts.

Hannah clasped her hands in her lap and scrutinized her surroundings, albeit uncertainly. The soldiers formed a small semi-circle around them, leaving Hannah's front view open. They seemed to be in another equally embellished area of the endless cave. More crystal warriors crowded the corners of the cave, likely keeping an eye on the three girls.

There was a smattering of distant footsteps, undistinguishable from who– or what– was roaming these halls. The thought alone sent a shudder down Hannah's spine, returning her attention to the crystal Orb that sat snugly in her holster pouch. Through the leather of the belt and the fabric of her pants, Hannah could feel the pulsating coldness washing over the sphere. Her anxiety tripped over itself, sending another jolt to her trembling heart. Just when Hannah thought she would drown in a sea of nerves, all the noise in her head ceased to whisper as a dark-haired boy sauntered towards her.

"I'm sorry you had to deal with this, Han." Jax gestured towards the crystal soldiers. "They don't seem to register sympathy. Mostly because they're crystal, but still."

"You may as well be crystal too," Hannah bit out, "Considering the non-existent sympathy you are basically *radiating.*"

She knew it was a lie; Hannah could see exactly how much Jax pitied her. But it still felt good to say it. The words gave Hannah a new electric charge inside, and she allowed it to power her confidence.

Jax tilted his head to the side, surveying her. "Let's not start lying to one another now, Hannah."

Rage zapped her. "*Lying?* You're telling *me* not to lie?" She released a bitter laugh, one that she never thought was capable of making. "Jax, don't make me laugh. You *cannot* talk to me about lying when that's all you've done for the past seven years."

Dee let out a supportive grunt through the tape.

Jax's cool demeanor crumbled, revealing brief, raw shock before he stepped back and cleared his throat.

"Those were all necessary, and someday, you'll understand why–"

"No, Jax, I need to understand *now*, before you are painted as a villain in my head and I have to train myself to hate you." Hannah allowed every ounce of pain to lace her words. Who cared if he pitied her? Let him feel exactly what he'd done to her.

But his gaze turned stony, rather than hurt, which thwarted her upcoming insults, letting them spark and fizzle out on her tongue, unspoken.

He crouched in front of her, bringing them face to face, his head shielding light that Hannah only realized was illuminating them before it was stolen away.

"You're ignorant, Hannah," He murmured, "I hope to change that."

Jax straightened and stepped back, letting the air rush back into Hannah's lungs. It was hard to think, hard to breathe when he looked at her like that. Like electricity had webbed together and caught her in its net. It left her head muddled and her senses in shambles.

Hannah cleared her throat and ducked her head, choosing to focus on a less... distracting object, such as the stone beside her shoe. Her hair formed a veil around her face, obscuring it from Jax's vision.

"What do you want?" She asked, her voice disturbingly strained.

"Listen," he said softly. His voice sent a shudder through Hannah's memory, accompanied by déjà vu; that was the same tone Jax had used when he had found her outside of the school, with her tear-stained face and shuddering little body. Hannah almost wanted to look up, to see the boy who was once her friend.

But was he?

"You already know too much. I can't let you go... but I can offer you a deal."

Hannah's head snapped up.

"I will not have you turned into crystal," he said, deliberately slow, "You can work with me. You can live here and help me gain control little by little in every country. We can expand our crystal army and gain dominance, *power,* and respect. The entire world will be at our hands, our mercy, ours to control as we so please. We're not encouraging chaos– we're containing it. And you won't have to live in fear or suffering or loneliness because you'll have me. And, if you really want, your parents."

Hannah was still, cemented into this moment with a frenzy of emotions chiseled upon her face.

Jax's softened. "You can have your parents again, Hannah," he repeated.

A sob lodged itself in Hannah's throat, but she pushed it down. "And my friends?" She clasped her shaking hands together. "What about them?"

Jax's gaze barely washed over the silent girls beside Hannah. He offered a small but harsh shake of his head.

"I will decide how I will deal with them later, but if you want to work with me, you need to forget about them. They mean nothing."

"No, I need to know now–"

"Hannah," Jax cut her off, eyes glinting dangerously, "Are you willing to risk your life, your future, and your *parents* over these people you've known for a *week?*"

Hannah stilled, her thoughts tripling their pace.

Yes, The word burned on her tongue. Her friends had fought with her, helped her, supported her, and–

Were they worth it?

Did she intend to preserve their friendship? Were they even really friends with her?

Yes! Her heart screamed, but it was drowned out by the clockwork of her mind. Jax knew exactly what he was doing when he placed the tantalizing prospect of her parents in front of her. He'd simply planted the seed, and Hannah's mind was watering it.

She was afraid that it would come down to this. She was walking a narrow, tightrope that was steadily fraying behind her.

Jax was watching her closely. She felt insignificant under his gaze, as though she needed to prove him. *They are your* friends! *They are worth it, they are beneficial, they* are *your friends! Say it!*

But the word that left her mouth was "No. I don't know. I don't care."

Instantly, Ara and Dee tensed beside her, as though paralyzed, and Jax's lips curled in a proud smile. He tapped his sword against the ground, and two crystal soldiers fell out of formation. Hannah ducked her head down and squeezed her eyes shut as her friends were dragged away.

No, not her friends. As Ara and Dee were dragged away. Two people she wasn't allowed to care for again. Two people who would hate her forever for the decision she'd made. Two people who were the closest thing to *true* friends she'd had in a while.

No, they weren't. A cold voice jabbed in her head. *And even if they were, you destroyed that, too.*

So Hannah ducked her head down, letting the last tear trickle down her cheek before she subsided to cold, hard resolve.

"Hannah," Jax said softly, prompting Hannah to look up at him. His eyes were comforting—sympathetic, even. He extended a hand for her, which she took after a moment's hesitation and rose to her feet, feeling a dense weight in her chest. Jax didn't let go of her hand, but rather, his grip tightened.

"You're making the right choice." He let the words hang there before he continued, "You're saving yourself and your parents."

There it was again. That weak, flimsy shard of her moral was bolstered by those words. She was doing this for her parents. Not for herself. *Her parents.*

Hannah managed a slight nod and slipped her hand out of his. Seemingly pleased, Jax turned and nodded to a crystal soldier, who stepped out of his position and marched toward Hannah. But instead of grabbing her, he sidestepped her and progressed into the cavern.

"Follow him. I'll meet you soon, Hannah. Just gotta finish some things first." A smirk twisted his lips before Jax turned away. "And don't worry. He's not leading you to the Beast."

Hannah watched him go, her footsteps treading after the soldier, almost wishing she was being led to her doom.

It would be much better than whatever mess she just created.

DIANA

Dee's heart was still thudding in her chest.

Good, because she wasn't sure anything else was working.

It was like her mind was lagging, because one minute she was bound and gagged, back to back with Ara and an unbound Hannah.

Then she blinked, and Hannah had suddenly denounced them of any importance, and sold them off to Jax.

And then she and Ara were being dragged off, stumbling behind crystal warriors like some *common prisoners*.

Not fun. Or cool. In fact, whatever confusion she'd had was steadily being succeeded by burning hot rage and hurt, making the front of her forehead throb.

Dee tilted her head to the side, catching a glimpse of an ashen-faced Ara. Her eyes were firmly on the ground they stepped on, and nowhere else.

Dee had only seen her cry once, and she didn't want to witness that again. The Ara she knew was a snobby, know-it-all pain. Not whatever *this* was.

As though Ara sensed Dee's thoughts, she lifted her head a bare inch, and their eyes clashed. A silent understanding shifted between the two, and Dee then glanced at all the soldiers in turn, noting their rigid gazes that were transfixed forward, to wherever they were marching in this dimly lit passage.

Dee flexed her hands, spreading out her palms to contract the muscles in her forearms. She widened them as much as she could, then aggressively ripped them out and away.

The bonds tore satisfyingly, and she whipped her hands to the front of her body and flicked her ring. The sword materialized within a mere second, and without a second thought, she sliced through Ara's bonds too.

The soldiers around them jolted to action, drawing whatever weapons they had, mimicking Ara, who drew her gun. Backs pressed together, the two girls spun in a slow circle, darting glares at any soldier surrounding them.

Dee parried a crystal sword that slashed down on her. She defended the jabs before she twisted and sent the blade clattering to the side. Dee spun around to narrowly deflect another sword similar to the previous, before it also tumbled to the ground.

She sank into that familiar pattern she'd learned to emulate every time she'd have to lift a blade. It was soothing in a brutal sort of way as she slashed, deflected, dodged, and twisted.

As the last soldier scrambled away, Dee whipped around, glaring. "Who's next?"

All the warriors were pressed against the side of the dimly lit passageway, their hands raised behind them, thanks to Ara. Dee glared at their crystal backs one by one, letting the hatred empower her.

Clunk. Clunk.

Dee rolled her neck, letting the muscles stretch, before turning around to face her next foe.

His skin was translucent and crystallized, like ice. His hair hung in frosty crystal threads atop his head, his face cemented in cold indifference.

A face she knew all too well.

Instantly, Dee's defenses dropped as she stared, horror-struck, at her brother's crystal face.

Distantly, she could hear Ara puff out an impatient breath, but she could hardly care because her brother was *here*.

Standing in the flesh– no, *crystal*.

The thought jolted her back to the painstaking reality where her crystal brother was charging at her, sword in hand.

"Whoa– Adrian!" Dee spun to the side, her sword raising instinctively as her brother whirled and swung his blade down.

Despite her knowledge of fighting, she barely managed to deflect his strike. She caught his sword with hers, gritting her teeth. A bead of sweat rolled down the side of her face.

Adrian drew his blade back and thrust it at a different angle. The tip of it nicked her neck before she ducked and parried.

"Adrian! Stop it!"

Her brother swung at her again, oblivious to her pleas and splintered heart. Dee would not harm him, but he clearly wouldn't offer the same grace.

Which was exactly the cause of her downfall.

She was too slow, blinded by dampening grief, when Adrian lunged for her sword, tugged her forward, and then spun her around, pulling Dee's back flush against his chest, like she'd seen Jax do to Hannah minutes before. But instead of releasing her, her brother raised his crystal fist and brought it down on the back of her skull.

Pain jolted through her, and her vision flickered. She barely heard Ara let out a panicked cry.

And then her vision dimmed entirely, letting her sink into an infinite pool of darkness.

CHAPTER 25

HANNAH

Hannah's stomach frothed with a tangle of nerves as her eyes traced over the boy in front of her for the millionth time. Begging, wishing she could take his mind and sort it out. She wanted to understand his thinking, his life, his motives. Because this was so far from the Jax that she knew. The Jax she knew was cheery, carefree, with a smile always plastered on the face she'd seen grow up. This boy in front of her was losing himself, stranded on an island of his construction.

Jax hadn't attempted more conversation, which both relieved and disturbed Hannah. She found herself wishing, again, that she could even begin to comprehend his thoughts. That hive of cultivating, scheming plans.

After the soldier had marched down the passage, it had led Hannah to a small cavern containing a mahogany four-poster bed, a humble set of drawers, a wooden table, and two armchairs poised beside it, all lit by a lamp offering pale, yellow light. It was a stark contrast to the lazily splattered coins everywhere. Each time Hannah stepped on one, she'd scowl, pick it up, and stack it atop the drawers.

Jax had walked in on her "cleaning" her new "room", and since then, they both had taken seats in the armchairs and hadn't said a word besides a quick "bring" to a crystal soldier. It promptly brought a tray of food, which Hannah consumed gratefully. When she was finished, she wiped her mouth with the silk napkin and set it down, then focused on Jax again, who was quiet.

Hannah cleared her throat, desperate to break the silence before it suffocated her. "Tell me why you're doing this."

Jax drummed his fingers on the table, seemingly distracted. "Reasons. A lot of them. And I won't sit here and explain all of them because it'd take forever."

"I have forever." Hannah pressed, "I want to understand what you are thinking. *Why*, Jax?" She leaned forward. "Why are you doing this? Your parents must be–"

"My parents are dead."

Hannah blinked, her words dying in her throat the second he'd cut her off. She furrowed her brows, attempting to mask her look of surprise.

"No, they're not. What are you talking about? Mr. and Mrs. Cartier–"

"Aren't my real parents," Jax said flatly, finishing the sentence in a way she never could have.

This time, Hannah did allow her face to reflect her shock. His words were so bizarre and disturbing at the same time. She wasn't sure whether to laugh or cry.

Hannah decided on a safe, concerned expression. "What do you mean?"

Jax sighed, his eyes focusing on his fingers, which had gone to fiddle with a splinter in the wooden table. With a pang, Hannah realized her fingers had also tugged out many strips of wood before they'd started speaking.

Jax's gaze was fixed on the splinter when he said, "They're my adoptive parents. My *real* parents have been crystallized already. When I was young."

He glanced up at her. "Almost as young as you when your father... You know..."

Hannah fought back the onslaught of emotions that crept onto her like she'd done a hundred times. They retreated soon enough, well acquainted with her repeated mantras to bat them away.

When the emotions had cleared, she blinked. Dozens of questions swirled in her mind, but one had ripped itself from her tongue before she could stop it.

"Why didn't you ever tell me?"

Hurt laced the words. Real, genuine hurt that surprised her almost as much as it had surprised him.

Jax pressed his lips together, pondering. "I... don't really know. I didn't like people knowing about it. Only my adoptive parents did. No one else."

The confession made sense, but the reality of it still stung. Hannah forced herself to accept that, since there was nothing else any effort could do.

Especially if more betrayals were coming up.

Jax let go of the splinter and leaned forward. "It's all precisely and perfectly planned out. The crystallizations are gradually increasing, but their distraught family members forget about them within a week. That is because the Beast eventually targets the whole family. Once the entire family has been crystallized, the adults are sent to fight– we provide the armor and weapons– and the children are sent to steal the money."

Jax talked casually, like they weren't discussing the lives of thousands of individuals. Hannah, on the other hand, had to fight the urge not to empty the contents of her stomach just by thinking of it.

"And me?" She mumbled, afraid to hear the answer. "What about me? *Why* me?"

He paused, allowing several emotions to flit across his face before it transformed into a confident grin. "Well, you were the perfect person I needed."

Hannah's breath hitched in her throat, and her fingers curled into a fist in her lap.

Jax continued: "You lived near me. You were also researching it, and, if I'm being completely honest, I've grown to care for you, Hannah. Which is why I won't let the Beast come for you. You needn't worry about that."

Worry about the Beast? No, she wasn't at all. Her thoughts were more occupied by the words uttered from Jax's mouth. The same one that had lied and cheated and comforted.

But the sincerity in his voice told her that every word he'd spoken now was the unfiltered truth, whether she liked it or not.

Hannah didn't know if she did.

"I also needed someone to *try* and stop me, just to test how infallible my plan really proved to be. You, Han, were the perfect test.

"And now, you'll be the perfect partner."

Hannah mulled over the words, letting them sink into her brain, brand itself on her skin. She was his *partner* now. Which meant that every move she'd make would be against humanity. Against the people she loved.

She already got a head start on it, then, considering what she did to Ara and Dee.

Whatever threads of guilt had woven within her chest were snipped away by scissors. Hannah chided herself for still worrying about them, since she was sure they wouldn't even care about her.

Jax snapped his fingers, and a soldier entered the cavern, a bundle of black fabric placed in its arms. Hannah raised an eyebrow.

Jax turned to her again. "I'll have you faded to a hotel room where you can change and shower, and do whatever else you need. Two soldiers will come with you, wherever you go. Once you're done, you'll fade back here, and then we'll discuss the plan."

Hannah nodded, unable to say much else before the world dissolved into a vortex of green.

***

Rivulets of water snaked down her skin, her hair, pooling onto the drain below. She sighed, her eyes fluttering shut as she soaked up the feeling. The water was cold, colder than she'd usually prefer, but the humid heat was the cause for this exception.

Two soldiers were poised in her hotel room, still as, well, statues. So she knew she was alone, at least for this moment.

Completely and utterly alone.

In more ways the one.

She wasn't with Dee and Ara– Hannah wasn't sure she'd ever be again. She couldn't be with Jax and risk being the downfall of humanity. She couldn't be with her parents; they were crystal.

And so was her heart. A tiny, translucent thing with the consistency of stone yet the appearance of something beautiful, but the color of ice. She pressed a hand to her chest, tilting her head down, and let herself cry. Letting loose all the bottled-up tears and screams that had been with her since the very beginning. Everyone and everything was turned away from her, reaching for something different, and she was caught in the midst of it. Stuck between two lands, she couldn't cross. She wept for her parents, her friends, herself, and even Jax. His betrayal had struck a thorn within her, and it had lodged deep.

Ara and Dee were gone, betrayed by her.

Jax was delusional and highly unpredictable, and she would *not* help him.

The tears swam down her face and mingled with the shower water, mimicking the downpour of emotions she was finally letting herself feel. Finally letting herself come to terms with.

She cried until she couldn't cry anymore. Until her emotions were stable and her breathing had calmed.

In a way, it was good she'd accepted Jax's help. Because now, she knew what to do.

***

The black bundle of fabric turned out to be an emulation of the crystal soldiers' uniforms, just clad in metal and fabric rather than crystal. Hannah slipped into the clothes, appreciating how the material felt on her skin— cold and flexible. The shirt sleeves ended at her wrists, and the cargo pants ended where her black boots began. The outfit allowed her to stay relatively cool in this blistering hot weather, which was a major plus point.

Hannah tucked her pendant underneath the folds of her top, trusting her recently brushed hair to conceal the chain. She strapped her holster back into place at her hip, sliding the dagger and Orb in moments after.

The Orb. Jax would ask her for it soon, so she had to come up with a plan to keep it far from his clutches. Finally, after checking and rechecking, she deemed herself ready enough, afraid that if she spent another minute wasted here, Hannah would never try to leave.

The image of the purple sphere lay heavy in her mind as she grasped a soldier's hand, her gaze as steely as her resolve as they faded away...

***

"Welcome back, Han." Jax grinned at her, approval flashing in his eyes as he surveyed her from head to toe.

"I'm through playing games, Jax." Hannah stepped forward, fists at her sides, "I need you to answer my questions now."

He raised an eyebrow. "Didn't I already do that?"

"Just answer them." She said, her words as frosty as her gaze.

His features cooled to match hers. "Depends if they're worth answering."

Hannah inhaled deeply, fighting the urge to clutch her pendant. "Tell me what happened to you. How did you become like this?"

She counted down the seconds until his barriers had risen, protecting Jax from her potentially devastating realizations. Protecting him, it seemed, from her figuring him out.

"Why do you need to know tha–?"

"Because I want to know how my best friend was forced to do something like this." Her face softened, betraying hints of emotion. "This isn't the Jax I remember."

Jax studied the floor, disturbingly tranquil for someone with such a challenging life. She almost thought his secrets would remain with him when–

"I was seven." He murmured, dark eyes still pinned upon the floor. "My parents had taken me to the park. There, the Beast found us."

He inhaled unsteadily. "Found them."

Fresh wounds were being torn in Hannah's frozen heart, reminding her of the pain she'd once felt. But the tears didn't restrict her to them this time. Her breathing continued normally.

Jax's didn't. "I ran away. I hid, and by the time it was gone, so were they."

He closed his eyes, continuing: "I was sent to an orphanage. I got adopted. Then a few years later, my foster parents nearly met the same fate."

Jax's eyes opened, letting her see all the emotion he'd clogged up inside him. None spilled out– calibrated to never do so.

"I found him– the Beast. I clung to him as he faded away. He kept me a prisoner here for a while. And then, I understood."

He quieted. "I understood..."

Hannah's hand wandered up and squeezed her pendant, letting the metal bite into her fist as she ejected all her pain into it, adding more weight to the tiny heart.

"I'm... sorry." She finished solemnly, her voice barely audible. "You didn't deserve that."

"Now everyone will." He glanced up at her, his eyes red. "We're going to start the countdown."

CHAPTER 26

HANNAH

Giant, white, holographic numbers had emblazoned themselves into the air, decreasing by the minute as more humans were morphed into crystal. Hannah forced herself to distance herself from any form of emotion. She was a pawn in this game, and she'd play it with a rigid face and straight spine.

"Isn't this wonderful?" Jax whispered, the glowing numbers reflecting in his eyes, "You'll get your parents back after everything is done, in fact... just for now," he whistled, and two soldiers stepped out of the ranks. One had long, crystalline hair flowing almost to her waist, a dagger identical to the one in Hannah's holster strapped to one on her waist.

She had the same features as Hannah, except older. Beside her was a man with a sword and clear crystal hair where it was supposed to be brown.

Her parents' faces were harsh and cold, alien to the ones Hannah was accustomed to.

Her breathing quickened.

No emotions, no emotions, no emotions--

Hannah stepped forward, tentatively reaching out to cup her mother's cheek. The soldier didn't flinch, didn't move. It just stared at her, as though seeing air where Hannah was standing. The crystal was cold, yet it didn't bother Hannah.

She let go and turned to her father. The dad she hadn't seen since she was six. She reached up to rumple his crystal hair, which looked white and frosty and felt surprisingly like frozen strings. His face was frozen into crystal. No hint of recognition flickered on it.

Hannah's heart felt like it was being beaten up before, but that was nothing compared to the pain she was feeling right now. It took every ounce of her willpower to bolster the trembling net woven to contain her emotions before it tore.

She retracted her hand, her eyes switching between her crystal parents, and exhaled deeply. The pendant on her chest weighed significantly more when she stepped away.

Jax cocked his head to the side curiously. "You don't want to be with your parents?"

Hannah's eyes tracked the two soldiers as they left to join their companions. "They are not my parents."

Jax's face was sad. "I understand how you feel." He turned back to the vibrant numbers, sorrow lining his face. "Jade..." He murmured, inhaling deeply.

"I must go, Hannah. I have more commands to give out. When I get back, we can discuss our next plans." He nodded to her once, then grabbed a soldier and faded away.

Hannah watched him go, not missing the way his eyes dimmed unnaturally before he left. That was strange, to say the least. And what did Jade mean?

She shook her head a little harder than she'd intended– she was here to rescue her friends. Not solve the puzzles of a person who was a mystery himself.

Hannah glanced around with a bated breath. Soldiers were positioned in the corners of this main dome-like cavern. They paid her no attention as she trudged into a secluded, darker passage littered with more soldiers. Bits of gravel were loose here, and she nearly tripped more times than she would've liked to admit. She was tempted to use Ozzie as a light source, but that might draw the attention she was going out of her way to evade. Her eyes struggled to adjust to the rapidly dimming light, and this time, she did lose her footing and ended up sprawled on the ground.

Sucking a breath through her teeth, Hannah placed her palms on the gritty sediment to haul herself to her knees. She swept her hands to clear the loose stones and bit her lip when her finger stung, burning like it had been cut.

She fumbled for the small item and pinched it. It felt smooth and flat, like a glass coin.

Her breathing hitched as the comparison resonated in her mind, and she pulled Ozzie out for light, panic unfurling within her.

The little glass was small and had a gold chain dangling off of it. Hannah clutched Ara's monocle, fighting the torrent of emotions pummeling her straining barriers. So her friends had come through here, and by the looks of the chaotic, broken sediments, they'd fought back.

But lost.

Hannah tucked the monocle into her pouch, along with Ozzie, and grappled for purchase on the uneven walls, trying to clear her screaming mind to no avail.

She was worried for Dee and Ara. But she had no right to be.

No emotions, no emotions, no emotions. She replayed in her mind. *Find them first.*

She could hear crystal bodies shifting up ahead, cluing her in as to where she was. Hannah was begging the heavens, pleading that she was correct.

That they were at the end of the tunnel.

There was a barely illuminated gallery up ahead, containing a plethora of crystal warriors. Children, by the looks of their height and faces. Her heart gave a quick twinge of sorrow before she smothered it.

No emotions, no emotions–

The crystal statues had stilled at her arrival, each head turning towards her in unison. She shuddered, her gaze landing on two individuals in the center of the room.

Dee and Ara were bound and gagged, back to back, unconscious. Shackles were rooting them to the ground, clamped around their wrists.

The sight left her breathless and pained. Red hot anger flushed her skin, but it immediately frosted over.

Jax hadn't done this to them.

Hannah had.

No emotions, NO EMOTIONS–

She waited until her lungs were functioning normally and surveyed her situation. Every crystal eye was trained on her, unmoving.

Just get them out of here, she reminded herself, ignoring the buzzing of her spine as she took a step forward.

Immediately, the crystal statues swarmed her, locking onto her legs and arms. She let out an alarmed shriek as the children dragged her back, away from Ara and Dee.

On instinct, she ripped her dagger out of the holster, but there was no other blade to counter. Just crystal bodies bent on keeping her away from the two people she needed the most right now.

One statue tugged her hair back abruptly, and Hannah cried out in pain. She whirled around and nailed the hilt of her dagger to the side of the child's crystal head.

The impact sent the statue flying backward, its crystal body shattering on the ground, thousands of shards crumbling to dust.

The attacks persisted, but Hannah froze. Her heart remained lodged in her throat as her mind replayed the scene ceaselessly, the crystal child shattering on the ground.

She'd just *killed* a boy. Someone's child, son, nephew, brother. He was gone, just like his crystal pieces.

Stunned tears clung to her lashes.

NO EMOTIONS, NO EMOTIONS–

She broke out of another statue's hold to brush away the tears, feeling that familiar numbness sink into her.

It's fine. She fabricated. *He'll just rematerialize as a crystal statue again later. But first...*

Hannah kicked away another statue and dragged herself forward, keeping her eyes pinned on the sleeping forms in front of her. She could feel the scratches of adamant statues on her neck, hands, and ankles, and found herself thanking Jax that he hadn't entrusted them with actual blades.

Hannah angled her blade tip down and sliced her friends' bonds, freeing them from their prison. All at once, every crystal child went still, then filed away from her, as though she'd never been here.

Hannah was thanking and cursing every lucky star by the time she dragged Ara and Dee out into the dark passage. Panting, she crouched in front of them as panic began to set in.

"Ara?" Hannah pressed her ear to Ara's chest, finding little relief at the beating of her heart, "Wake up. Please." She moved toward Dee, repeating the same pleas and actions. Hannah shook their shoulders and pinched their arms. But every attempt to wake them up was futile.

They were out cold.

Hannah's attention landed on the metal shackles still clinging to their wrists. Annoyed, she tugged them off.

As though freed from some curse, her friends began to stir. After a few painful seconds of Hannah barely breathing, Ara opened her blue eyes groggily.

"Hannah?" She whispered, her voice hoarse from disuse.

Relief spread through Hannah, dousing her in its abnormally bright feeling.

"It's me," Hannah confirmed, eyes turning a little misty.

Ara's expression hardened, every bit of warmth in her look extinguished. "Get away from me."

Hannah's heart thudded, and hurt crawled into her swarming feelings. *No emotions,* She reminded herself. *This was expected. You deserve it.*

She opened her mouth to apologize, to explain, to beg for forgiveness, but she was cut off by a loud groan from the girl beside her.

Dee blinked, her eyes droopy. Her eyes were unfocused, but they slowly fixed on her and widened. Hannah grimaced at the look of outrage on her face.

"Hannah? What the–?" She glared, scooting back against the wall as far as her still-waking body allowed, "What are you doing here?"

Hannah smothered her crushing heart and went to explain when–

"You're bleeding," Ara said, more of a statement than a question. Hannah squinted down at her wrists, which were covered in scratches deep enough to have thin streams of blood pooling out. Hannah sucked a breath and wiped the blood off with the hem of her cargo pants, loathing the stickiness it now contained.

"How'd that happen?" Ara asked, still in that unwavering, quiet voice.

Hannah swallowed. "I... got you out of that room."

"After you basically had us sent to it?" Dee demanded, crossing her arms. Despite their current hatred for Hannah, they made no effort to leave.

Yet.

The thought was little comfort as Hannah flattened herself against the other side wall and shrank, despising her idiocy.

She sighed and rubbed her eyes. "I know you'll probably hate me forever. And I don't blame you." Her hands dropped into her lap along with her gaze. Her throat constricted to hold back tears and feelings as she said what she should've said a long time ago:

"I was an idiot. I was confused and tired, and so, so scared. I didn't know what I had to do. Jax had been my friend since forever, but you guys... You guys have only known me for a week. And still..." Hannah choked back tears that were now on the verge of spilling out, "And still you supported me. You fought with me. And I... I sold you off to the enemy in an instant. I'm a terrible person for doing that to you, and I understand if you never want to see my face again. But I realized how wrong I was, and I *need* you." She squeezed her eyes shut. "I need you guys. And I'm sorry. I'm so, so, *so*, sorry."

Painful seconds ticked by. Hannah fisted her pendant, drowning in the agonizing silence that followed. The tension was thick, leaving Hannah to pin down swelling sensations that were strangling her. She swallowed for the millionth time, preferring whatever they would say next to this stillness. Let them scream at her, yell at her, turn their backs on her.

Fresh blood still dotted her ankles and wrists, but Hannah made no effort to clean it off, afraid any movement would interrupt their silent pondering.

"Hannah," Ara began softly. Hannah trembled, eyes still pressed shut as tears began to roll down her cheeks.

"I'm sorry," She whispered, tilting her head down as more tears swam down her face, "I'm sorry, I'm sorry, I'm sorry–"

Someone placed a hand on her shoulder, and Hannah looked up to a misty-eyed Dee. She kneeled beside Hannah, her gaze soft and etched with emotion.

"I believe you." She mumbled, "I don't think I was ever mad at you."

Hannah froze. "B-but, I sold you out–"

"And you still came to get us," Ara murmured, offering a tentative smile, "And no doubt you did that against Jax's will." She pointed at Hannah's recently attained injuries.

Suddenly, the cuts didn't hurt as much. "I should've never done that to you," Hannah murmured, staring up at the two of them.

"But you fixed it." Ara insisted, "And though it might take some time for us to get over it, we still love you, Hannah."

Fresh tears arose. "Me too,"

Dee gave a watery grin and wrapped her arms around Hannah, who leaned into the hug, pouring all the unfinished apologies and worries into it.

And it seemed Dee put in forgiveness, too.

**

After the tears and mushiness had subsided, as Hannah was now calling it, her heart felt strangely light. Not completely unburdened, but alleviated of a great pressure.

She quickly got them both up to speed with whatever she'd learned about Jax, which was close to nothing, but it still felt relieving to talk about it to someone.

Ara seemed more closely guarded, which was probably Hannah's doing; she expressed little emotion, and her tone was flat. But Hannah didn't miss the way her eyes lit up with gratitude when her monocle was returned, and that gave Hannah the hope she was clinging to.

For the most part, Dee was blatantly furious with Jax, and the murderous gleam in her eyes every time her eyes fell on her sword was distinct. She listened to Hannah carefully, occasionally pausing to throw in a promise for revenge, before twirling her ring between her fingers. She didn't seem upset with Hannah anymore– or at least, she didn't show it.

"Okay," Hannah sat criss-crossed on the floor, her face bathed in Ozzie's green glow, "Jax said that Yin is bonded, but not to him. So what if it's physically separate? We just have to find the purple Orb, destroy it, and then we're set."

"How are you gonna find the purple Orb?" Dee asked, the green light reflecting in her irises.

"Ozzie turns purple every time it gets near it, correct?" Hannah waited for Ara's confirming nod before continuing, "Then Ozzie will lead me to it."

Ara raised an eyebrow. "And what about the army and monster?"

"We'll do our best to evade them." Hannah fabricated, hesitant to imagine any army or monster charging at them, "The purple Orb. Get to Yin."

"What about Jax?" Ara asked, studying Hannah closely.

Hannah bit back a grimace, meticulously schooling her features into indifference. "What about him?"

"You're betraying him."

Hannah flinched at the hurt those words triggered. She pinned her eyes onto Ozzie, avoiding her friends' gazes when she said: "He betrayed me first."

"But will you be able to harm him if necessary?" Dee questioned, her gaze dropping down to Hannah's dagger.

Hannah's voice was devoid of any emotion when she said, "I'll have to be."

CHAPTER 27

JAX

Jax was fighting.

That's all he seemed to do lately.

Fighting back a torrent of emotions pummeling his insides, he waited until Hannah's face blinked out of view in a swirl of green, then exhaled in relief.

He barely recognized when he was spat out into the room. Hardly felt his hand slip out of the crystal statue's as it turned to guard the door.

Jax padded toward the stack of drawers and opened the first one. It contained two flimsy bracelets composed of small rubber bands woven together. One was light green, the other dark brown. Jax delicately placed them aside and dug past old records and papers. He barely glanced at his adoption files, having seen them a hundred times previously.

His fingers paused at the feel of glossy paper, his throat constricting, as he lifted the forgotten photograph. He brushed away the veil of dust and stared at the image.

It contained a young, dark-haired boy swinging at the playground. Beside him was an identical girl, her eyes gleaming with excitement as she prepared to leap off her swing. The boy had a competitive look, carving his face as he prepared to trump his sister's oncoming jump.

Scrawled in the corner of the photo were the words: *Jax and Jade– the twins*♡

The paper flinched, a bead of water rolling down the glossy texture. Jax hadn't realized tears had formed in his eyes until they were rolling down his face.

He tucked the bittersweet photo into his chest pocket, wanting to keep it as close to his shell of a heart as possible as he attempted to clear his thoughts.

But now that the ball was rolling, memories sifted through the front of his brain relentlessly. Jax could remember every second of it like a movie he was forced to watch.

Unlike what he told Hannah, his parents hadn't been crystallized. Jax never even knew them. He and Jade were dropped off at the orphanage when they were seven years old after a freak accident involving their aunt.

Jax remembered the day his sister had clung onto his shoulder and wept until she'd fallen asleep. That was the first day in the orphanage.

And the rest weren't much different, until the day he got adopted.

Jax didn't think he'd ever sobbed that much any other time.

His new foster "parents" had arrived to pick up their new child. Neither he nor his sister had predicted that they only wanted a son, not a daughter.

The staff had to rip Jade away from his fingers to pull them apart, and Mr. and Mrs. Cartier were oblivious to Jax's cries for her. For Jade.

The last memory of Jade was her horror-struck, heartbroken face as Jax was dragged away from her, fighting every individual he could to claw himself back to her.

"*Take her too! Please!*" He had screamed, thrashing against his new father's grip on his wrist as he led Jax to their car. "*Please, she's my sister!*"

"*Now, now,*" His foster mother had said, smiling down sympathetically at him, "*It's just an attachment, Jax. You can break it.*"

"*No– Jade!*" He struggled against the confines of the arms that lifted him into the car. "*Jade!*"

And with a slam of the car door and the screech of wheels, his entire life was uprooted, leaving behind a broken boy, his other half lost behind.

First, he fought against his adoptive parents, refusing to eat or sleep. They treated him like a temperamental toddler, coaxing small bits of nutrition into him by offering the tantalizing temptation of getting his sister for him.

"*Now, Jax,*" His mother had said, handing him an apple slice, "*Being starved won't be so good if we bring your sister, now, will it? She'll have to see a very sick brother then.*"

And so, only for the promise of finding Jade, he begrudgingly accepted food and the sleep that clawed at him every night.

Sleep– a mere, cheerful illusion of the nightmares to come.

Soon, Jax was enrolled in a school, a whole other form of torture. It was lung-crushing not to see Jade with him during lunch or by the swings. It was terrible not seeing her at all.

But on the first day, he'd met a little girl on the stone stairs. Her face was pinched in an effort not to cry, yet tears had already begun streaking down her face. She had light brown hair and hazel eyes too innocent to bear pain.

Seeing the girl, Jax was reminded of Jade. Too young, too innocent, too wholesome.

He stopped to talk with her, maybe cheer her up. Her name was Hannah. Jax smiled and introduced himself.

Her father had been crystallized. It was uncommon, but not impossible, according to the rumors circulating on the internet. Jax didn't want her to be burdened with this responsibility, so he lifted it from her hands. He would help Hannah.

The day he had met the Beast was an unusual one.

His father had taken him to a park in hopes of "lighting some spirit" into Jax. Jax only went because he doubted he could withstand another hour of his mother discussing how skinny he was.

Jax had found a crystal duck so beautiful he knew Jade would love it. Maybe he could find a way to send it to her.

As he was pondering, his father shouted his name from atop the hill. Disgruntled, Jax had turned around to see a mass of gray fur.

He screamed as the *thing* turned around, and instinct alone prompted him to latch onto the back of the monster's fur, which instantly dissolved into purple particles, clouding his vision. When the world had rematerialized, he lost his grip on the monster's fur and swung into the water.

Bubbles erupted around his head, and his lungs thrashed, unprepared to be submerged. He kicked upward, sputtering, and managed to haul himself onto the riverbank. Jax inched toward the massive stone dome and leaned against it, his lungs contracting as they fought to pass air.

Jax had glanced around, unfamiliar with this lush meadow, a stark contrast to the dull park he'd been in moments before. Here, there were no people, no buildings. Only grass, wildflowers, and the giant stone dome towering above his head.

And the monster.

At first, Jax was a prisoner. He wasn't allowed to leave the infinite borders of the cave and meadow. He was confused, lonely, and upset. Every morning was the same. Wake up on a pile of highly expensive, stolen fabric. Take a quick swim in the river as an excuse for a shower. Stare at the monster that seemed equally afraid of him as he was of it. Pass the hundreds of crystal automatons aimlessly meandering about.

The monster seemed lonely and intrigued by Jax. And as time passed on, Jax understood the potential this monster contained, yet there was no system, no plan for achieving dominance. It just teleported arbitrarily, crystallizing whoever witnessed it.

But not Jax.

He was still alive.

The Beast expressed no sign it could understand human languages, yet when Jax had requested it to teleport him to the orphanage, without a moment's hesitation, the Beast took him there.

But Jade was already gone.

He sought records as to where she'd been taken. Another orphanage, by the looks of it.

And he teleported there. But she was gone.

Ceaselessly, Jax searched for his twin. But Jade was missing, given a fake identity, he presumed, lost to the whole world.

And he'd fought. He'd fought for so long and hard that Jax had collapsed, finally giving in, lowering his barriers, and slumped against the Beast, tears clinging to his lashes as the pure, unfiltered agony pummeled him in waves.

He missed his sister.

The next day, he'd approached the Beast, eyes set and red, resolve steely. His plan was simple, and it would be carried out with the utmost precision.

For it to work, he required a proof-check, which meant he couldn't remain missing. Jax asked the Beast to teleport him to his house, where he provided a long-winded explanation of a kidnapping. After a few weeks, he had crystal soldiers build the secret library, manipulating their teleportation powers into transforming it into a mini nook filled to the brim with books about the Beast he'd made them collect. Some, he had even written himself, based on his observations of the Beast.

And now he was so, so close. Jax would find his sister, uprooting every corner of the Earth if he had to.

Perhaps that's why he cared so greatly about Hannah– whenever he looked at her, Jade was the person he saw.

Thundering footsteps knocked Jax out of his stupor, and he hastily shoved the drawer shut, swiping at his eyes in an attempt to look presentable.

Not that it mattered. The Beast had already seen him at his worst, and even though it was strange to feel self-conscious of his appearance next to a literal monster, Jax despised being caught off guard.

The Beast stepped through the door, and Jax angled his gaze away from him instinctively, even though he knew he was exempt from crystallizing. He cleared his throat and extracted his sword, dusting off any imperfections from the crystal blade.

"The mission went well?" He asked, his voice painfully hoarse.

A confirming growl.

"Anything else you need to tell me?"

The Beast growled again and faded away. Jax sighed, rubbing his temples. At least nothing out of the ordinary happened– yet.

As if on cue, a crystal soldier shuffled forward. His arms contained dozens of crystal shards lazily swept together. Jax's jaw tightened.

"Which one was it?" He questioned, glaring at the soldier.

The soldier ducked his head, leveling one crystal hand near his waist. So it was a child. A young statue was shattered into pieces.

Shock clawed its way towards him. The children were supposed to guard Hannah's former accomplices. And if one of them was broken...

Jax took a step back, breathing heavily. Hannah had rescued them from that room. But she was naive, underestimating Jax's careful preparation and planning that went into this. She had betrayed him when all he'd ever done was try to fix this dismal world that loathed this wretched, broken boy.

She had betrayed him. And now Hannah was nothing to him, as insignificant as a mosquito on the bottom of his shoe.

A slow smirk crawled its way to his face. Hannah had no idea Jax was aware of her betrayal. And if she wanted to play a game of secrets, then so be it.

Because if there was one thing Jax had mastered, it was secrets.

CHAPTER 28

HANNAH

Ozzie's glow pulsed in the abandoned passageway, now one-fourth of the way bright purple. The other three-fourths of green smoke was distinctly avoiding the other alien color, both forces repelled by each other.

Hannah frowned. The Orb had just recently gained its extra color and its chilly feel, signaling their increasing proximity to the purple Orb. Hannah barely breathed as they padded down the passage, imprisoning any mounting hopes before it was jinxed.

Ara and Dee flanked either side, equally silent. They both had their respective weapons clutched in their hands, prepared to strike at the most microscopic of actions. Hannah glanced back briefly to survey their body language. Ara's face was pale in the dim glow, but her jaw was set, her gun hefted in her hand, prepared to shoot. Dee's fingers were wrapped around the handle of her sword, and a sharp glare set her features, only briefly softening to offer Hannah a nod of acknowledgment. Exhaling, Hannah turned to focus ahead.

Ozzie shuddered violently, its temperature going from cool to frigid, causing Hannah to nearly drop it. Now, half of the smoke was purple.

She squinted up ahead, making out a tiny prick of light at the end of the tunnel. That must be where the purple Orb was kept. Ozzie's brother.

Hannah flexed her fingers, ignoring the sweatiness of her palm, as she tested its functionality. She was afraid that the moment she hefted her dagger, fear would ice her limbs.

A familiar face surfaced in her mind: Jax. The moment he'd viewed the falling numbers, the awe in his eyes. But within those shields he always cloaked himself in, there was a tiny fissure. And when Hannah had peered in deeper, a broken boy was visible. Broken, like half of him was missing, a stranger to this world.

The name Jade popped into her mind as well, and she seized all her thoughts and twined them together, creating a mental folder of information. What did she really know about Jax? Taking into account his excellent skills in lying, it could be that she knew nothing at all.

The thought turned Hannah's stomach sour– he trusted her, didn't he? Jax's largest secret was his parental status, and now that was cleared up, he had nothing left to hide.

Right?

Cold shot up her hand, sending ice through her veins and momentarily numbing her palm. The interruption saved Hannah from her thoughts, but unfortunately put her in another, rapidly approaching predicament.

Ozzie was now three-fourths of the way purple, and the smoke swished faster. The entrance to the purple Orb's home was closer now, the light it contained almost dizzying. Hannah sucked in a breath, Ozzie's biting temperature beginning to sting.

She halted abruptly and turned around. Dee and Ara both paused, their eyes on the Orb.

"Hold this for me." Hannah dumped Ozzie into Dee's hand.

Dee jumped back and cursed colorfully. "Why is it so cold? I'm not holding this."

She clumsily half-dropped and half-threw it to Ara, who was completely unprepared. Ozzie tumbled between her and Dee's fingers and plummeted to the ground.

It floated up at the last second and drifted over toward Hannah, who had just realized she could've let it float in the air in the first place. Hannah shook her head, focusing on her task at hand, pretending like she didn't see Ara just smack Dee upside the head.

Hannah glanced at Ozzie, muttering a quick "sorry" before she tore off the fabric that originally contained Ozzie as a pouch. Hastily, she fashioned a makeshift fingerless glove for her right hand and grasped the Orb again.

And again, they began their silent, tensed walk through the tunnel.

"Do we have a plan for if we encounter the Beast?" Ara asked quietly.

Hannah gulped, feeling Ara's eyes on her. "No... but hopefully it won't come to that."

"And the crystal army?" Dee added.

The crystal boy exploding filled Hannah's mind. "Just... try to fight around them. All we'll have to do is find the purple Orb and destroy it, and then it all ends."

Hannah tried to convince herself as much as them, grasping onto the words and hugging them to herself. Thankfully, her friends didn't pressure her into answering their abundance of unspoken doubts.

The pocket of light ahead neared, coaxing Hannah and her friends to step through into this secluded, tiny cavern. Hannah held her breath, raising Ozzie higher, as they stepped over the threshold of their destruction...

Simultaneously, five things happened.

Number one, whatever remaining heat on and surrounding Ozzie vanished, and the Orb froze Hannah's exposed skin on her fingers.

Second: its color completely surrendered to amethyst purple that churned as though caught amid a hurricane within the barriers of the crystal orb.

Third: thousands of crystal soldiers faded into view, clad in their signature crystal armor and military-worthy rows before them. At the head of the group, with a callous smile, was Jax, watching Hannah with an amused, sharp glint in his eyes.

Fourth: thudding, heavy footfalls echoed behind them, presumably sealing the exit for their escape.

And lastly, no purple Orb was here, and this was no secluded pocket containing it. No, it was the same, giant area they'd started in, with the stone dome towering above it. With the countdown of humans crystallizing over the entire world, glowing above it.

They were trapped.

And they were about to die.

AMARA

Ara's throat tightened, and she had to remind herself to breathe.

Then, at the reminder of the monster towering behind her, her lungs froze again.

Jax, the intolerable, inconsiderate *worm* that he was, smirked toward them, but there was a new sense of callousness in his eyes directed towards Hannah. As though he was witnessing revenge being served to him on a silver platter.

His gaze flickered over his former friend to Dee first, then came to rest on Ara, who glowered at him. Amusement was threaded in his expression when he took note of the gun clutched in her hands.

"You made a big mistake, Hannah." Jax drawled, focusing on Hannah again. Hannah, whose face was white and whose body had frozen from terror.

Jax's expression hardened. "What, no words left? Did you use them all up when figuring out how to *betray me?*"

The last two words were shouted, and Hannah looked like she would've flinched if her body hadn't been encased in fear.

Jax breathed heavily. "Honestly, how stupid do you think I am?" A lunatic smile stretched his lips, displaying a dimple on his left cheek. "You have *no* idea the planning, the resources I have in this. And– what?" A sharp laugh exited his still-smiling mouth. "You thought you could change– do *anything* about it?"

Ara watched as Hannah moistened her lips, her eyebrows creased in the obvious turmoil crushing her.

"Jax... what you're doing... It's wrong." Hannah said, her voice barely audible. In her hand, Ozzie glowed brighter.

"Wrong?" Another crazed laugh. "I don't *care* if it's wrong. I don't *care* how awful, how horrible, how immoral it is. *You* will not stand in *my* way."

Hannah's gaze hardened. "I will. I am." Her voice was steely, her spine straight, as though she'd momentarily forgotten the threat encircling them. Half of Ara wanted to cheer on her boldness, but the other was tempted to hide. Yes, Ara was defiant, but she wasn't stupid. She could tell when they were outnumbered.

And this was one of those times.

Jax raised an eyebrow. "You've changed," He murmured, dissolving into thought. His expression was a multitude of emotions.

And then his next words were: "Finish them. Get the Orb."

Ara stiffened, her grip on her gun tightening as the soldiers marched forward. Her eyes jumped onto Hannah instinctively, expecting her to say something.

Hannah gulped, retreating, horror weaving in and out of her eyes, a stark contrast to her earlier determination. "B-but, you said you never wanted to hurt me!"

"Yes, and that was before you betrayed me." Jax's eyes flashed with a lust for murder. "And now you can spend the last few minutes of your life wishing you hadn't."

He backed away as his soldiers marched forward. Ara hefted her gun, ready to aim for a soldier's leg or arm, when–

A sharp, smooth touch ran across her neck, brushing her hair aside as a deep growl resonated through the cavern, issuing from *it*, which was right behind her.

Her breath froze in her throat as what she assumed was the Beast's claw swiped through her blonde strands. She squeezed her eyes shut just as the nail dragged from the nape of her neck to her throat and paused. A large shadow draped over her, and Ara had to bite her lip to suppress a scream. She could only hope that Dee and Hannah had enough sense to shut their eyes before the Beast turned to them as well.

Crystal hands latched onto her arms and legs, locking her in place just as the Beast pressed on her throat with his claw.

Ara fought back a whimper as agony dug into her neck. The Beast was testing her, dragging her to the limit where she would give in, open her eyes...

Crystal hands locked her neck in place while others began to loosen Ara's vicelike grip on the gun. But if they were relentless, so was she.

For how long, however, she wasn't sure.

HANNAH

Ara's in trouble, Hannah's brain screamed, drowning all other thoughts as she jerked off the crystal fingers reaching for her, attempting to snatch the Orb from her fingers. Dee had unsheathed her sword the moment the army had swarmed forward, and now she was intent on keeping Hannah and Ozzie safe.

Ara's in trouble, Hannah repeated, elbowing a random crystal arm swinging towards her face.

I have to keep Ozzie away until I manage to find the purple Orb.

Suddenly, tearing that pouch Ozzie had custom-created was the worst decision of her life.

Well, that among other things.

Hannah batted away another limb and extracted her dagger, slipping Ozzie inside the holster instead. It managed to remain inside the extra material, but with any jerky movement, the Orb would go flying out.

Ara's priority, too, Hannah reminded herself as the familiar battle instincts washed over her. She dropped to one foot and spun, sweeping every near crystal soldier off their feet.

She leaped up again and fled the recurring crystal hands, praying Dee could prolong them. Hannah's heart crawled up her throat as her eyes scanned for Ara.

A flash of blonde hair caught her eye, sending instant relief, then terror, circulating within her.

The good news: Ara was still alive.

Bad news: Crystal soldiers swarmed her, clutching her limbs to restrain her movements.

Even more bad news: A giant, hairy, gray *thing* towered over her, pressing its jagged claw against her throat, torturing her to coax her to open her eyes, give in...

Ozzie pulsed near her hip, freezing even more, but even as Hannah whipped her head around, no purple Orb was in sight.

Ara first.

Hannah hefted her dagger, sprinting, and without a second's worth of thought, jammed the blade into the monster's back.

The Beast let out an angered growl and spun around just as Hannah snapped her eyes shut, keeping a vice-like grip when it turned. She felt the blade slide out of the monster's flesh and had to bite her tongue to keep from crying out. Her breathing quickened as the monster stomped closer–

And then, next thing she knew, there was a burst of agony at her side, and suddenly she was hurtling backward through the air.

Her back connected with what felt like the stone wall of the cave that exploded apart moments later, sending pain so raw that red spots danced in the darkness of her eyelids. The momentum of her crash sent her splashing into the water.

Her lungs screamed with the lack of air and the abundance of freshwater, unprepared for a swim.

Bubbles rose near her nose and mouth, and Hannah hastily froze her lungs, wanting to preserve whatever air she had left.

She was still sinking, slower now. Carefully, she peeled open her eyes, ignoring the sting of water against them, and looked up. She could see a watery film separating the air from the water, and from the borders of sediment, Hannah could tell where she was.

She had fallen– probably because the Beast had swatted her– and broken through the cave wall right beside the river.

Her hair drifted around her head, blood swarming her scalp in tow. As though reminding Hannah of it, her head throbbed in protest, whining about the numerous injuries it had managed to attain. Hannah batted it away, fingers brushing against her now-empty holster.

Panic grasped her as she whipped her head around, her eyes scanning for Ozzie in the clear water. The erratic beating of her heart lessened slightly at the sight of her dagger— which she quickly shoved in the holster— but didn't disappear.

Her lungs tightened. Air was running dangerously low.

But as Hannah glanced back up, a strange shudder rippled through her, as though a watery finger was sliding down her neck. Taunting her... prompting her...

What would happen if she remained down here, let the last breath of air leave her lips as water replaced it? If Hannah liberated herself from the crushing weight of the responsibility she'd taken.

What was left for her anyway?

How was she supposed to complete such a daunting, impossible task?

Dee wouldn't have chickened out. She was fighting, even now. Even Ara's stubbornness would've rescued her from even contemplating the decisions laid out for her.

But Hannah... Hannah wasn't sure.

She still remembered the loathing, the disgust Jax's eyes contained when he had seen her. When the last bit of the boy she remembered surrendered to the person he was now: a person drowning in a sea of his own downfall.

There was still a veiled piece of goodness when Hannah had seen him before. Before she'd hefted the dagger Jax had given her and plunged it into his own back.

Then that little piece, that little light fighting to burn in this dark world within him, went out.

Hannah exhaled, her remaining air abandoning her, as water began to wrap her in its unforgiving embrace, nothing like its gentle touch before. She was presented with a choice now, two shimmering jewels, each offering a different curse.

And Hannah chose to fight.

She kicked upward and broke the surface, her lungs expanding at the raw air flooding them. She gasped, tugging herself to the riverbank and collapsing against the grassy earth.

Hannah hoisted herself up, pushing aside her hair, which was dry. In fact, it seemed that as quickly as the water drenched her clothes and body, it had filtered out. She ran a finger on her neck, relieved to find the comforting chain of her necklace, and tucked it back in her top. She fished out a rubber band from her pocket and swept her hair in a loose ponytail, eyes tracing the massive hole in the cave wall she'd caused and fallen through.

Finally, murmuring a quick prayer to the heavens, she drew her dagger and stepped through the opening, ignoring her mounting heart rate.

A massive flash of gray barreled towards her, and before Hannah could even react, she was pinned up against the wall by her throat, her feet dangling a yard over the ground.

She clawed against the Beast's unforgiving grip, all thoughts momentarily gone as she stared at it, their faces level.

It had shaggy gray fur covering every inch of its eight-foot-tall body, resembling a yeti crossed with a wendigo. Its head had one black-lipped mouth and, where eyes and a nose were meant to be, was a giant orb with green smoke revolving within. It had bone-white, curved horns sprouting from its skull.

Hannah's nails dug into the Beast's leathery black fingers, shock seizing her. She had just assumed the Yin Orb they'd come to destroy was like Ozzie, a physically unbound entity. But this Beast wasn't a protector of the Yin; it was bonded to it.

With another jolt of surprise, Hannah realized she wasn't turning into crystal. Her mind still belonged to her. Her body didn't morph into translucent crystal.

She was immune.

"Ah, yes," Jax's voice wrenched Hannah from her overload of shock, bringing her back to reality where the Beast was still pinning her by her throat against the stone wall.

With effort, she managed to twist her neck to see him sauntering towards them, a cold smirk curving his lips. In his palm was an agitated Ozzie.

The Beast's Orb and Ozzie both reacted distressingly, seemingly recognizing each other's proximity. Ozzie was now all the way purple, and the Beast's eye was green.

Jax's smile fell. "What are you waiting for? Why isn't she crystallizing?"

The Beast grunted and turned back to Hannah, and she braced herself.

But nothing.

Jax's eyes widened, and he glanced at the hole she'd fallen through. Rage contorted his face, and he tucked Ozzie into his pocket.

"You fell into the water?" He bit out, glowering at her.

Hannah choked, air struggling to pass through her windpipe.

"Release her."

Hannah plummeted to the ground, landing on all fours as she gasped, clutching her throat. Her dagger clattered to the side, just out of reach.

"Did you fall into the water?" Jax pressed, his voice laced with venom.

Hannah nodded mindlessly, inching forward and grabbing her dagger. It slid into her holster with a rustle against the leather.

"Do you even know," Jax stalked forward, forcing Hannah to back away, "what you've done?"

Her voice was hoarse when she straightened and said: "Step back. Get away from me before you receive a knife in your stomach."

He laughed hollowly. "That's an empty threat, Hannah, and you know it." Jax slowed to a stop, but malice still glinted in his eyes. "You don't have the guts to hurt me."

Hannah hefted her dagger, refusing to admit the truth wafting off the words. "Oh yeah? Try me, Jax."

His grin was cruel. "Gladly."

Hannah glared, ready to block a strike, when the Beast stomped between them, shielding his master. Hannah glared up, moistening her lips, as the Orb glared down at her.

"Coward!" She shouted, withdrawing her steps, "You didn't even tell me about the river!"

Jax barked out a sharp laugh. "What more do you need to know? It provides immunity to the Beast's gaze– or anything, really. It also heals most wounds, though you weren't in there long enough. So sad you won't live long enough to celebrate your *first* achievement."

Hannah squeezed her dagger. "Maybe. But at least I'll live long enough to tell someone else."

Jax frowned. "What–" Realization dawned on him. He yelled, "Seize her!" At the same time, Hannah turned on her heel and began sprinting away.

Her hair sailed behind her as she scouted for a cluster of crystal soldiers. Where there were soldiers, there were likely to be Dee and Ara.

"Ara!" She shouted, flailing her arms in hopes of gaining their attention, "Dee! The river!"

Her friends turned to her, halting their struggle against the crystal soldiers, a mix of shock, relief, and confusion flitting across their faces. Hannah jerked an arm to the cavity in the wall, doubling back to lead the Beast away from the hole.

"Grab them! Why isn't anyone getting them?!" Jax screamed, his voice echoing through the cavern. Hannah flinched, ducking as the Beast swiped his arm at her head, then springing up again, willing her legs faster.

Out of the corner of her eye, she witnessed Ara and Dee make a break for the river, at least a thousand soldiers clamoring after them. Ara made it to the gap and sprang into the river. Dee copied her, leaping out just as a crystal soldier snatched her ankle from the air. They locked their arms around the struggling girl and hauled her away.

Hannah cursed under her breath, losing her footing and stumbling into a crystal soldier. She murmured a quick apology, then berated herself for apologizing to a statue, and shoved it in the way. The Beast tossed it aside like a rag doll, but Hannah was already sprinting again, unwilling to witness another statue shattering into pieces.

Footsteps thundered after her. A stitch ran up her side, turning her breath ragged. She pivoted to the left, her sneakers screeching on the stone. Time for another tactic.

Hannah snatched her dagger out and dropped to the ground between its legs. The Beast ran forward, and she sprang up, aiming for a slice at its back when it pivoted, directing its horns at her.

The world dissolved in a blur, all focus aimed at Hannah and the Beast. In the back of her mind, Hannah worried for her friends, hoping one of them could get Ozzie back. Or even just stay alive.

Ara had to get out of the river.

Dee had to escape from the crystal soldiers.

Hannah had to best an eight-foot-tall, invincible monster bent on drawing her blood.

So far, chances were far slimmer than she would've liked.

CHAPTER 29

DIANA

Dee was blinded, drowning in a sea of crystal limbs.

She was wrenched back by at least a hundred or so crystal warriors who lugged her away in an awkward dragging competition. For her struggles, she received a nice bruise on her jaw, courtesy of her closest soldier.

Tasting blood, Dee swallowed as a crystal sword poked her in the back. Her ring was still on her finger, but it was dangerously close to sliding off, and then she would be weaponless.

Well, not entirely. She still had her voice. But what good would those powers do when she could barely control two people, let alone an entire army of crystal automatons?

Dee bit her tongue, glaring, as her ankle got nicked by another crystal blade. Fine. If they wanted to manhandle her, she'd make it as difficult as she could muster.

Dee gave up on walking and dropped to the ground. The soldiers around her paused, then attempted to grab her again. As their crystal abdomens bent to reach her, Dee front-kicked one soldier in the face. He toppled backward, colliding with another, which collided with another...

Creating the most satisfying domino effect Dee had seen to date.

She spent an extra minute admiring her handiwork before taking off on a run. She knew where the opening leading to the river was, and even though she wasn't sure why Hannah had urged her and Ara to jump inside, Dee trusted her enough to listen.

She pounded across the stone, ignoring the crystal limbs pursuing her, her mind focused on the crumbling hole in the cave side.

Dee let out a psychotic laugh. She was going to make it. The opening was right *there*. She just had to jump through...

Crystal soldiers filed in, blocking the hole with their bodies.

An annoyed growl tore itself from Dee's throat as she skidded to the side, avoiding collision with the warriors as she continued sprinting, darting right into a tunnel. That was all she seemed to be doing lately: running and making others run.

Fine, Dee snatched a flickering lantern off its post and bounded into the passage, her eyes pinned forward as crystal feet stamped after her. *If they want to run, I'll give them a run.*

AMARA

Ara didn't know how to swim.

Less than fortunate for her, because she was currently submerged in the river, her eyes pressed shut and her lungs frozen, her body still.

When Hannah had urged her and Dee to jump in the river, Ara hadn't considered the fact that blindly leaping into water wasn't the best idea. But she had simply prolonged the realization and bounded into the water, believing she'd deal with the issue when the time came.

The time came.

And now she was cursing herself.

It wasn't necessarily her fault that she'd never learned to swim: Ara had always been shifting due to her father's work, which denied her any time to start something new and stick with it.

And she hated it. Hated that her life couldn't be stable enough to learn a skill. Although the prospect of flinging her arms and legs in water never seemed very appealing, and honestly, terrified her more than she would've liked to admit.

Ara was stuck in a situation she had created for herself. And this river wasn't even assisting her like a regular body of water would. She should be floating near the top due to density differences, but something about the river kept her sandwiched between the bottom and the surface.

And she *couldn't* swim.

Ara exhaled through her nose, and bubbles tickled her face. Was this how her life would end? Drowning in a river, so close yet so far away from what she'd been fighting for. Yes, she wanted to see Goldie again. But the temptation to see her mother was equally as strong, and more in favor now that she was trapped by the strangling arms of death in this river.

Cautiously, Ara peeled her eyes open, ignoring the coolness of water stinging her irises as she addressed her surroundings. Her gun was still tucked in the waistband of her pants– loosely, now– and would surely be gaining water damage with every passing second she spent here. With a jolt, she also realized her glasses were missing. *Very* inconvenient for her.

Where was Dee? Ara realized suddenly, glancing up. There wasn't a second splash, no tornado of bubbles. It was just her in the river, alone.

Close to being helpless.

Tired.

Exhausted enough to consider making this river her final resting place.

Ara blinked, a few tears from straining her eyes mixing with the river water and the loss of her glasses. She was presented with two options now.

Ara looked up, the sun beaming down on her, the rays distorted by the water.

She tilted her head down at the clear river bottom.

Her blonde hair floated into her eyes, and she swiped it away, the cool liquid filtering through her fingers. Ara paused, ignoring the gnawing pinch at her lungs, and swiped up, kicking her feet at the same time.

Her friends needed her. Which is why Ara crawled up to the riverbank, her lungs expanding with gratitude as they fought to process air.

She dug her nails into the soil, spluttering and choking as Ara collapsed on her back. Despite her current inability to breathe normally– or see that well, though it wasn't horrible– a triumphant smile curved its way to her face. No matter how clumsy or chaotic, she had still swum.

Ara sat up, her now-calm breathing overshadowed by the pounding of her heart. She crawled to her feet, strangely dry, excluding her waterlogged pistol. With fumbling fingers, she extracted her gun and unloaded it. She pointed it into the distance, opposite the dome wall, and drained the water from it. After a less-than-thorough inspection, she deemed it usable enough.

Her pistol could rust, but that was the least of her worries.

Two crystal soldiers were standing in the opening, their backs to Ara, their faces pinned on somewhere inside the dome.

Well, that was convenient.

And increasingly annoying.

Ara hefted her gun, ready to fire a warning shot, when–

"Out of my way!" Someone snapped. Jax shoved one soldier aside, his face fuming.

"Did anyone else get through here?" He bit out to the other, which shook its head.

Ara hitched her breath. They were unaware of her presence. This proved to be the perfect time to steal Ozzie–

Jax stepped through the opening, his face cold. "Of course, they missed one."

Ara furrowed her brows, concealing her surprise and gun, as she took a step back. "They're pretty dumb." She agreed.

"Exactly," Jax nodded, scrutinizing her, "So you would've been an excellent crystal soldier. Maybe some smarts would actually *remain* with you. But unfortunately..." His eyes fell on the rippling water behind her, "You jumped in, didn't you?"

Gears began turning in Ara's head, and puzzle pieces began to click together. "I did,"

Jax smiled, a strangely attractive grin if it weren't in this scenario, and hefted a crystal gun. It was beautiful and expertly crafted, too.

"So you understand why I can't let you live, right?" He twirled the gun between his fingers.

Ara swallowed, taking another step back, her heels teetering on the edge of the riverbank. "Oh, I understand perfectly."

His smile turned pleased as the gun leveled at her forehead. "Then we understand each other."

Ara shrugged. "Nearly."

Before he could pull the trigger, Ara ducked and tackled him into the grass, the two of them tumbling on the land before they came to a clumsy stop, Ara splayed atop him.

He grunted, shifting to sit up, and Ara darted her hand into his pocket, retrieving a freezing Ozzie. She stumbled to her feet and dashed over to the opening, barely managing to fling Ozzie in before she was jerked back.

Ara yelped, whirling around to face a disheveled, fuming Jax. He let go of her hand and smacked the barrel of his gun against her temple.

Agony, colored red, clouded her vision as she stumbled back, landing splayed on the riverbank. Jax towered over her, his eyes bearing unspoken maliciousness.

He looked so unlike the person who had leaned over Hannah when she had fainted. Who had checked over her pulse serenely and waited for her to regain consciousness. Now, his dark hair was disheveled, his eyes containing anything but peace. Smudges of dirt and blood speckled his face and clothing. An assortment of weapons was strapped to his waist.

"Know-it-all Ara, huh?" He taunted, repositioning his gun. Now it was aimed at her. A fatal shot.

All the bravery from Ara was melting away, symmetrical to the broken girl collapsed on the ground, barely able to keep her eyes focused above as she propped herself on her elbows.

Something warm and wet trickled down the side of her temple, dragging a trail down her cheek and dripping onto her neck. The sun glared into her eyes, forcing Ara to squint at the weapon aimed at her and the face behind it.

"Is that what you've been reduced to?" She rasped, clearing her throat in hopes of her vision doing the same. "Killing someone just for the pleasure?"

Jax's eyebrows furrowed. "You think I'm doing this for pleasure?" A strange, unnatural laugh came from the tormented boy dominating her. "It has *never* been for pleasure, Ara." His voice was strangely bitter, mirroring the steel in his eyes.

The safety of the gun released again. "And now, you're gonna regret even talking."

HANNAH

It wasn't enough that she was in the midst of a brawl with the Beast. No, she had to get nailed in the head by something, too.

Hannah staggered to the side, her skull already throbbing with the memory of the object that had hit her as she grappled for purchase on the gravelly earth. Swallowing back curses, Hannah whirled around to find what had hit her.

A small, purple Orb winked back at her.

Relief spread through her, igniting the fireworks of her hope, which skyrocketed faster than she could douse them. Hannah snatched Ozzie up, preparing to duck another blow, when–

The Beast let out a growl, unlike those he had made before, and stomped back. Hannah paused, her grip on her dagger loosening, as fatigue started to catch up with her.

And it seemed the Beast was plagued with it, too. That, or maybe a hint of fear that had flickered upon his face, which was impressive itself with features like that. Still, Hannah stepped back, clutching her arm, panting.

The Beast looked at her through its massive crystal eye-slash-orb– now green. Pain tore through Hannah's arm, which she had realized had been impaired by the Beast's horns; a massive slice traveled down the length of her arm, leaking blood and soaking the already-shredded fabric of her top.

Gritting her teeth, she forced back the pain and stared at the Beast, her breaths still shaky and uneven. The Beast stared back, locked in some sort of staring contest.

One eye locked on two.

Ozzie remained chilly in her covered palm. Was the Beast feeling that, too? Except it was embedded into his face, freezing its eye socket.

What would happen if I had tapped into Ozzie's powers? Hannah wondered. *If I truly kept it, used it, and accepted it?*

An image drew itself in her mind. She would become faceless, then, burdened to carry one crystal orb as an eye. No nose, no regular hazel eyes. Just a blinding, smoky Orb, and pink lips, dulled by the essence of her morphed being.

Hannah shuddered. Was that what the Beast's life was like? Was he a creature– granted, a very *abnormal*, unreal one– before he had been cursed with the Orb? Was there a memory, a shell of the sentience he'd once possessed trapped within? What *was* it before it had bonded with Yin?

The Beast gave a mournful, steely growl, as though daring her to defy it again. But it sounded half-hearted, like it had already come to terms with the idea of death.

CHAPTER 30

DIANA

The muscles in Dee's legs screamed, likely on fire now, by how much she'd stressed them into carrying her forward.

Forward. Run.

Her thoughts were reduced to those two words, revolving around her brain like the moon's orbit. She barely registered where she was going, only having a vague idea of the tunnel she was sprinting through, her only light source coming from the flickering lanterns zooming past her.

And the one clutched in her hand, flame already out.

Not-so-distantly, crystal soldiers stampeded after her, zeroed in on their singular task: catch her.

After being captured *twice*, Dee refused to make it three. And her stubbornness alone kept her sprinting ceaselessly, barely realizing when the lanterns nailed to the dome walls disappeared, and she was sprinting through darkness, with no sense of where she was heading.

Or did she really have no idea where she was?

Dimly, she recognized the cracked floor here as her footing slipped not once, but *three times*. Either she was morphing into Hannah, or she'd already been here. With the same company.

Except this time, she was unbound.

And if Dee was correct, there would be an opening right...

Dee sprinted into the entryway of the mini cavern, the same one she'd been held hostage in. Like before, when she'd peered out of her heavy eyelids that she pried open after being knocked unconscious, there were mini crystal statues here, rooted to the ground. That was all she'd managed to glimpse before the shackles had been snapped to her and Ara's wrists, sending them into an instant coma.

Now she had *plenty* of time to view her surroundings. Dee coughed at the irony of the situation, taking into account the arched ceiling and sconces circling it, each containing a little ball of fire. Her eyes fell on the crystal children frozen in place.

Her throat tightened, knowing that somewhere in here, there was a girl about eight years old, with crystallized hair and eyes that would bear no emotion until her older sister sorted out this mess.

With that thought in mind, Dee dropped the lantern and eyed the mini cavern, hoping to find a spot to hide to figure out what to do next. But the walls were smooth stone here, leaving her in the inevitable predicament.

She was trapped.

Dee spun around to meet the sight that had been approaching her all along. She winced, fisting her hands so that her nails dug into her skin, as a crystal sword pressed against her stomach.

"So..." She said blandly, staring at the crystal face threatening her. "You caught me."

It looked back with its blank stare.

More soldiers poured into the room, flooding the only exit and framing the dome walls. The familiarity of the situation was almost funny, but Dee didn't dare laugh.

Yet.

Deliberately, she took a step behind, out of the reach of the crystal statue, which didn't pursue her with its sword, but did keep a watchful eye on her. Hands up, Dee held her breath, inching back, as her eyes washed over the room again, taking into account anything she could use.

Crystal couldn't melt... right?

A giant sconce flickered above the entrance, containing the largest flame. Stone couldn't be lit... but whatever was fueling the fire within its carrier could.

An impulsive idea sprang into her head, and without giving it a second thought, Dee put it into action.

She ducked, unraveling her sword, and slammed the flat end of the blade against the statue's legs, which toppled to the side. The soldiers were spurred into fighting, and they charged for her from all angles. Dee broke into a run *towards* the soldiers, hoisting her sword like a javelin, aiming for the main sconce above the warriors' heads.

She reared her arm back and let it fly.

There was a satisfying explosion of crystal as metal struck through it, peppering the ground with microscopic shards of the sconce. Dee barreled into the warriors, fighting to get to the exit as they resisted.

Panic flared through Dee.

She had to get out of here before–

CRACK

The remaining crystal gave way, scattering its contents and blocking the only exit. Wood shavings rained down in piles, soon igniting once the fire graced it.

Smoke unfurled as the mounting fire increased, its wispy hand unraveling to dauntingly waft over to Dee, grasping her throat with its hand of ruin.

She choked, still struggling against the soldiers, who seemed unaware of the mounting flames.

But then again, they were immune to fire. And they wouldn't be against her being roasted to her imminent end.

Definitely one of her topmost *idiotic* ideas.

"Let me go!" She shouted, the smoke clouding her vision as she began coughing violently. Dee ducked, and the soldiers quickly rearranged their grip on her, now pinning her down.

"Please!" She screamed, the fire arching against the dome wall, continuing to be ignited by the wood shavings. *"Please!"*

A blank-faced soldier stared down at her, extracting his dagger. It gave her a well-sized gash on her face, drawing the midnight blue blood Dee knew would be spilling down her face.

There was no way she could call back her sword, which was probably engulfed in the flames right now. No way she'd survive if she didn't use her powers. No way she'd survive because her powers were weak. And even if her life miraculously prevailed, there was no way she'd be able to hide the truth of her origin.

Her origin.

She was a siren.

She was born a siren.

Lived a secret siren.

And would die a siren.

And Dee was done hiding it.

Pure desperation fueled her as she tapped into her power, this time letting the words flood to her throat, become doused in strength before they rolled to and off her tongue.

"Let me go!"

The soldiers closest to her froze, but more kept surfacing, charging towards her. Dee's eyes stung with tears from the smoke, her skin angry and red from being manhandled. Her throat felt scratchy, but still she screamed:

"Let go of me!"

The command burst into the open air, bouncing along the stone walls, twirling and twisting its way into crystal ears.

All at once, the statues stilled. Dee scrambled back, her lungs tightening with the effort of breathing. Her throat was in splitting pain from the fumes, and she had to get out of here.

But the fire rippled relentlessly, blocking her only path outside. *And it still had her sword.*

Growling in frustration, she pushed back the now-sweaty strands of her sticking to her face and urged herself to think. Crystal contained fire, as seen by the sconces. So if she...

Dee cleared her throat, standing up, and tossed out another command.

"Stomp out the fire."

The soldiers jumped to life, satisfyingly compliant to her words. Delayed awe crept to Dee when she realized she could command the soldiers to her bidding, even more so with her newly revived power. Soon, there was just a jumble of soot and ashes and a whole lot of smoke in the thick air.

Dee forced her aching legs to exit the mini-dome and take measured steps into the passageway. Her head throbbed and her vision swam, but surprisingly, her throat didn't hurt.

She leaned against the passage wall, anticipating when her lungs would be clear. She gulped down fresh air gratefully, wiping away the blood that had trailed down her face.

Midnight blue blood.

Dee glanced back at the soldiers, who were still awaiting their next order. With a sudden, giddy thought, she realized she could have them carry her. March her in like a princess.

Gosh, I'm turning to Pelli now.

Dee activated her voice and said, *"Follow me."*

At once, the soldiers were jarred to life, and obediently, they followed her. One reached for her sword and brought it to her.

Dee grinned, her smirk widening as she noticed the tip of the blade was still smoldering with the remnants of fire. The metal seemed to absorb some of the fire. A thin curl of steam wafted into the air, dappled with evaporating sparks.

Dee hoisted her sword on her shoulder and marched forward, down the path, soon emerging in the main chamber.

She did it.

She won.

She–

Was being stared at by a pair of eyes she knew all too well.

CHAPTER 31

AMARA

Ara had previously wondered how Death claims people. People meet him in all sorts of unique ways– disasters, illness, injuries, to name a few. Once, when she was younger, Ara even questioned herself about how she would meet him.

Face-to-face with a crystal gun was not how she'd expected it to be.

"Jax," She breathed, arching her neck as far back as she possibly could. Not that it would matter. He had a clear shot.

"Listen," Ara was afraid speaking loudly would trigger him to fire, which he was about to do. "She wouldn't want you to do this."

Jax's mask cracked, and he stepped back as though Ara had burned him. "How do you know about her?"

Ara gradually sat up, darting a careful look at him. "What? Of course I know her."

She was talking about Hannah, of course, but something on Jax's face signified he was alarmed. Even defensive.

But then he relaxed enough to bite out: "You mean Hannah?"

Ara nodded stiffly.

He glared. "I couldn't care less what Hannah thinks about me. She should've realized breaking my trust only results in this."

"But what about the trust you broke first?" Ara glowered at him. "She really cares– cared about you, Jax."

"You're not in a position to be lecturing me right now." He growled, refocusing the gun.

Ara's heart rate spiked, and she blurted one of the many jumbled thoughts swirling in her head.

"Who's Jade?"

This time, Jax dropped the gun in shock.

His face was gaunt, hollow, as he stared at her. "How do you know that name?"

Ara swallowed. So she'd exploited a crack in his armor.

"Hannah heard you say it. And she told us."

A muscle ticked in his jaw, paralleling the turmoil in his eyes. While he was processing, Ara, deliberately slow, rose to her feet, ready to sprint the second he reacted.

But there was no shout, no lunge to grab her. His vision had clouded over, like memories were flooding past his eyes, fisting Jax in its unforgiving grip. He seemed stunned, so obviously Jade was important to him.

Ara's speculating ended when her gaze landed on the crystal gun hidden among the stalks of grass. This was her opportunity to seize it before she ended on the wrong end of it. Again.

Steadily, Ara took cautious steps toward the gun, which, in all fairness, were also steps toward him. She schooled her features to the closest thing to sympathy she could muster before saying,

"Listen, I know whatever you've gone through–whatever you're going through, is difficult."

Jax's eyes snapped onto her, and Ara wanted to glower, sneer at him, even. But she kept her face neutral and her tone soft when she continued.

"I also lost people very dear to me. It hurts, doesn't it?"

Ara knew what she was doing: manipulating him. Giving him a reason to feel compelled to trust her, for at least this moment. She was offering Jax a person who understood his pain to some extent. Someone who could empathize with the mental torment he had obviously been through.

So even though she knew his conscious mind didn't trust her one bit, his subconscious did agree with her. That's why, when he tilted his head in the bare suggestion of a nod, victory erupted within her, threatening to blow Ara's scrupulously conceived plot.

She was practically standing on the crystal gun now; could feel it under her shoes. If she just managed to kneel and reach it...

"Who did you lose?" Jax asked, his face still rigid. But his voice was hoarse, and his eyes contained a still fire.

Ara's breath hitched, pain blooming atop her shoulders. Undeniable weight that had burdened her for quite a while now. She forced her knees not to buckle as Ara swallowed, shifting into her monotone voice.

"My mother. Heart disease. I was only ten."

Ara was surprised by how much the words ached. She hadn't spoken aloud about it for a while now.

Jax's face didn't change, but Ara knew he meant it when he said, "I'm sorry for you."

And I'm sorry for you. Ara had to stop herself from speaking. This time, she did let her knee tremble and jerk her down with a grunt.

Jax stiffened, his body tensing further. "What—"

Ara's fingers closed around the crystal hilt, and she whipped the gun up, directing the barrel straight to Jax's face.

He backed away, holding his hands up, startled. His eyes widened with recognition, then closed off as he sank into his signature barriers. Except these were more exceptionally built, guarding him with higher walls, tinier cracks.

It was probably Ara's fault he'd closed up even further, but she couldn't really bring herself to care at the moment.

"You're done." She panted, "If you move, I shoot."

Jax's lips pressed together, falling silent. His body was pulled taut, like every muscle was humming with energy, waiting to be spent. He stared down at her, where she was still kneeling on one knee, the gun pointed at him.

"Don't. Move." She repeated, her eyes pinned on him as she rose to her feet.

Jax's eyes tracked her as she straightened, following the tiniest movements. His arms were still raised, his body still.

"You're gonna turn around," Ara said slowly, squeezing the hilt of the gun, "And–"

Before she could complete her sentence, Jax lunged forward and spun around, grasping her wrist and angling the gun up just as Ara squeezed the trigger. The crystal bullet exploded from the muzzle and zoomed up, disappearing into the sky.

Ara released the gun from her grasp, instead whirling around to face Jax as she extracted her regular pistol and aimed at him.

Time screeched to a halt as they stared, breathless, their guns positioned at each other like a duel.

Jax was the first to break the silence. "You have nerve," He mused.

Ara scoffed. "Not the first time I've been told that."

Jax smirked. "I'm sure. But do you know what else you've probably been told?"

Ara cocked an eyebrow. "What?"

Time slowed as Jax pulled the trigger and ducked, tackling Ara to the ground before the bullet delved into her. They landed in the opening of the dome with a thud.

Ara's vision went fuzzy as she blinked, her head disoriented with its recent physical trauma. She was half in, half out of the dome, and Jax had sat up so he was now straddling her, positioning a mini dagger above her face.

"You're weak." He derided, "And you hide your emotions because you're not sure how to feel them. You find contentment with Hannah because she's emotionally driven, contrasting with you, who cannot feel at all. Secretly, you envy her, admire her even, even though you know you shouldn't."

Tears sprang into her eyes, an aftershock of the agony seizing her, as she looked around, desperate for any help.

Any.

Her eyes clashed with gray ones exiting a passageway.

Dee marched out of the tunnel, her sword a bright beacon now that the tip had been dipped in what appeared to be flimsy flames. Behind her was an array of crystal soldiers, unthreatening and unmindful.

And the *blood.*

Midnight blue blood smattered Dee's wrists and neck, and had tangled her hair. More of it painted a trail down her left cheek, where she was sporting a massive cut.

Instant relief flooded through Ara, more so when Dee's eyes widened in recognition and she halted. Her eyes scanned over the situation, where Jax had also taken notice of the newcomer.

"Well, hello." He grinned. "Want to watch?"

Jax paused, his eyes narrowing as he observed the soldiers behind her. "What is wrong with them?"

Dee stepped forward, ignoring his question and brandishing her sword. "Let Ara go."

Jax pursed his lips. "No, I don't think I will. Considering your friend here..." he dragged the tip of the blade from Ara's cheek down to her throat, "got me aggravated."

Dee raised an eyebrow. "It's not very difficult, you know?"

Ara cleared her throat, reminding the two of her *very* uncomfortable state. "Jax, please..." She muttered.

The tip of the dagger dug into her neck harder. He smirked, bowing his head so she had no choice but to stare at his smug face.

He clucked his tongue. "Aww. Did over-smart Ara make a mistake once in her life?"

A tear bubbled out. *"Please,"*

"Get off her."

Ara's eyes snapped back to Dee, whose face had transformed into undeniable malice towards Jax, who had become rigid. He turned to look at her slowly, his eyes unfocusing, her breathing shallower.

"Get. Off. Her," Dee repeated. The sides of her face sharpened, each cheek sporting three smoky lines layered atop each other. Ara shuddered.

Jax sluggishly climbed off Ara, who sat up carefully, her gaze darting between him and Dee. Dee padded forward, angling her sword at his heart.

"Step away." She instructed. Jax didn't move, his eyes clearing, turning sharper. His lips tilted up in a smirk as he blinked once, then twice...

"Fancy power you have." He nodded to her.

Dee's stern demeanor warped. "What–?"

"Shame you won't be able to use it anymore." Jax whistled sharply, and a tremor shuddered through the cave, followed by thudding footsteps. He stepped back, his arms twined behind his back.

Dee rounded on him. "What did you do?!"

He shrugged, his eyes twinkling mischievously. "Say your goodbyes."

Dee growled in frustration, opening her mouth to give a new command, when–

Jax's hand closed around her throat, lifting Dee into the air. He pinned her against the back of a soldier, closing out her air.

She choked, the sword tumbling out of her fingers to land with a clatter on the ground as she dug her nails into Jax's hand, attempting to pry it away. Ara stumbled to her feet, her vision spinning. Ara leaned against the dome wall, breathing heavily, when something crunched under her feet.

She swept away her blonde hair, her eyes widening at the sight of her now-fractured monocle, which she snatched up. Heart thudding, Ara brought it to her eye.

A blend of smoke drenched the air: blue, purple, green, and red. They were all warring with one another, repelled by the other colors.

Purple smoke stayed distant from green– the two resisting each other's proximity. Red and blue, however, constantly swarmed each other, attempting to cancel out their opponent. Ara's gaze shifted toward Jax, whose hand was still strangling a gasping Dee. His eyes were covered by a thin veil of the blue mist, and a weak string of red crackled against the barrier, a stark contrast to the purple smoke practically pummeling his face.

Something told Ara that if she looked at herself, the blue mist would be immunizing her from the Beast's purple magic, too.

And the red smoke was feebly drifting from...

Dee's sword.

With a gasp, Ara lost her grip on the monocle, and it shattered upon the ground. Jax turned to stare at her, a frown on his face.

"What?" He questioned.

"Ara–" Dee wheezed. Jax squeezed tighter, and her eyes widened further.

"Help,"

"What are you doing?" Jax demanded.

With loose fingers, Ara snatched up Dee's sword and raised it, channeling the mounting determination and adrenaline spinning through her veins.

Jax released Dee, who collapsed on the ground and turned to Ara, fire in his eyes.

"Whatever you're doing–"

Before he could finish the sentence, Ara plunged the sword tip directly into his face.

It connected a millimeter away from his eyes before Dee's sword melted away, leaving three shocked people, and the smashing of crystal reverberating through the cavern.

Uncertain breaths shuddered through Jax as he stared, unsure. "Ara?" He asked slowly, ignoring the nearing thuds of footsteps, "What did you do?"

Ara didn't have to look through her monocle to know what had happened to the blue mist that had covered Jax's eyes.

Dee lifted her head, eyes watery, as she glanced at the unspoken, stunned exchange between Ara and Jax.

"What did you *do?*" Jax repeated, stalking forward.

All thoughts screeched to a halt as a sudden shadow fell over them. Jax and Ara whipped their heads toward the Beast in unison.

The giant, gray Beast towered over them, his eye flashing purple. Time froze.

Dee shielded her eyes with her palm.

A scream tore from Jax's throat.

Ara's mouth went dry.

She whirled around in time to see the color drain from Jax's body, literally, as purple fog blanketed him. His eyes were wide, and whatever light twinkled in them, no matter how malicious, dissolved from his essence. His skin turned translucent, his face carved with shock before the purple light enveloped him, then faded. It left behind a crystal statue where a boy once was.

The effect of the crystal gaze.

Right in front of her.

Ara felt all her strength dwindling and a lump form in her throat as Jax– no, the *statue*– shuffled to join the other soldiers.

The Beast let out a mournful growl and stomped away. Ara watched, transfixed, as his gray figure lumbered away to the other end of the dome.

"Is it gone?"

Ara's head snapped to the huddled figure on the ground. Dee peered through her fingers.

Ara swallowed. "It's gone." She confirmed.

Dee staggered to her feet, clutching onto Ara for support. She wiped her mouth with her sleeve, her breathing ragged.

"Jax–?"

"Don't." Ara planted her feet firmly, refusing to let clashing emotions upend her. The red smoke, the remnants of fire, seemed to have a cancellation effect. Where water presented immunity, the fire denied it.

Dee peered at her. "You okay?"

Ara cleared her throat. "Fine. Just... overwhelmed."

Dee's face softened. "You don't have to hide your emotions, you know? You do that a lot. It can't be good for you."

Ara scoffed, turning her face away to conceal the bubbling tears, but her voice was still thick when she said: "I'm fine. Just—"

She yelped in surprise as Dee tugged her back and embraced her.

Ara froze, her muscles tensing.

"It's called a hug." Dee murmured in her ear, tightening her arms around Ara, "You should try it sometime."

Tentatively, Ara reciprocated the hug, allowing Dee to bolster her. A few tears leaked onto her face, and she sniffled, her body relieving itself of tension.

Ara sniffled, pulling back and swiping at her face, an uncertain smile on her face. "Maybe I should." She agreed softly.

Dee beamed. "Where's Hannah? She has to see this. She's gonna be so excited."

CHAPTER 32

HANNAH

Hannah was *not* excited.

Or joyful.

Or anything close to the sensation.

Her limbs ached with every movement as she slumped against the wall, her breathing labored as her eyes fluttered shut.

She had been diverting the Beast, attempting to tire it out so it would quit pursuing her. Hannah had hoped she would be able to generate a plan. Find a way to destroy its eye.

But all she managed to do was enrage it further until a sharp whistle rang across the opposite side of the dome, and the Beast had bounded away readily.

Hannah breathed heavily, searching for any remaining traces of adrenaline within her, something to sustain her enough to continue opposing the Beast.

Her spine stiffened at the strangled scream echoing from across the dome. Hannah's skin crawled as she stepped away from the wall, horror uncurling in her throat.

Who yelled?

Her heart pounded in her throat as she squinted past the gold piles.

Are they okay?

Denial had her in a headlock, refusing to believe it was Dee or Ara who had shrieked like that. She couldn't– wouldn't allow that.

Please let them be okay. Her mind was dissolving into desperation and mounting anxiety.

Please. Her skin buzzed with electricity.

Hannah looked around aimlessly, trying to find something to bolster herself with. She could hear her heartbeat roaring in her chest.

Every sound singled and separated, a cacophony of noises merged together to create what Hannah had originally perceived as background vibrations. Every clink of crystal. Every tremble across the earth as footsteps ceaselessly pummeled it. She zeroed in on everything and nothing at all as the world transformed into a swirl of gold and agony. Green and anxiety. Purple and danger.

Absently, her fingers curled tighter around the hilt of her dagger, jarring her out of her spiraling mentality. She stared down at the lethal weapon, noting the piles of gold reflecting within the crystal blade.

Noticing the reflection of her eyes.

They were wide and scared. Young and lonely.

Various bruises and scratches adorned her face. Hannah swiped at her cut lip, blood smearing to the side.

Vaguely, she drew out the freezing Orb. It iced her skin even through the flimsy fabric covering her palm.

For the first time since Hannah had left her home, her mind was unfavorably blank, refusing to provide any ideas to defend herself.

A roar rumbled from the opposite end of the dome, followed by recurring tremors in the ground. The Beast was approaching.

Hannah's muscles went taut, her body humming with the newfound epinephrine flooding her senses. She only had one shot at this, and judging by the way the Beast stalked towards her, she wouldn't have much time left.

Hannah inhaled sharply and reinforced her grasp on the dagger, a new kind of fire igniting within her eyes. Her gaze tracked the mass of gray as it stomped towards her.

She hoisted up Ozzie, spine straight, posture unflinching as the Beast glared at her Orb.

"Come and get it," She breathed, daring it to heed her.

The Beast reduced its pace, prowling toward her. Hannah didn't move.

Its claws lifted, close enough to graze the agitated Orb...

Impulsively, Hannah shoved her crystal blade into its stomach, releasing the handle as its face leveled with her when it doubled over. Hannah raised Ozzie–

And smashed it into the Beast's crystal eye.

A high-pitched whine screamed through the air, mixed with another, symmetrical screech. The Beast joined the two with its own earth-shaking roar.

Hannah stumbled back, cupping her ears, which were ringing and shrieking with the sea of noises. Her chest was constricting, and something was muffling her face. She was sure her ears were bleeding, her tears were drowning her, and everything was collapsing–

Hannah was thrust back into reality as the Beast collided with her, its claws snatching her body as they both crashed into the stone wall.

Into, and through, like the opposite dome wall Hannah had flown through.

But this didn't lead to the outside meadow, which Hannah would've been overjoyed to see. No, this one broke into another secluded cavern, where the Beast lost its grip on Hannah, and they both sprawled in separate directions.

Spots danced in Hannah's vision. Her breathing was uneven as she crawled to her feet, inching away from the Beast, who had tumbled all the way to the tip of the ledge.

Hannah swallowed as her vision stabilized. Ignoring all the warnings issuing in her mind, Hannah padded toward the monster, her heart twinging with untold grief. The shattered Yin Orb that was once his eye lay steaming in its empty socket, its particles mixing with the fragments of a once-whole Ozzie.

Murmuring apologies, Hannah retrieved her dagger, refusing to look at the Beast. Refusing to acknowledge the fact that it was dying before her. All because of the very thing that had brought it powers.

Hannah turned to the ledge, which widened into a chasm. It was at least a hundred-foot drop, prompting Hannah to shudder and step away– away from the Beast and ledge.

A tiny thought nagged at the back of her mind, and realization struck her; Hannah had made it. She was alive. She had survived. Both Orbs were destroyed. She had defeated the monster, freeing herself– and everyone– from the burden of the crystal plague.

Slowly, enormous weights were being lifted, up and away from her. For the first time in a long time, a true idea of a smile quirked her lips.

Even more so when the nearing footsteps behind her turned out to be Ara and Dee, their faces banged up and bloody, but sporting the most outrageously positive grins.

Hannah's lips did truly split into a true smile at the sight of her friends, and she held out her arms for a hug, anticipating when they stepped through the new opening and–

Every thought, every feeling, winked out in a second as something tight clasped around her ankle. Alarms flashed through her head as she whipped around, barely gaining enough time to see the Beast toppling over the ledge, into the drop.

And it was bringing Hannah along with it.

She let out a petrified scream as she was wrenched backward, barely managing to catch a glimpse of her friends' freezing faces before she and the Beast hurtled down into the abyss.

CHAPTER 33

HANNAH

It was fast.

Too fast.

They had won, hadn't they?

And yet Hannah was falling, tumbling through the chasm with no correct sense of up or down. Of left or right. The wind whipped at her face as she plummeted. Hurtling to the ground below like a raindrop would.

In a way, she was like a raindrop. One out of millions like her that she had saved.

Whatever tears had managed to cling to her lashes were stolen away by the velocity at which she was still falling.

Falling.

Falling.

Falling.

Fear had seized her throat, locking in any screams or sobs or anything else that would also be stolen away by the wind once let out. The Beast's hand had released her ankle, but it was of no use now.

She didn't thrash. Didn't cry. Hannah doubted she even could. Her eyes remained squeezed shut.

Her pendant clung onto her neck, attempting to tear itself away from her as it zoomed up. But the chain kept it bound to her, leaving one thing she'd have before Hannah died.

With that thought in mind, she fisted it, desperate to find stability–something she couldn't be offered. Time seemed to slow as her life flashed before her eyes.

That was all ending now because she was falling.

Falling.

Falling.

Falling.

There was a massive thud below, and she flinched, biting her tongue in an attempt not to scream. The Beast had found its way to the bottom.

Soon she would too.

Falling.

She didn't want it to end.

Falling.

She wanted to see her friends again.

Falling.

Hannah wanted to see her parents again.

Falling.

She wanted to feel their arms around her, encasing her in a protective embrace. If she'd had the chance to, she'd never let go.

Falling.

But it was all ending. Here. Now. She'd die a broken girl.

Falling.

Falling.

Falling.

I'm falling–

The sudden rush of air froze, hitching her breath as the velocity ended within a second. The inertia of her past movement tugged her down feebly, dissipating moments after.

Was she dead?

There was no impact, no screaming, no arcs of pain racing within Hannah. Tentatively, she pried her eyes open.

They immediately locked on her splayed hands, which now had small glows of pink thrumming on her palms. A thin sheen of sweat had arisen on Hannah's skin to keep herself suspended in the air. A veil of pink light washed over her body, enveloping her in its barely perceptible glow. Hannah's hair had drifted off her neck and now haloed her head. Her ankles drifted a foot above the Beast's broken body.

Swallowing down a bout of nausea, Hannah craned her neck up to view the ledge from which she had pitched off. Tiny humanoid figures were above, no doubt confused, and in more than a little stress. With that thought, Hannah pressed her eyes shut and focused on that distinct buzzing at the top of her spine. She let the humming travel to the rest of her limbs, and suddenly, the darkness inside her eyelids burst pink. She thrummed with power, and slowly, with bated breath, when Hannah dared to open her eyes again, she was shooting up-- up so high and fast it was like gravity had reversed.

The wind whipped at her hair, and her veins glowed pink. She drank in the feeling, the sensation of having control. Of being powerful.

Hannah concentrated on that feeling as she shot up, soon coming to stand before Dee and Ara. Hannah was breathing heavily, her eyes wide. The light around her had faded, leaving behind a prominent buzzing at her spine and a load of shock shared between the three girls.

Ara blinked.

Dee's jaw fell open.

Ara blinked.

Dee rubbed her eyes.

Ara blinked.

Hananh's gaze flickered between the two of them, an uncertain, stunned smile spreading across her face.

Dee was the first to hug her. Her arms encircled Hannah in a firm hug that Hannah readily returned. The relief between them was unspoken, yet palpable. They clung to each other, and Hannah sniffed, allowing the embrace to ground her.

But she peeled away for a minute to look at a still-stunned Ara. Hannah bit back a watery laugh and extended an arm, which Ara quickly stepped into, returning the hug to her.

The three of them held each other, not caring that they were bloody and battered. Not minding their awkward positions. Just content to share stability and trust.

They didn't let go even as their surroundings dissolved into gray mist. Didn't let go as the world rematerialized into familiar shelves containing books from the Grand Rapids Library.

Until finally, Hannah pried away, a watery sob bubbling from her lips. She smiled at her surroundings, her heart easing.

Books really did know how to make her feel better.

***

It was an achy, albeit short, walk to Hannah's house, where they all unanimously decided to go first. The second Hannah had stepped in, tears welled up in her eyes again, and immediately she sank into the couch, wrapping a blanket around herself. Dee waddled over to the opposite side and collapsed on it, stretching her sore limbs. Ara retrieved an ice pack from the freezer and placed it on her head, sighing in contentment.

The three of them sank into a comfortable, restful silence.

That Ara interrupted.

She sat up slightly. "So... I feel like we need to address the new... developments we've seen."

Dee and Hannah nodded sluggishly, sitting up only after Ara shot them pointed looks.

Hannah cleared the thickness from her throat. "Dee goes first."

Dee whipped her head to Hannah. "Hey! Why me?"

"You're older." Hannah nodded, prompting her to speak, not missing the dark blue stains on her arms and neck.

Dee followed her line of sight and winced. "Right...
okay,"

She straightened, rubbing her neck awkwardly. "I... am
a siren."

DIANA

Ara and Hannah took the news surprisingly well.

Granted, at first Hannah had blinked as though in a
stupor, and Ara had simply frowned at her. But later,
considering the things they had witnessed as of late, they
seemed to believe her.

As she unloaded her story—Melumora, leaving it,
settling down here—bizarre looks crossed over their faces,
mostly Ara's. Especially when she pleaded with them to
safeguard her secret. When she was finished, an uncertain
silence hung damp in the air.

Dee cleared her throat. "So... yeah," she repeated,
hoping to jar them into speaking.

Ara, of course, was the first to speak. "So you have
midnight blue blood? And the monsters from the Grocery–"

She paused, contemplating, then repeated her original
question, noticeably avoiding the next part.

Dee nodded anyway, swiping her wrist against her
cheek to accumulate some of it, then tilting it towards them.
Hannah's lips were pressed tight, nearly turning them white.

"And you have magic powers?" She asked tightly.
However, pure curiosity lined her words.

Dee shrugged. "Sort of. I've been told that every siren
has a different power. Mine is control."

Hannah's lip tilted up, hinting at a smirk. "Prove it."

Despite herself, Dee smirked. Both of them looked at Ara.

She glanced between them. "Hey. Hey-nuh-uh. I'm not going through that–"

"*Lift your hand,*" Dee commanded.

Instantly, Ara's face went slack. Her arm hovered in the air.

Hannah giggled. "Okay, that's freakishly cool."

Dee grinned. "*Slap yourself.*"

As told, Ara gave herself a hard strike on her cheek. And when Dee let the powers fade, she looked furious.

"Next time you do that, I will use your sword against you." She snarled, hostility sealing her promise.

Dee and Hannah only snickered, and when Ara sank back into the couch, muttering under her breath, Dee's abdomen was threatening to burst from laughter.

Her heart felt strangely lighter, relieved from the iron fist clenching around it. Even she had enough common sense to be aware of how much more their adventure had affected Ara and Hannah, so to see their faces– Hannah's smiling one and Ara's begrudgingly amused one– free from tension? It warmed her insides, making her feel lighter than ever.

Or maybe the feeling generated from the fact that Dee had finally told them her heavily guarded secret. And they didn't seem repulsed, terrified, or even perturbed. No, their energies welcomed Dee as she was, swathed her in their acceptance. Maybe that's why she was light-headed with giddiness.

Well, either those things or the lack of nourishment she'd faced in the past week or so. Dee was certain all three of them were responsible.

"So Adrian's a siren too?" Hannah questioned, her eyes gleaming with intrigue.

Dee nodded, confirming her thoughts. "And so is my sister and mom. But we don't know Pelli's powers yet."

"What do you think it could be? And– oh! When will you find out?"

Dee smirked, amused by Hannah's interest. "Maybe in a couple of years. But for now, her power is making everyone annoyed."

"And what about your battle training?" Ara interjected, adjusting her ice pack. "Why did you have to learn that?"

Dee frowned as she dug into her memories. As always, they turned fuzzy, until she could barely remember what Melumora looked like.

Strangely, despite all her memories, sword-wielding never explicitly approached her. It was never emblazoned in her recollections. A silver-blue thing was blurred in her thoughts, but didn't magnify enough for her to latch onto it.

It drifted away, sinking back into her consciousness, nestled in the froth of thoughts, concluding her evocation.

"I barely remember." She admitted, pretending to ignore the disappointment etched on Ara's face. "It was a long time ago. And sirens were... weird."

Despite her despondency, Ara sighed and felt her scalp for any signs of ease.

"Dee's super lucky," Hannah murmured enviously, "She at least has her sword."

"You have your dagger." Dee pointed out.

"Yeah, but I don't know how to use it. Ever since we destroyed the Orbs, it's like the magic has... died out. Whatever was guiding me through the fights just disappeared."

"True. But now you have that weird, freaky magic to control the dagger, too! Who cares if you can't hold it? Hold it with that pink blob of light you somehow generate."

For added effects, Dee wiggled her fingers in the air, successfully pulling another grin to Hannah's face.

Ara sat up again. "Yeah, what even is that?"

"I don't know. When I was falling..." Hannah abruptly went silent, her eyes widening, her breathing quickening. She clenched her eyes shut, fisting her pendant at her chest before continuing:

"I just kept thinking how I didn't want to die. I... wasn't ready to accept that yet. And... I dunno... the magic took over."

She pried her eyes open again, and Dee quickly mouthed.

You okay?

Hannah nodded, fidgeting with her necklace. When speaking about her infamous fall, something had triggered her. And she looked extremely perturbed, as though memories were flashing beneath her eyelids.

Worry sifted through Dee, but in an attempt to ease both her and her friend, she said:

"Prove it."

Hannah's lips tilted into a smile that didn't necessarily reach her eyes, but she bit her lip, concentrating on Ara's direction.

Her arm lifted on its own a moment later.

"Why do you guys keep experimenting on me?" She complained, dropping it down after Hannah released her control.

Hannah giggled. "You're a very easy–"

The doorknob rattled aggressively.

"–target."

Uneasy silence rendered all three girls speechless as they all glanced toward the door. At the second rattle, they sprang up from the couch.

"Who the–"

Hannah shushed at Dee as she inched towards the door...

HANNAH

Hannah was having difficulty being afraid.

Sure, her heart was pulsing a little erratically than normal, but she was also exhausted, and as the doorknob rattled again, Hannah stupidly wondered if the Beast had somehow come alive to finish her off.

She glanced briefly toward Ara and Dee, both of whom had stiffened, embodying the fear she vaguely felt. They were a couple of paces behind her, watching warily as Hannah padded closer toward the door.

Her brain was spiraling out of control, overthinking every possible scenario that could happen. Maybe the Beast was here. Or Jax– even after being crystallized, as she was told by her friends– had somehow managed to gain enough strength to end her. Or maybe the cops were here to cart her off to custody. Or–

Cutting her stalling to an end, Hannah pulled open the door and poked her head out tentatively.

"Hel–"

Her greeting faltered as her eyes fell on the person standing before her.

A woman was perched on the porch. She had waist-length brown hair, green, distraught eyes, and faint lines etched on her face, making her seem older than she was.

Her frame was thin, even slimmer than before. Her hands shook at the sight of Hannah.

A sob choked Hannah's lips, and tears bubbled into her eyes, mirroring her mother.

"Oh, Hannah–" Mrs. Thorne's words were cut off as she clasped her arms around her daughter, who had already turned into a sobbing mess. Tears streamed down her face, soaking her mom's cardigan, as Hannah buried herself in the warmth she'd missed for far too long.

Mrs. Thorne pulled away enough to step back, sniffling, her eyes crinkling with excitement as another figure came into view.

Forget time.

The universe itself stopped.

It ceased to exist.

The world blurred into shades of gray.

Except for the man in front of her.

He had stringy brown hair and eyes so full of emotion. Emotion Hannah hadn't seen since she was six years old.

In the past years, Hannah had grown so she was nearly as tall as him. Her features were a blend of his and her mother's. She had her mom's light brown hair, but her father's hazel eyes.

Her father attempted a small smile. He chuckled at her paralyzed posture.

"Hannah?"

That was it for her.

This wasn't a phantom. This was real.

He wasn't crystal. He was real.

Hannah threw her arms around him, allowing his arms to wrap around her. The light pouring inside her intensified once her mother joined the hug, too.

Hannah was just a girl. A girl turned warrior, returned girl.

And nothing close to crystal.

***

After many tears, sobs, confessions, promises, and an abundance of catching up, Hannah's parents left her, Dee, and Ara in the kitchen while they went upstairs. Hannah watched them go, convincing herself they'd be with her again.

The once-crystal soldiers seemed to have foggy, distorted memories from their time as warriors. Rather like those one would attain from a dream. Hannah didn't have the heart to confirm her mother had, indeed, attacked her in the forest. For now, that would remain her secret.

Dee cleared her throat, snapping Hannah's attention to her. "Do you mind if... if I use your mom's phone to call my mom?"

Hannah sprang to her feet and retrieved her mom's phone, handing it to Dee. "Please. Check on them to make sure they're okay."

At the first few rings, Dee waited, her knee bouncing restlessly as her eyebrows furrowed with anticipation. Once the phone was answered, she sighed with relief and left the room to talk.

Hannah suspected there were many teary questions passed back and forth.

Ara's eyes followed Dee as she left the room, and her face was mournful; she was probably wishing there was a parental figure who would care enough to answer their missing daughter's call. Hannah felt a twinge of sympathy, and she wordlessly sat beside her. It was the best she could offer: an unspoken promise of support.

Dee returned a few moments later, grinning widely. She set the phone down and looked at the two girls with giddy excitement, dimpling her face.

"They're back!" She hauled both of them to their feet and did a small dance, which both Hannah and Ara laughed at.

"We did it! They're all back!" She exclaimed, holding up both hands for a high-five.

Hannah lifted her hand and high-fived her. She turned to Ara, jerking her head to follow through.

But Ara just stared. She looked at Hannah, then slowly toward Dee. Her eyes were wide, as though a realization had struck her.

"Everyone's back." She echoed, any remaining phantoms of her previous joy evaporating. Hannah furrowed her eyebrows, concerned.

Dee waved her still-hovering hand. "Come on, girl, don't leave me hanging."

"Put your hand down."

Dee's grin faltered. "Why?"

But Ara had already moved on. "Hannah, don't you get it? Everyone is back."

Hannah nodded slowly, chewing on the inside of her cheek. "Yes... I thought we already... figured... that out..." She trailed off as her face shifted to mirror Ara's.

"Guys...?" Dee asked weakly, her eyes flicking between both of them, still utterly perplexed.

Hannah stumbled back a step, her chest constricting as panic erupted through her senses. "That means... oh, no..."

"Guys, you're starting to freak me out," Dee said uneasily.

"If everyone came back... that means..." Hannah inhaled sharply, forcing out the next few words.

"That means Jax is back too."

The atmosphere shifted, plunging into sickly silence. The three girls stared at each other, locked in a staring contest, begging the others to break the silence.

Hannah could hear the thundering of her heart in her ears, but still, after calming her pulse, she said:

"You know what? It's fine. He doesn't have any resources. No family. He can't do anything to hurt us."

Ara tilted her head, nodding slowly as if letting the words rush through her as well. A slow smile spread to her face.

"You're right. So, how about we just ignore that, yes?"

As if on cue, Dee wrinkled her nose. "You say 'yes' like a founding father."

Ara scoffed. "Just proves I'm smarter than you."

"Are not,"

"Are too,"

They began bickering as usual, throwing out their regular insults like water balloons. Hannah felt herself grin as she stepped away, heading outside.

The driveway looked perfectly normal, sitting there as pavement would, containing no evidence it ever bore two crystal soldiers on it.

The sidewalks were overshadowed by the slowly swaying trees, displaying no trace of crystal animals.

The world had sunk into a comfortable, beautiful atmosphere, with the five p.m. sun preparing to climb its descent into night and let the moon outshine the stars.

There was no trace that there had ever been a crystal apocalypse.

And Hannah studied the beauty of it all, the wind tousling her hair, sweeping it into her still bruised face. The cool string of air curling around her body gave her pleasant shivers that crawled up her spine.

She'd saved this. Hannah and her friends. And she'd attained a special gift out of it, too. A very pinkish, magical one.

But for now–

There were no remnants of the crystal apocalypse.

CHAPTER 34

JAX

The world had sunk into a mess of battles.

The memories replayed ceaselessly.

Jax could barely pick out what had happened when he was a crystal soldier, but he knew he never wanted to feel that again.

And out of all the faces that stood out to him from the flooding memories, there were two most prominent ones.

Jade.

Hannah.

Those were the two names revolving around his head, spinning around like a top that refused to clatter upon the table. Spinning like the Earth that refused to pause to breathe.

And those were the two names he had embedded into his mind as he snatched back the two rubber band bracelets. One brown. One green.

Because he was leaving. Tonight.

And Jax had fought.

For so long.

And so hard.

Constantly tormenting himself with battles he both had and hadn't picked.

His next one, however, would be intentional.

Make sure you're ready, Hannah.

There's a fight coming.

THE END OF BOOK I

AUTHOR'S NOTE

I got the idea for this book when I was ten years old, sitting on my bed, about to read a book.

I know. *Shocker.*

(Or maybe you are shocked — I can't really tell.)

It took me years to finally write it, mostly because I could only work on it during summer vacations, and the story had fluctuated drastically. At some point, I had changed the whole thing. And to make matters worse, I had stopped writing in December of 2023 entirely. After getting back into my love for literature, I made up for lost time by writing nonstop from December 2024 to June 2025.

(If any Hamilton fans got the reference, you're my new favorite people.)

Those seven months were the most productive I've been in writing, and this book is now ready, finalized, and awaiting sequels!

But anyway— no matter how long it took, this story has never felt more alive. Thank you so, so much, dear reader. The time you've spent with these pages means the world to me.

ACKNOWLEDGMENTS

They say writing a book is a pretty lonely process.

And while a lot of it is done solo, it wouldn't be possible without so many people quietly cheering me on, encouraging me, and sometimes just putting up with my endless chatter about plot twists and character ideas.

To my family: thank you for listening, especially when I rambled about story details that probably made no sense.

To my friends: for all the late-night brainstorming, meme sharing, and those "You've got this!" texts when I needed them most. You helped keep me going.

Thank you to every teacher, librarian, and book lover who inspired me to keep reading and writing. Shout out to Amanda Merrill, my seventh-grade English teacher, who was so kind and never interrupted me when I was buried in drafts during independent reading time.

And finally, to you, the reader: thank you for picking up this book and sharing this story. Without you, these characters would still be stuck in my head. To express my gratitude, I'll leave a little gift for you. Turn the page to see!

BOOK 1.5 TEASER

PREFACE

Jax clenched his teeth, slamming his eyes shut. Arcs of agony raced across his spine and limbs, but he didn't dare struggle against his bonds. A sharp gaze pierced him nearby, fueling his tolerance to withstand the hold.

His vision rimmed red when he opened his eyes. His mouth felt raw and heavy, like blood was pouring out of his gums.

Still, this was nothing compared to the pain he would feel when switching dimensions. That thought and Jade were the only things keeping him upright.

Many times, he'd considered himself a broken human. Maybe he was.

And maybe while this force of power was destroying him, it was also steadily rebuilding.

It wouldn't be *him*.

It would be an entirely different being, capable of too much.

Destruction was spiderwebbing across this dimension, and he would be at the lead of it, ruling with an iron fist, slamming against the fabric of reality.

The mirror behind him pulsed feebly, offering a glimpse of a haunted soul inside, quiet and somber. This may be the last time it works.

The power swarmed through his vision, turning the remnants of it into pure swirling gold.

Not the pretty, dainty kind, no.

The insatiable, unstable kind that emerged from the depths of desperation and everything tormenting.

Jax welcomed it, embracing it with open arms.

Because that was what he'd been reduced to. A bottomless pit of desperation–

And everything tormenting.

ABOUT THE AUTHOR

Harshika has always believed in the quiet power of imagination—and the strength that comes from facing the unknown. Fascinated by elemental forces, parallel worlds, and emotional journeys, she began writing stories that combine fantasy and heart at a young age. *The Crystal Gaze* is her debut novel and the first in an elemental series exploring courage, connection, and the choices that shape us. The world-building of Rick Riordan and the emotional depth by Leigh Bardugo inspire her.

When not writing, Harshika can be found wandering book stores, reading, and doing all the things a teenager would. She lives in a small city in Michigan and dreams of meeting her favorite authors someday.

www.ingramcontent.com/pod-product-compliance
Lightning Source LLC
Chambersburg PA
CBHW051945240626
47153CB00005B/1630